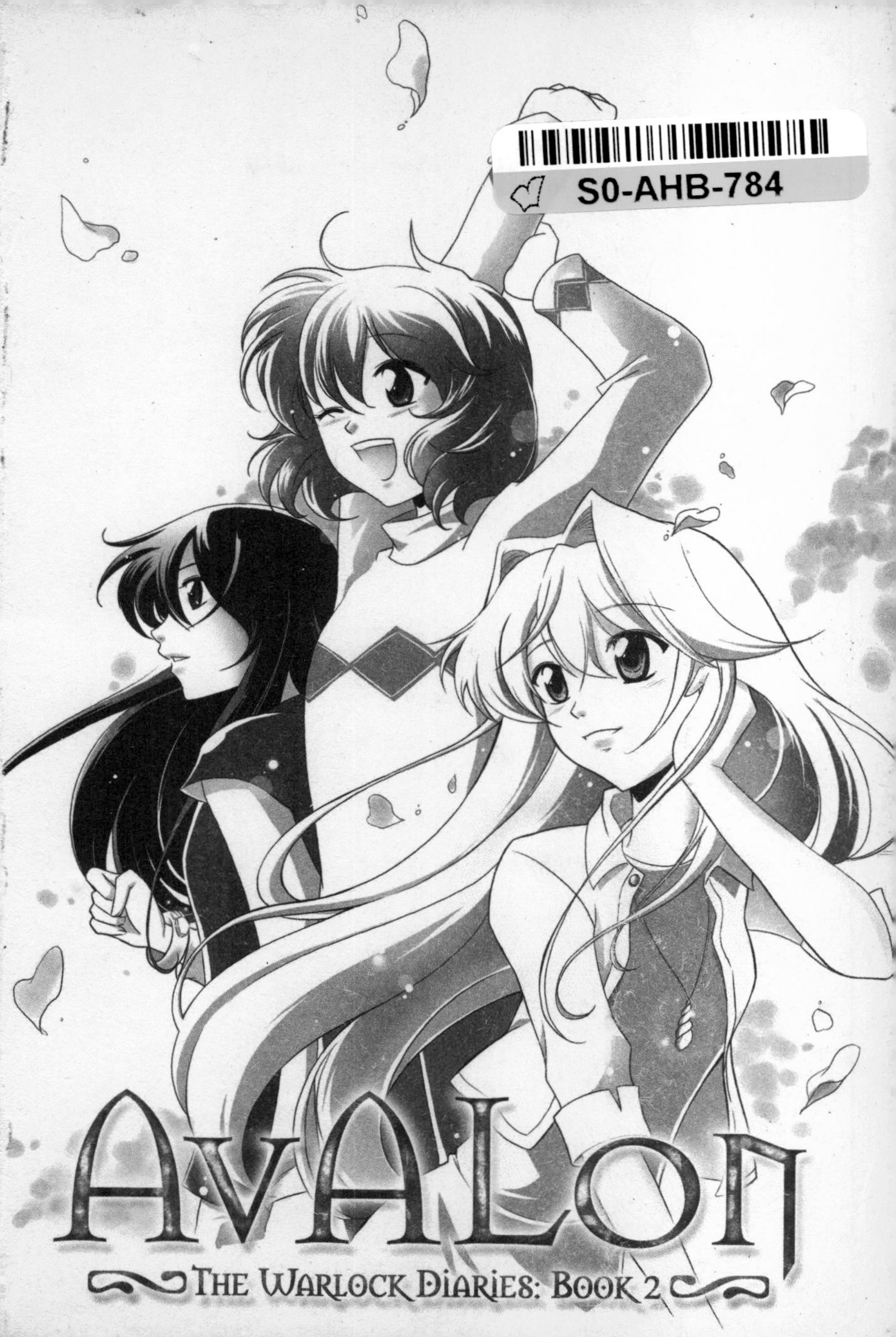

AVALON

THE WARLOCK DIARIES: BOOK 2

AVALON

THE WARLOCK DIARIES: BOOK 2

story by Rachel Roberts   art by Shiei

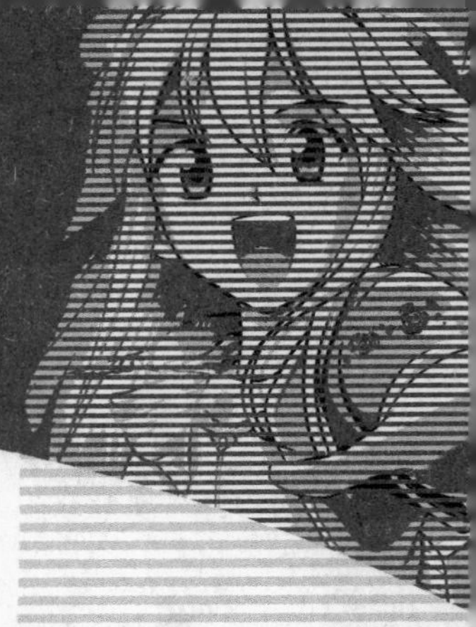

STAFF CREDITS

toning **Rhea Silvan**
lettering **Nicky Lim**
sketch art **Edward Gan**
graphic design **Nicky Lim**
layout **Adam Arnold**
cover design **Nicky Lim**
editor **Adam Arnold**

Publisher **Jason DeAngelis**
Seven Seas Entertainment

Explore a world of magic at www.AvalonMagic.com.

Seven Seas

ISBN: 978-1-934876-67-1

Printed in Canada

First Printing: November 2009

10 9 8 7 6 5 4 3 2 1

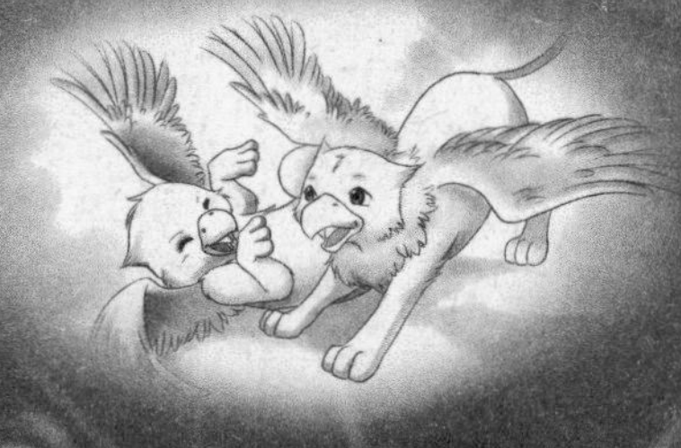

Once magic flowed freely along a vast web, the Magic Web, connecting many worlds.

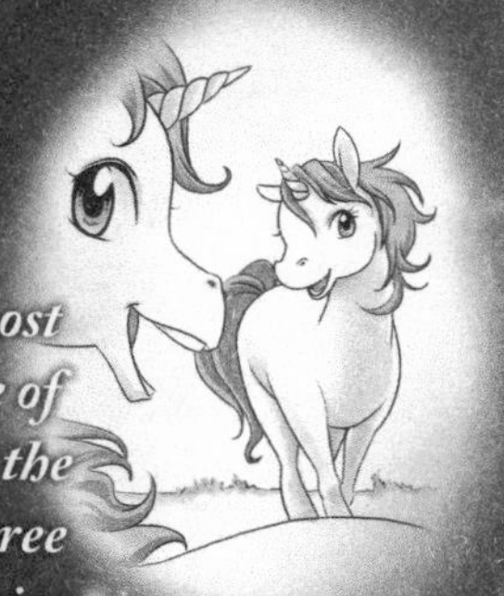

Now the magic has almost vanished. The only hope of renewing it and saving the magic web falls upon three mages—a healer, a warrior, and a blazing star.

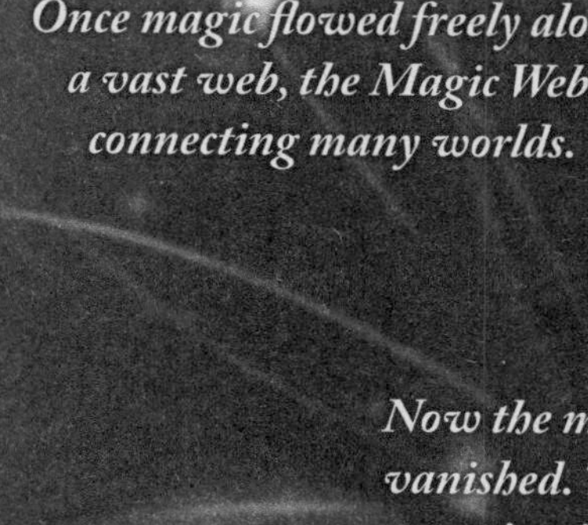

Together with their animal friends, they are on a quest to find the lost, legendary home of all magic: **Avalon.**

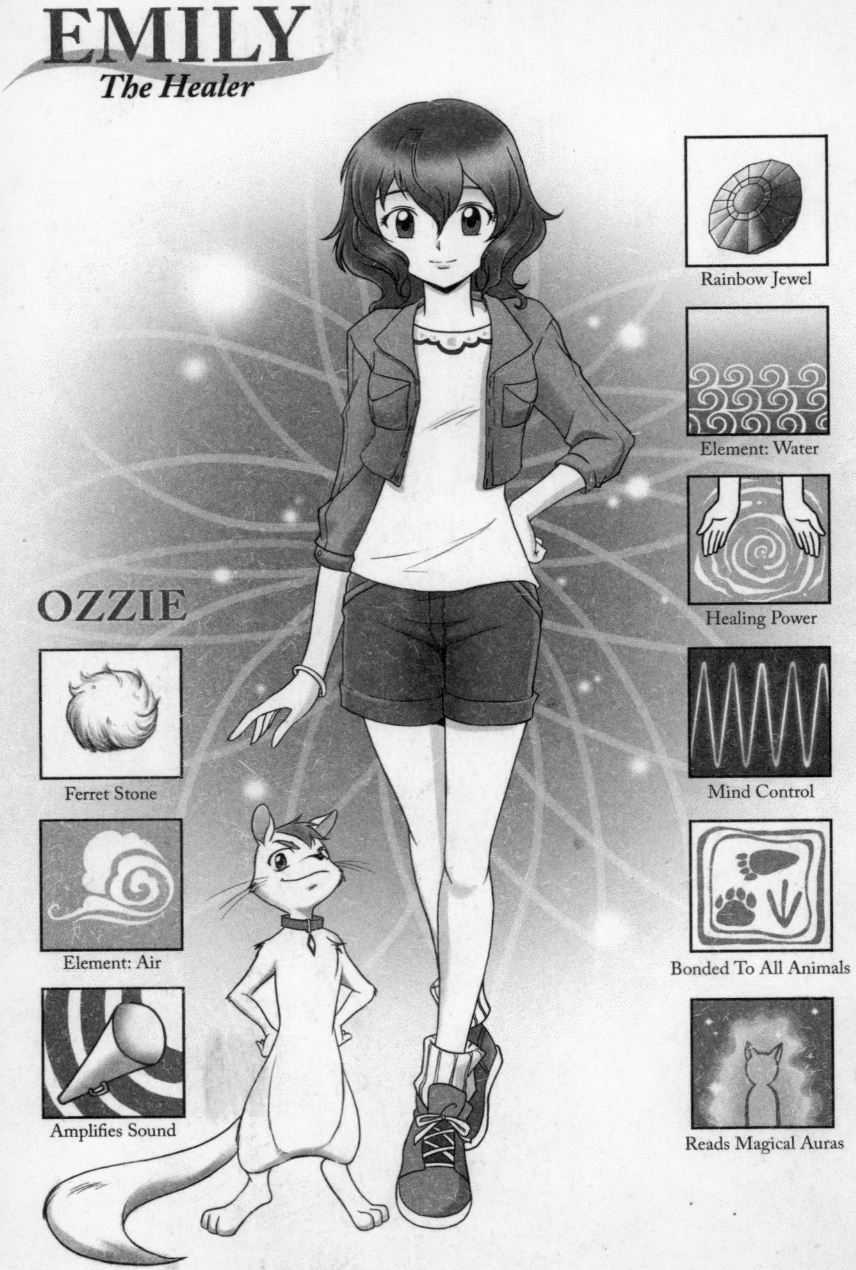
EMILY
The Healer
Rainbow Jewel
Element: Water
Healing Power
Mind Control
Bonded To All Animals
Reads Magical Auras
OZZIE
Ferret Stone
Element: Air
Amplifies Sound

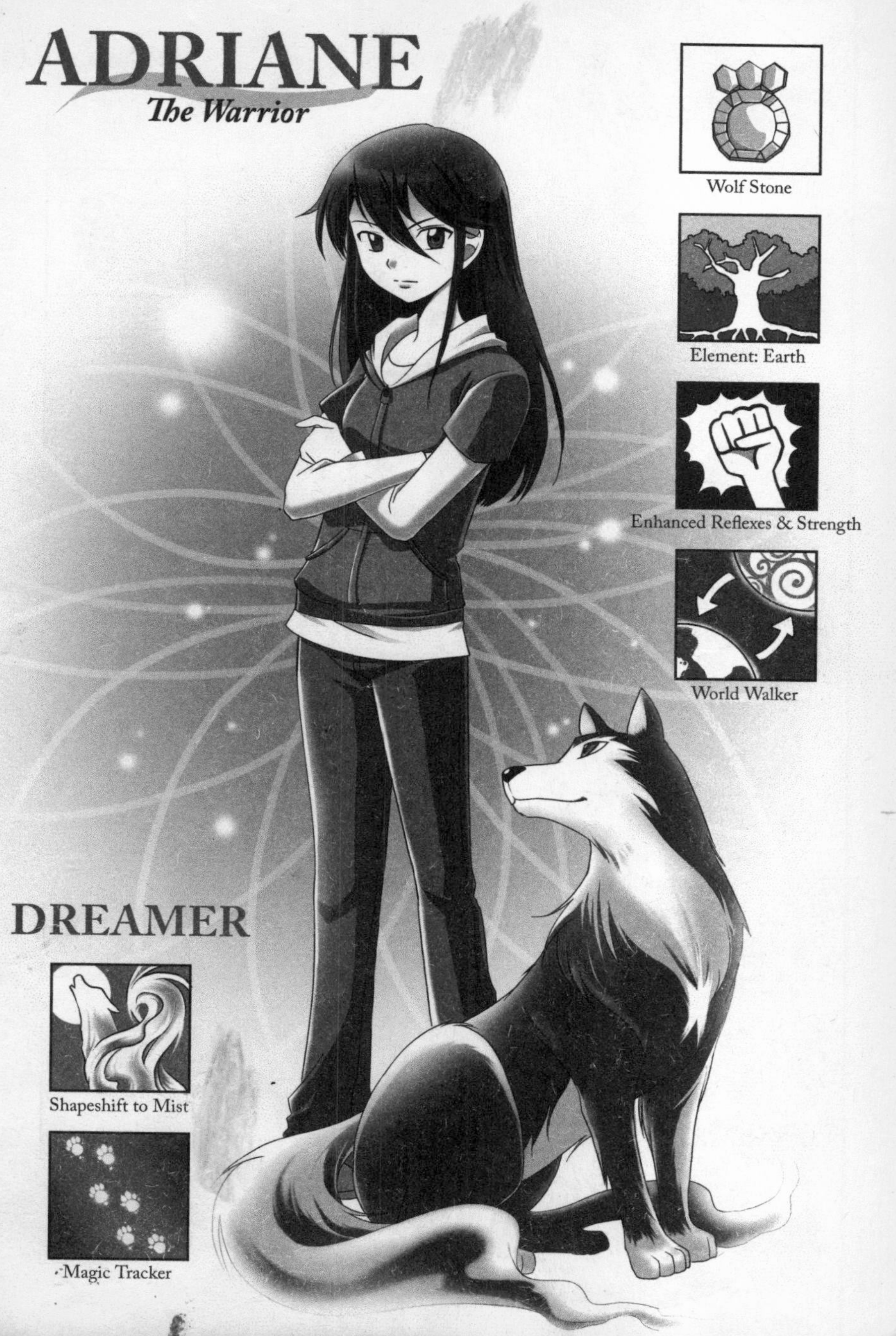
ADRIANE
The Warrior
Wolf Stone
Element: Earth
Enhanced Reflexes & Strength
World Walker
DREAMER
Shapeshift to Mist
Magic Tracker

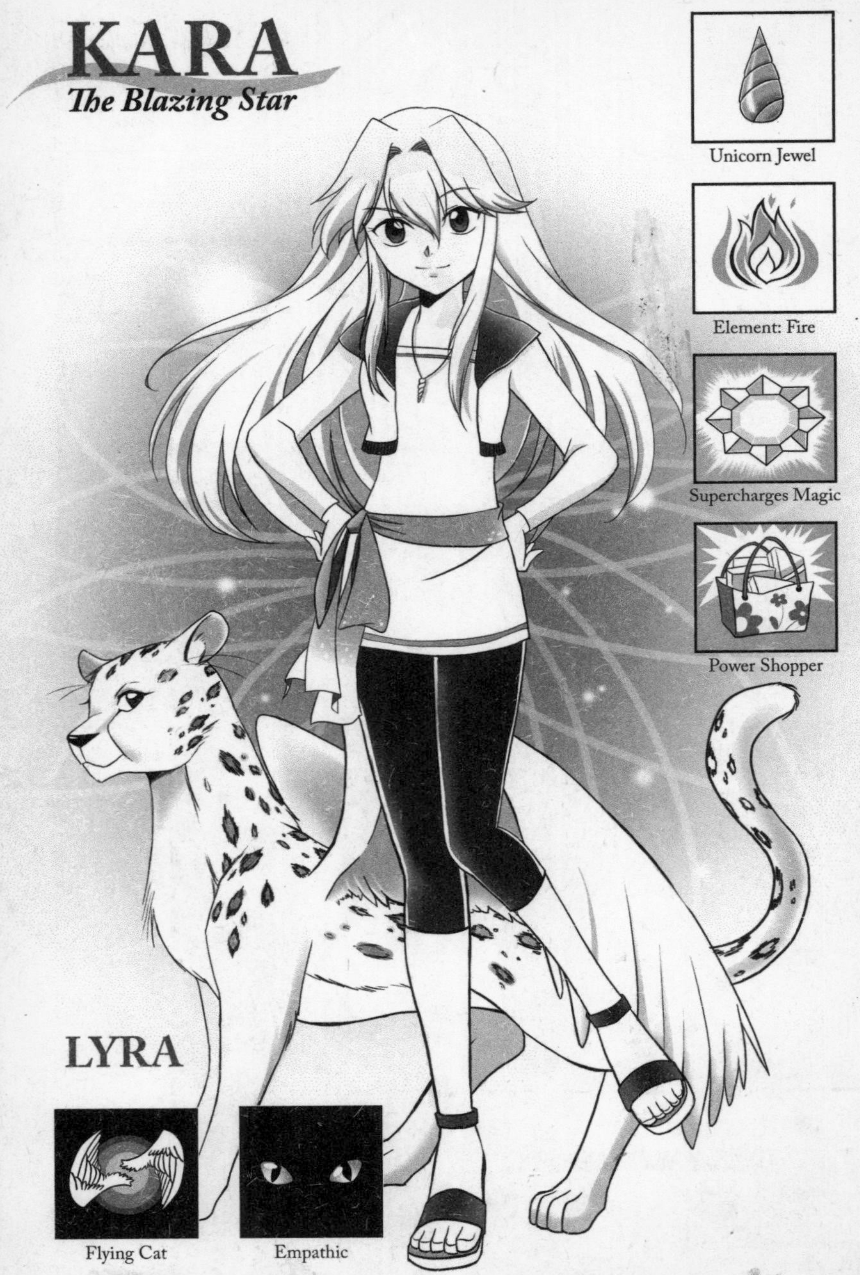
KARA
The Blazing Star
Unicorn Jewel
Element: Fire
Supercharges Magic
Power Shopper
LYRA
Flying Cat
Empathic

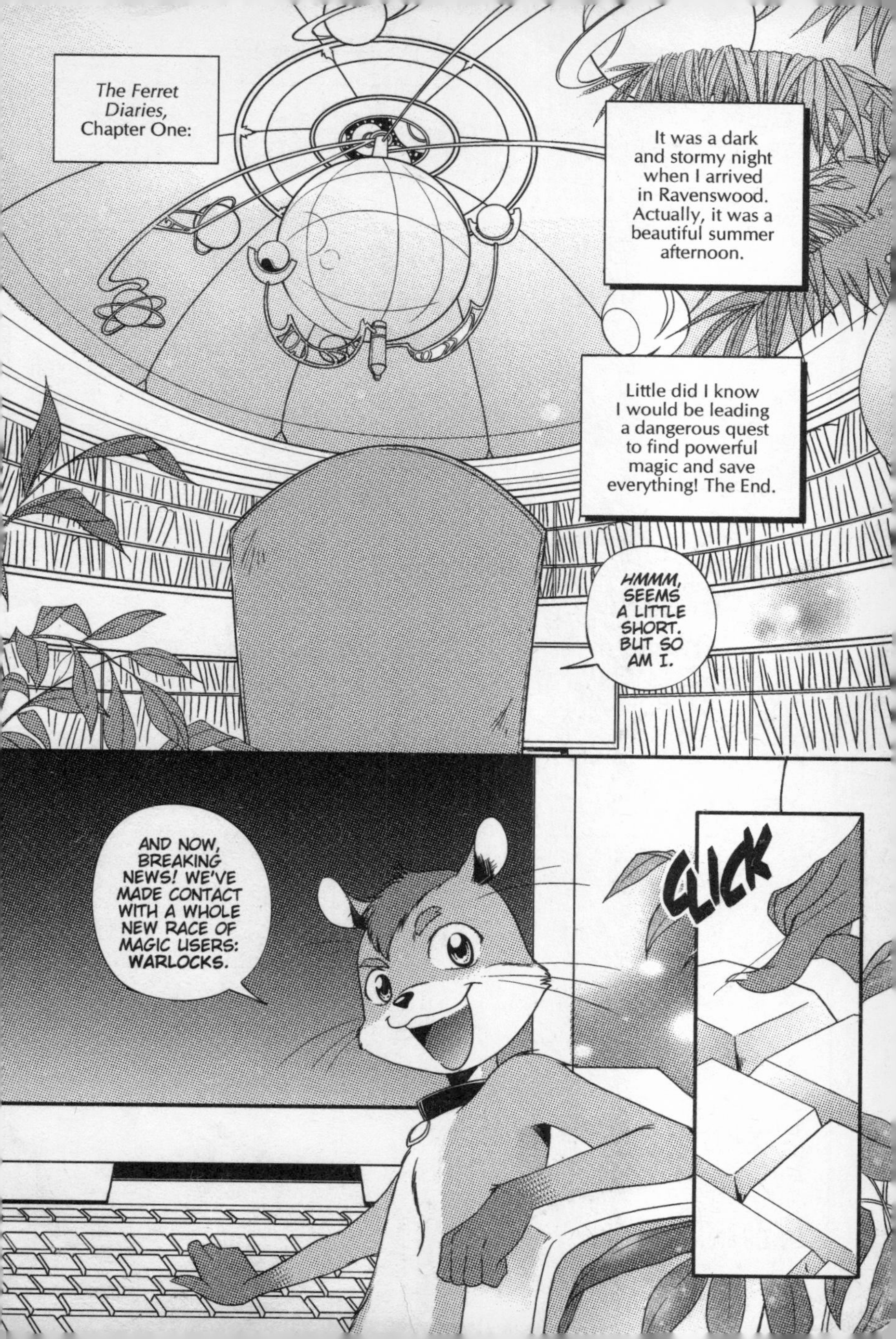
The Ferret Diaries, Chapter One:
It was a dark and stormy night when I arrived in Ravenswood. Actually, it was a beautiful summer afternoon.
Little did I know I would be leading a dangerous quest to find powerful magic and save everything! The End.
HMMM, SEEMS A LITTLE SHORT. BUT SO AM I.
AND NOW, BREAKING NEWS! WE'VE MADE CONTACT WITH A WHOLE NEW RACE OF MAGIC USERS: WARLOCKS.
CLICK

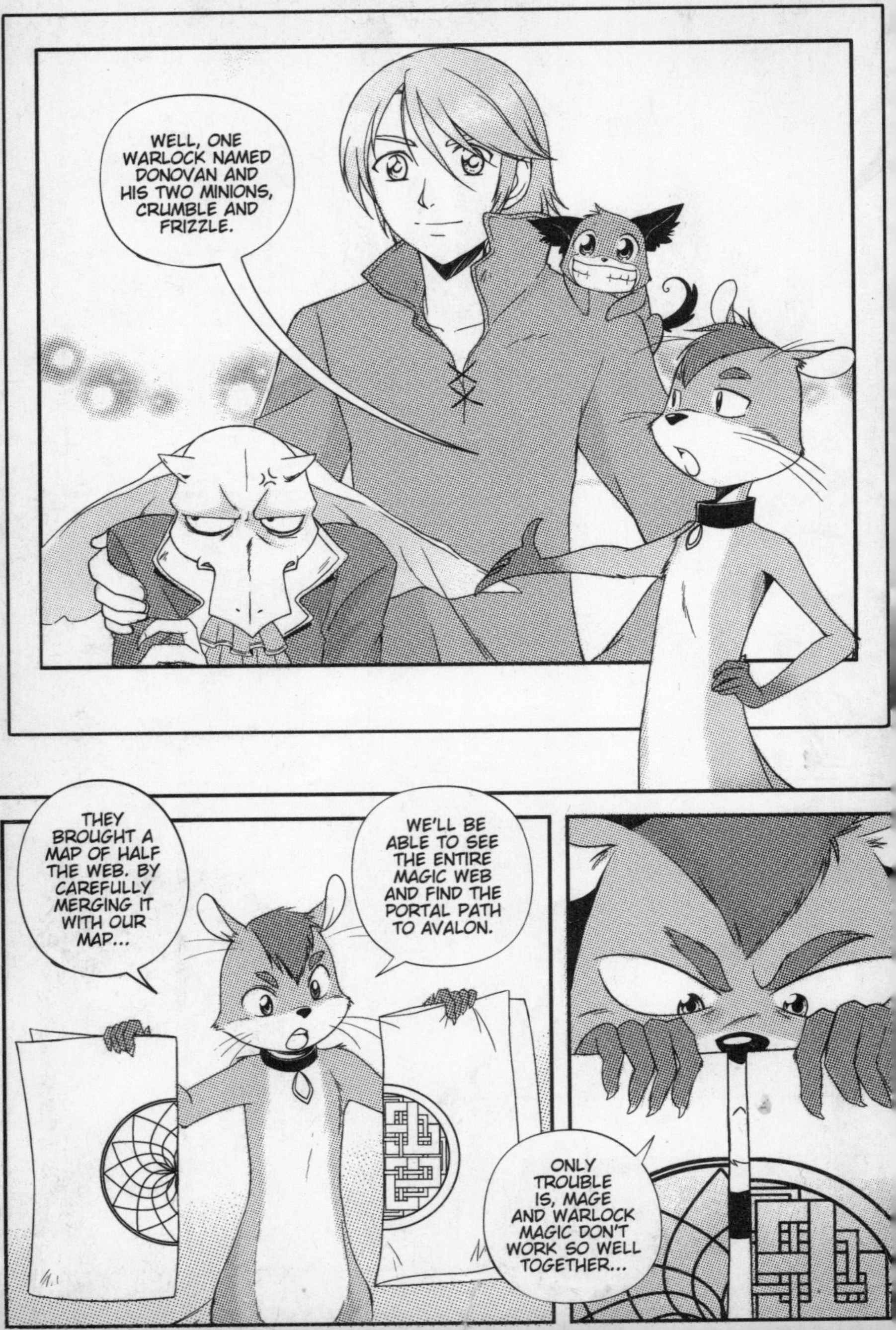
WELL, ONE WARLOCK NAMED DONOVAN AND HIS TWO MINIONS, CRUMBLE AND FRIZZLE.
THEY BROUGHT A MAP OF HALF THE WEB. BY CAREFULLY MERGING IT WITH OUR MAP...
WE'LL BE ABLE TO SEE THE ENTIRE MAGIC WEB AND FIND THE PORTAL PATH TO AVALON.
ONLY TROUBLE IS, MAGE AND WARLOCK MAGIC DON'T WORK SO WELL TOGETHER...

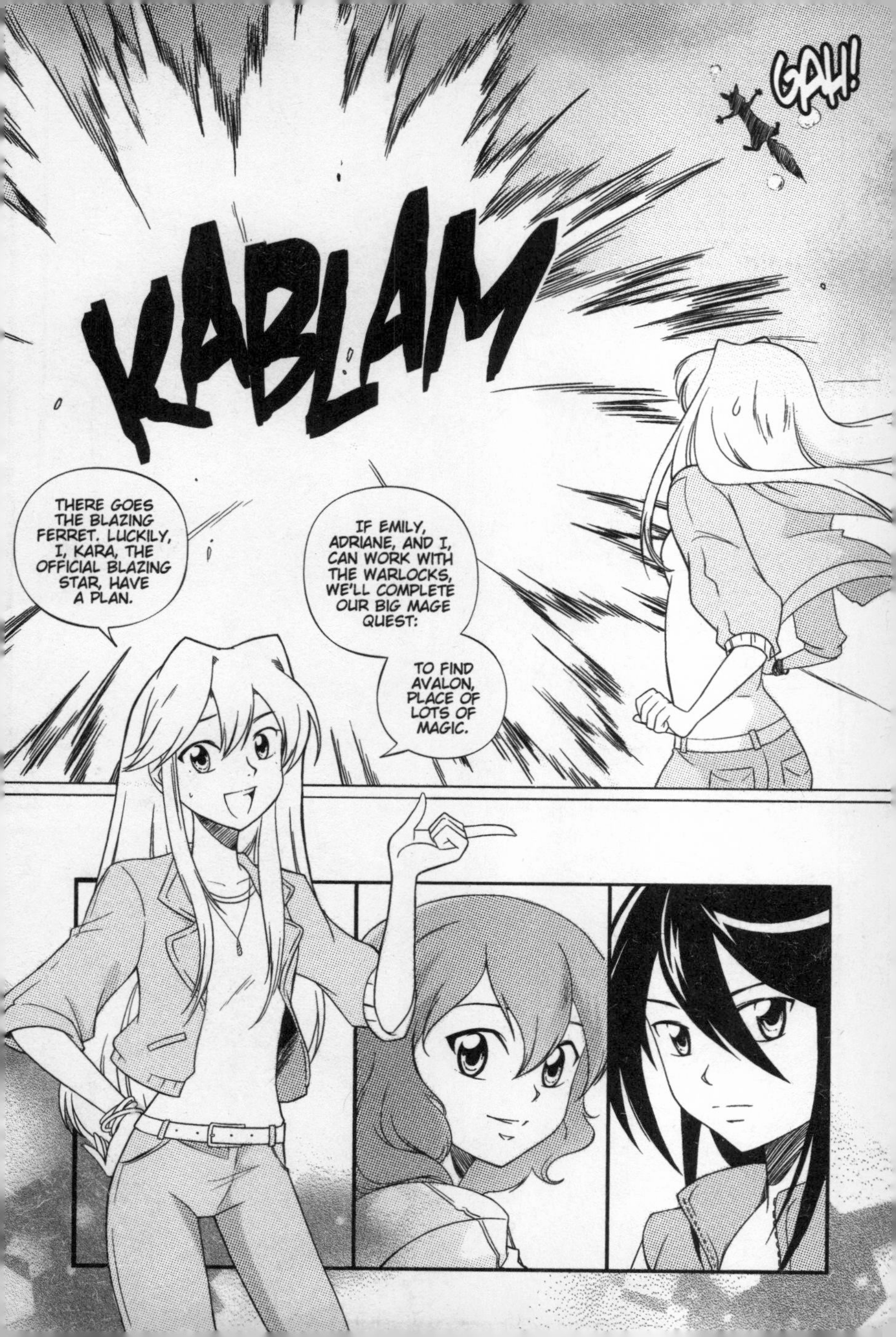
GAH!
KABLAM
THERE GOES THE BLAZING FERRET. LUCKILY, I, KARA, THE OFFICIAL BLAZING STAR, HAVE A PLAN.
IF EMILY, ADRIANE, AND I, CAN WORK WITH THE WARLOCKS, WE'LL COMPLETE OUR BIG MAGE QUEST:
TO FIND AVALON, PLACE OF LOTS OF MAGIC.

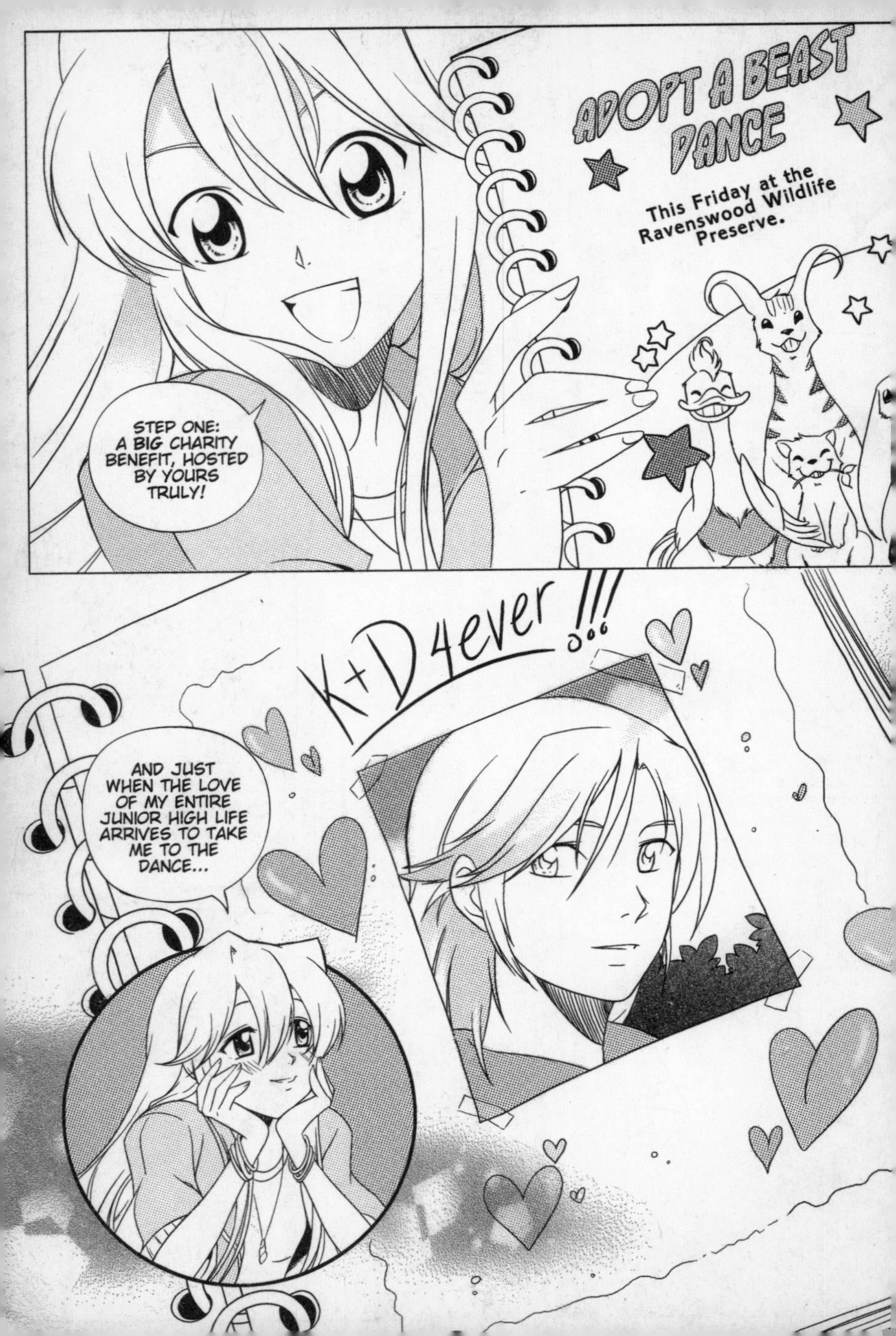
ADOPT A BEAST DANCE
This Friday at the Ravenswood Wildlife Preserve.
STEP ONE: A BIG CHARITY BENEFIT, HOSTED BY YOURS TRULY!
K+D 4ever!!!
AND JUST WHEN THE LOVE OF MY ENTIRE JUNIOR HIGH LIFE ARRIVES TO TAKE ME TO THE DANCE...

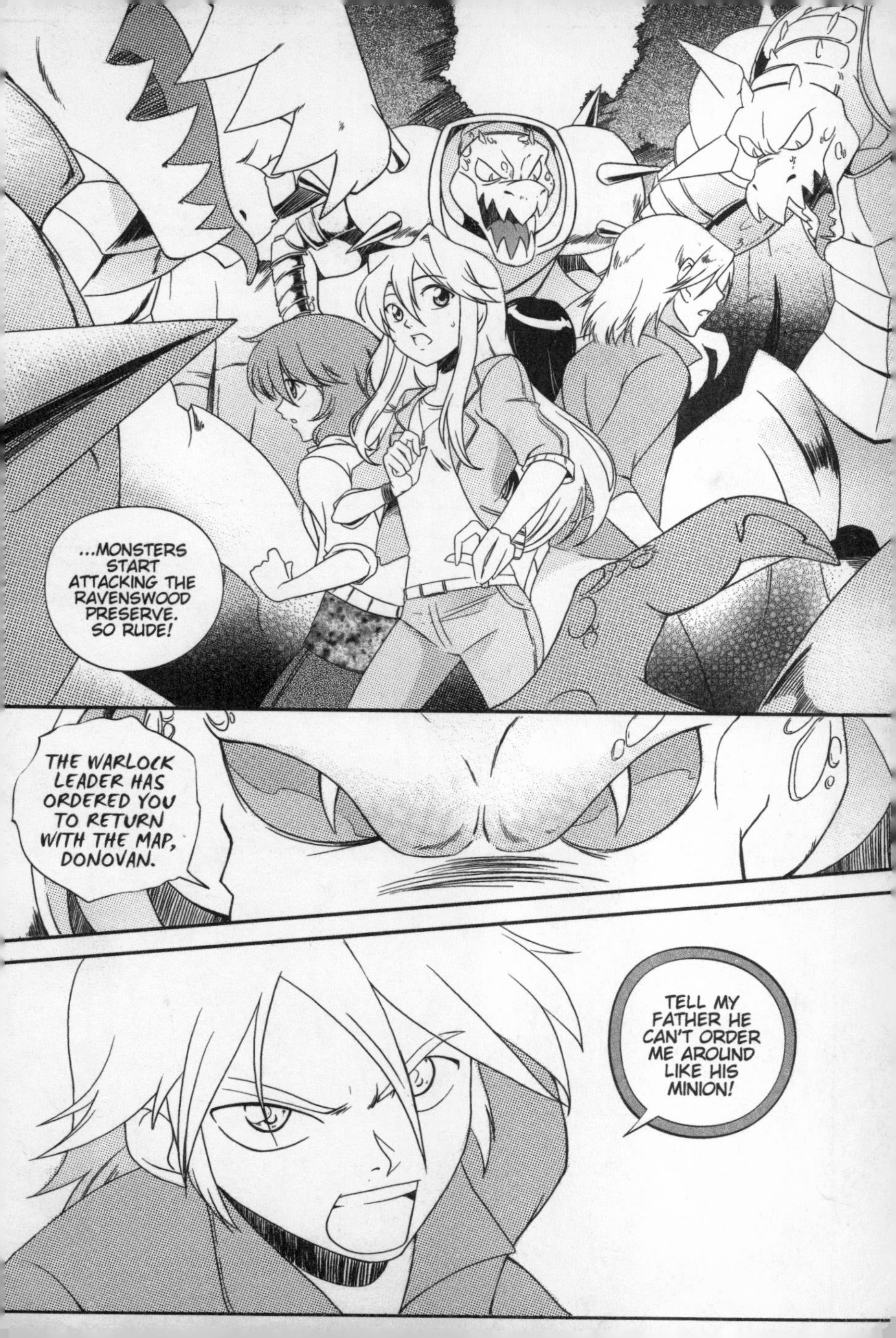
...MONSTERS START ATTACKING THE RAVENSWOOD PRESERVE. SO RUDE!
THE WARLOCK LEADER HAS ORDERED YOU TO RETURN WITH THE MAP, DONOVAN.
TELL MY FATHER HE CAN'T ORDER ME AROUND LIKE HIS MINION!

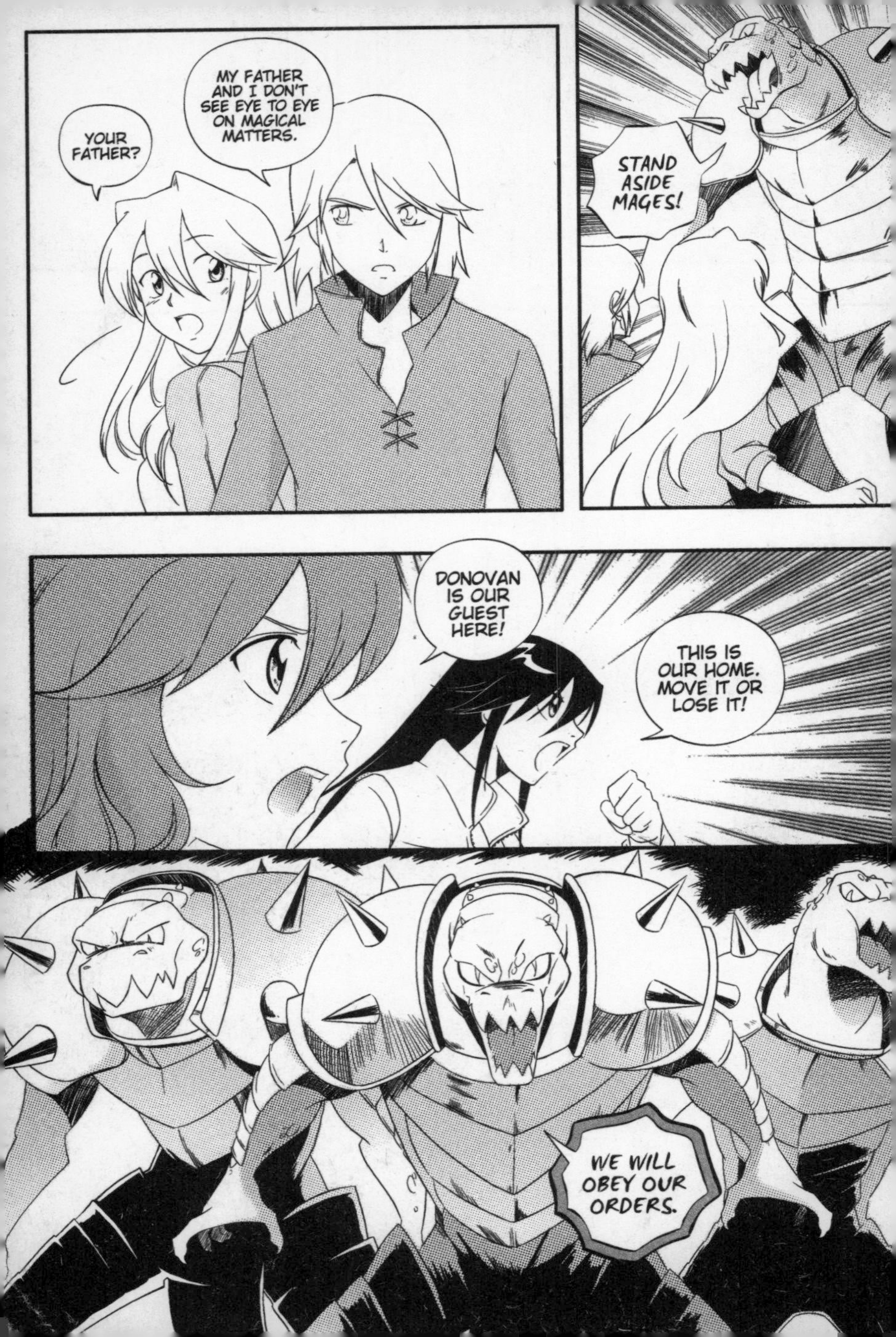
YOUR FATHER?
MY FATHER AND I DON'T SEE EYE TO EYE ON MAGICAL MATTERS.
STAND ASIDE MAGES!
DONOVAN IS OUR GUEST HERE!
THIS IS OUR HOME. MOVE IT OR LOSE IT!
WE WILL OBEY OUR ORDERS.

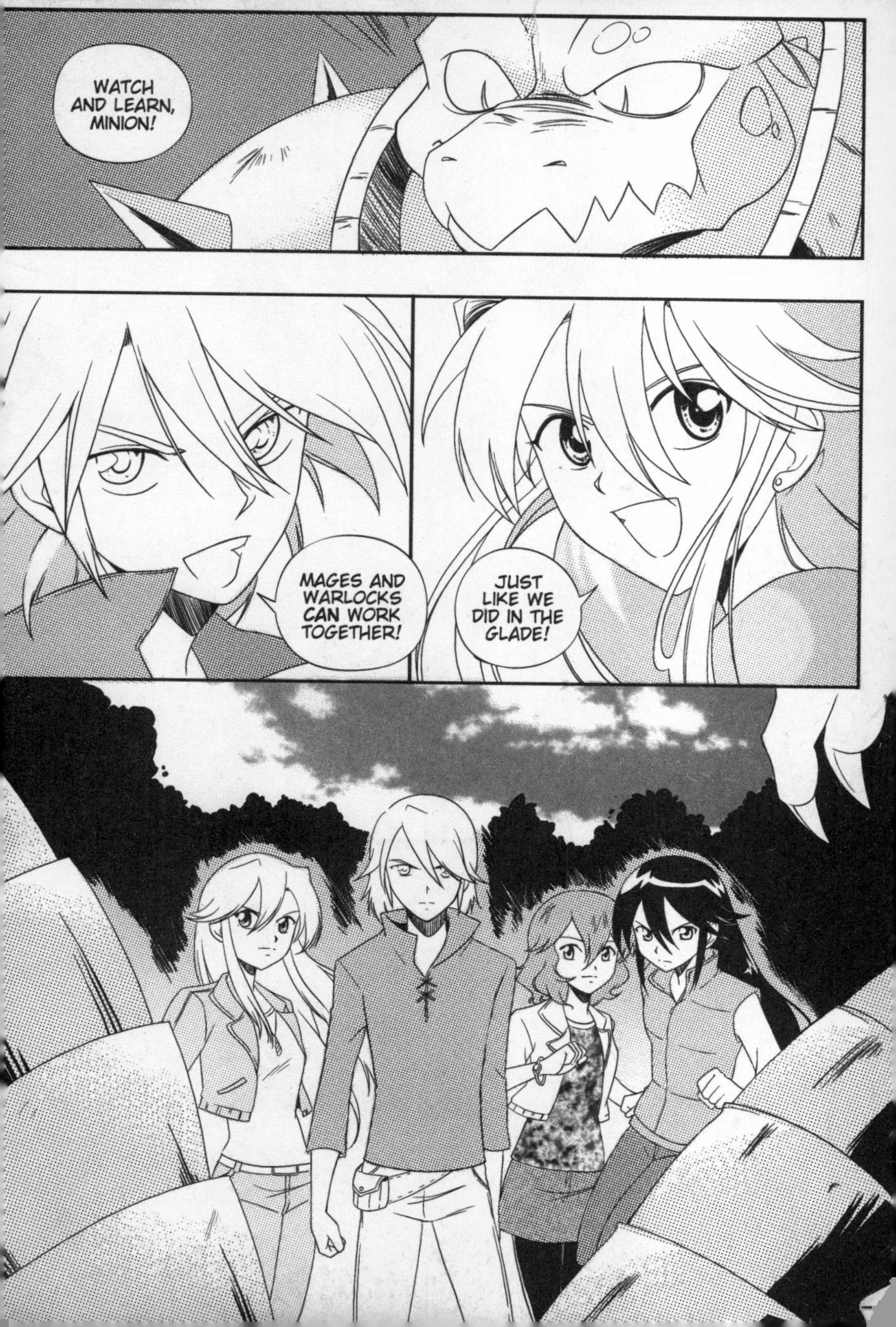
WATCH AND LEARN, MINION!
MAGES AND WARLOCKS CAN WORK TOGETHER!
JUST LIKE WE DID IN THE GLADE!

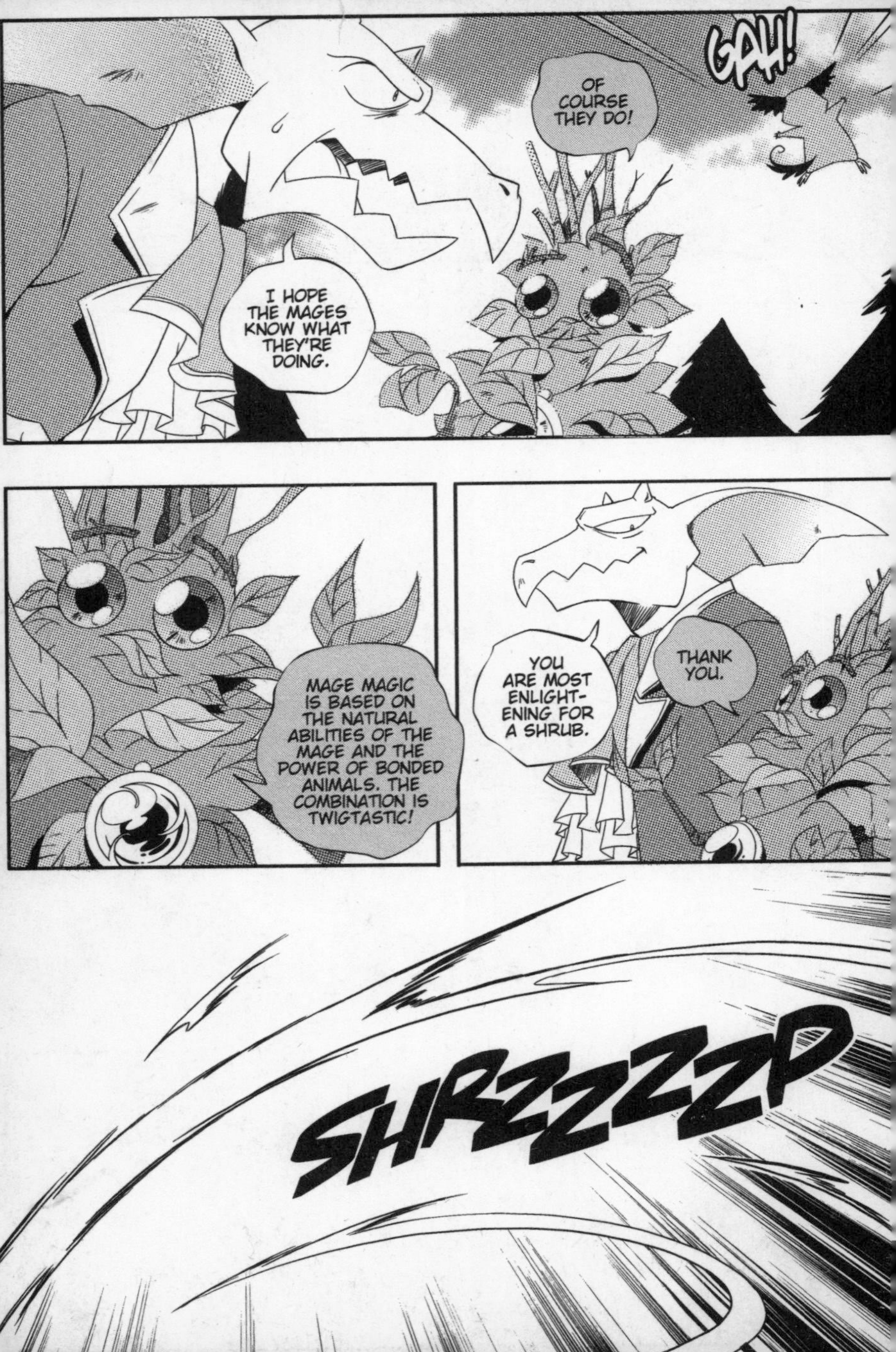
GAH!
OF COURSE THEY DO!
I HOPE THE MAGES KNOW WHAT THEY'RE DOING.
MAGE MAGIC IS BASED ON THE NATURAL ABILITIES OF THE MAGE AND THE POWER OF BONDED ANIMALS. THE COMBINATION IS TWIGTASTIC!
YOU ARE MOST ENLIGHT-ENING FOR A SHRUB.
THANK YOU.
SHRZZZZP

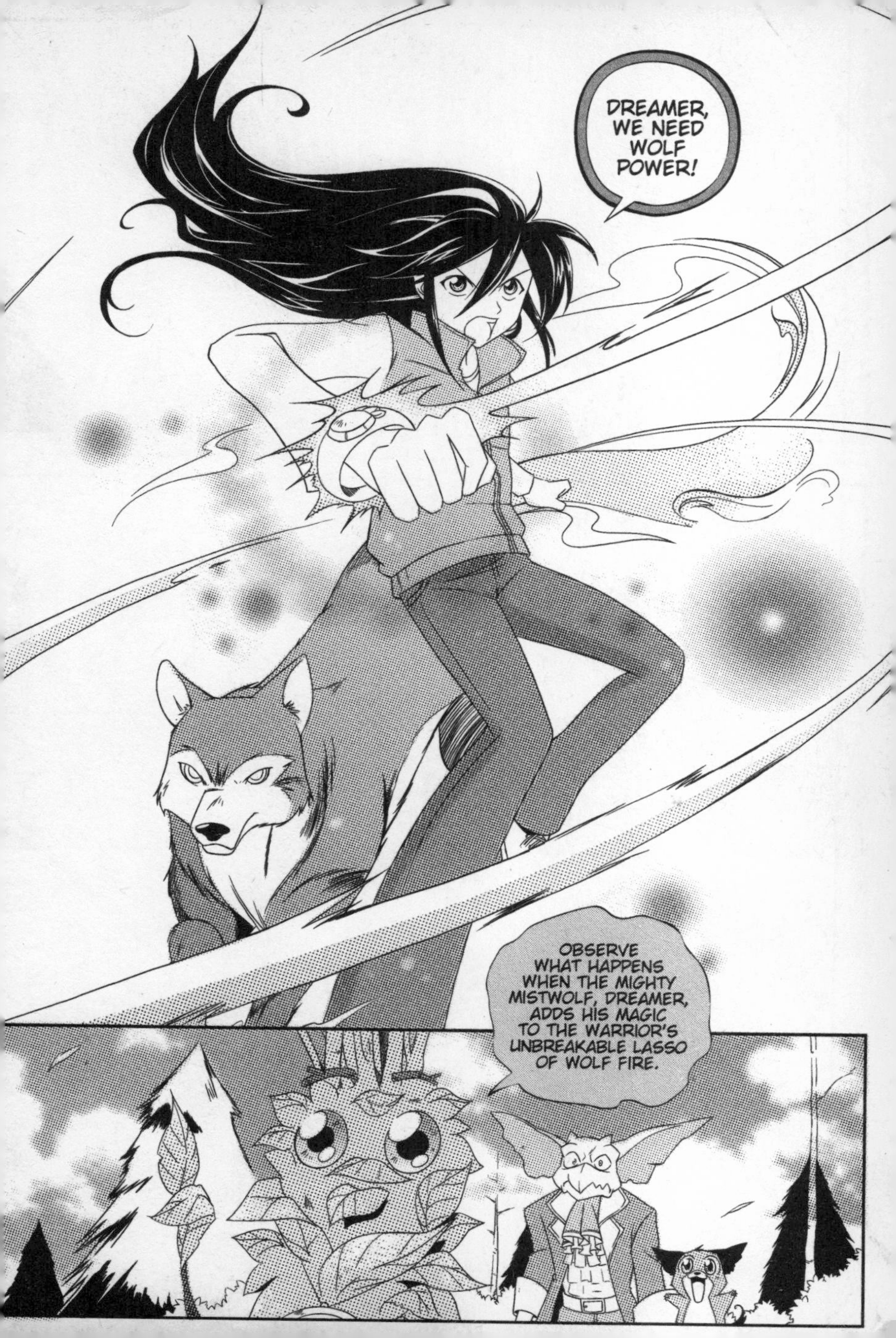
DREAMER, WE NEED WOLF POWER!
OBSERVE WHAT HAPPENS WHEN THE MIGHTY MISTWOLF, DREAMER, ADDS HIS MAGIC TO THE WARRIOR'S UNBREAKABLE LASSO OF WOLF FIRE.

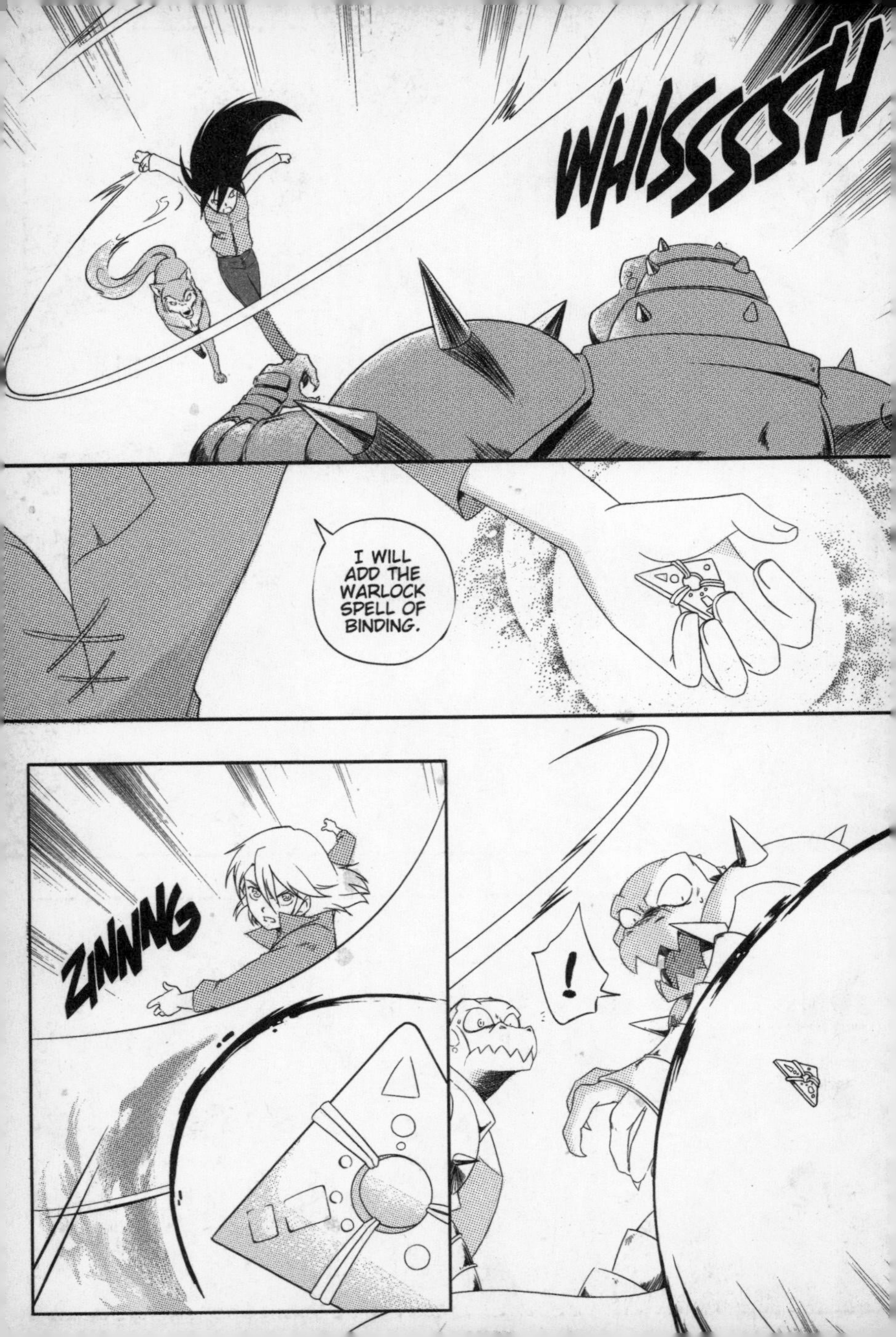
WHISSSSH
I WILL ADD THE WARLOCK SPELL OF BINDING.
ZINNNG
!

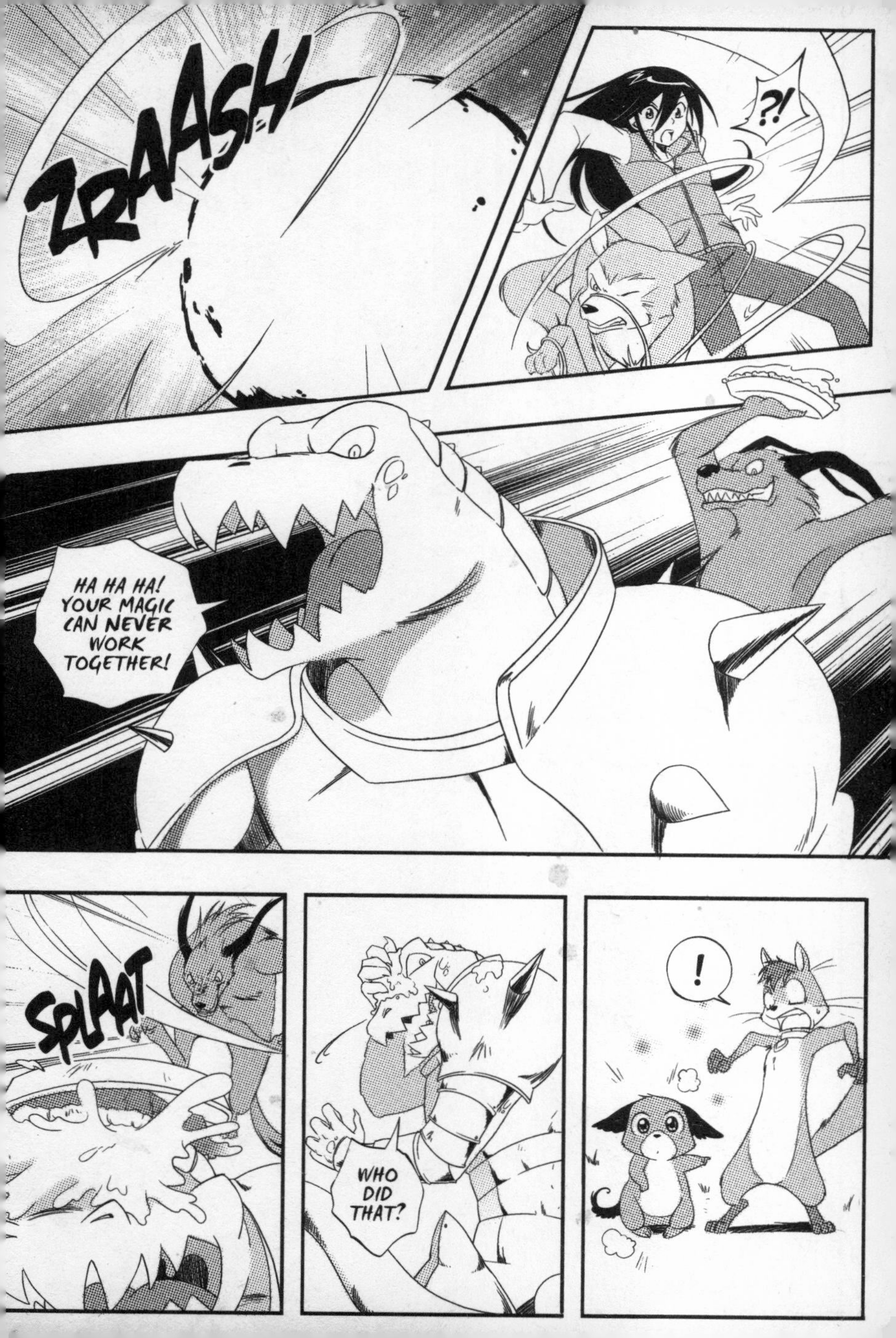
ZRAASH
?!
HA HA HA! YOUR MAGIC CAN NEVER WORK TOGETHER!
SPLAAT
WHO DID THAT?
!

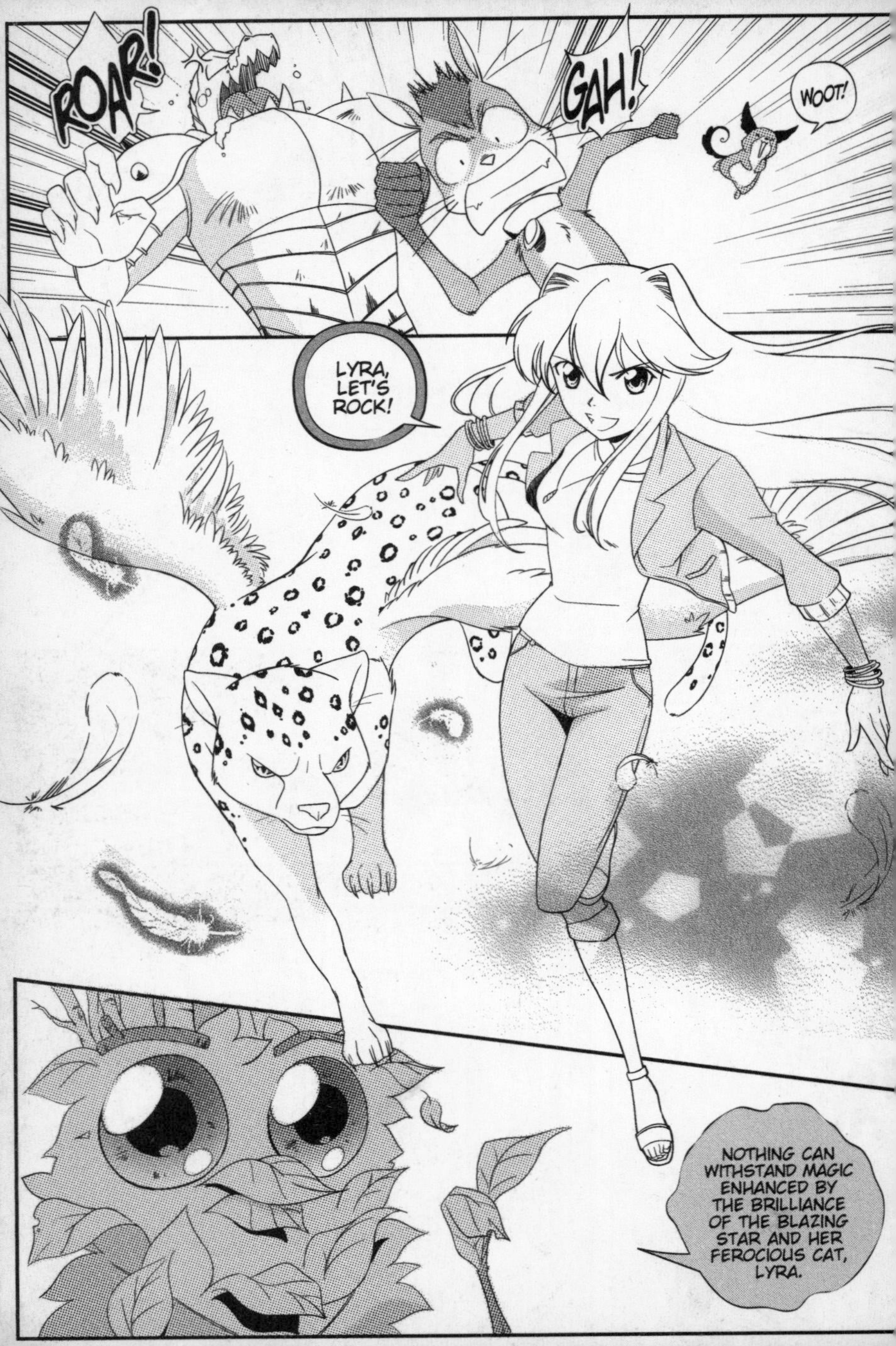
ROAR!
GAH!
WOOT!
LYRA, LET'S ROCK!
NOTHING CAN WITHSTAND MAGIC ENHANCED BY THE BRILLIANCE OF THE BLAZING STAR AND HER FEROCIOUS CAT, LYRA.

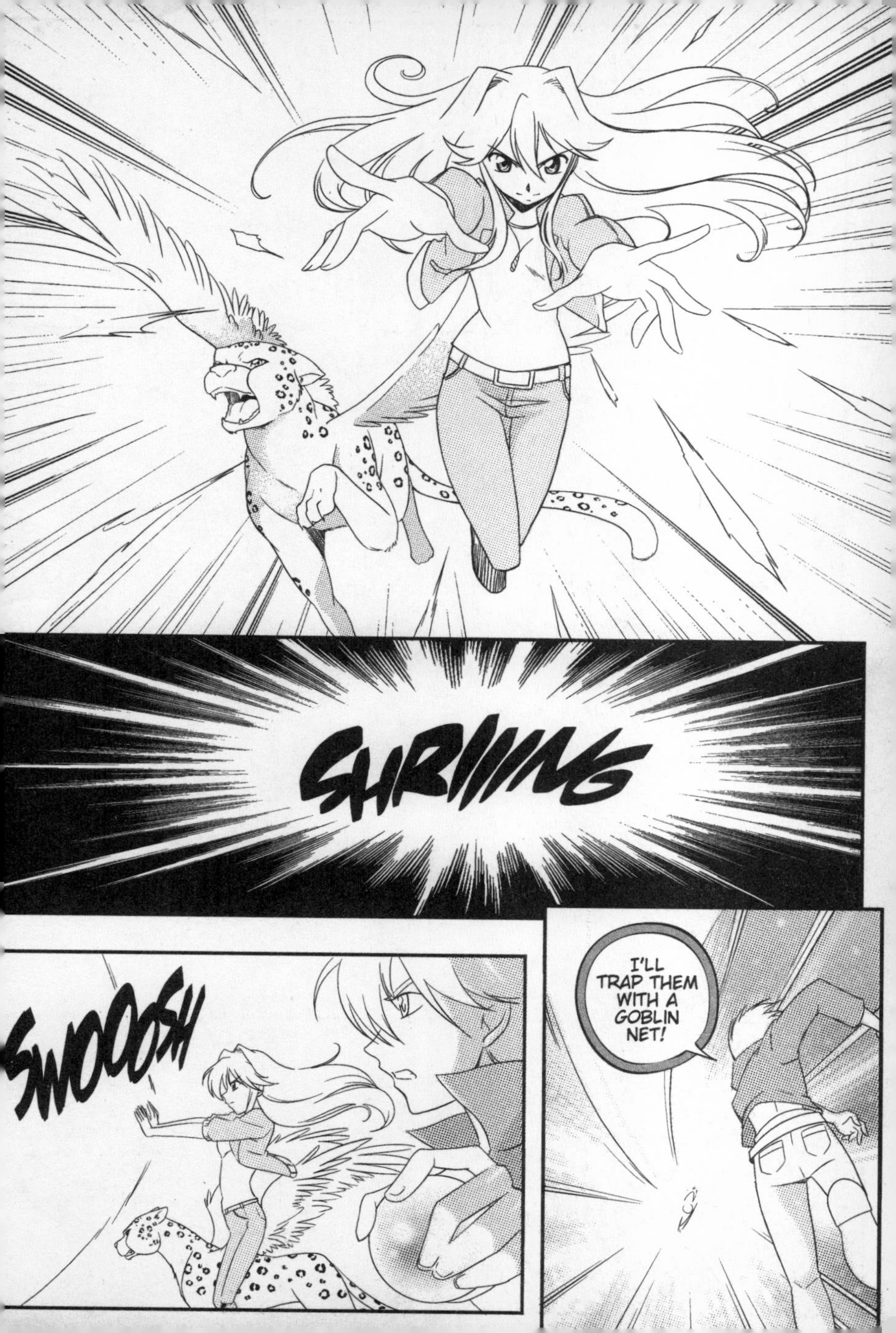
SHRIIING
SWOOOSH
I'LL TRAP THEM WITH A GOBLIN NET!

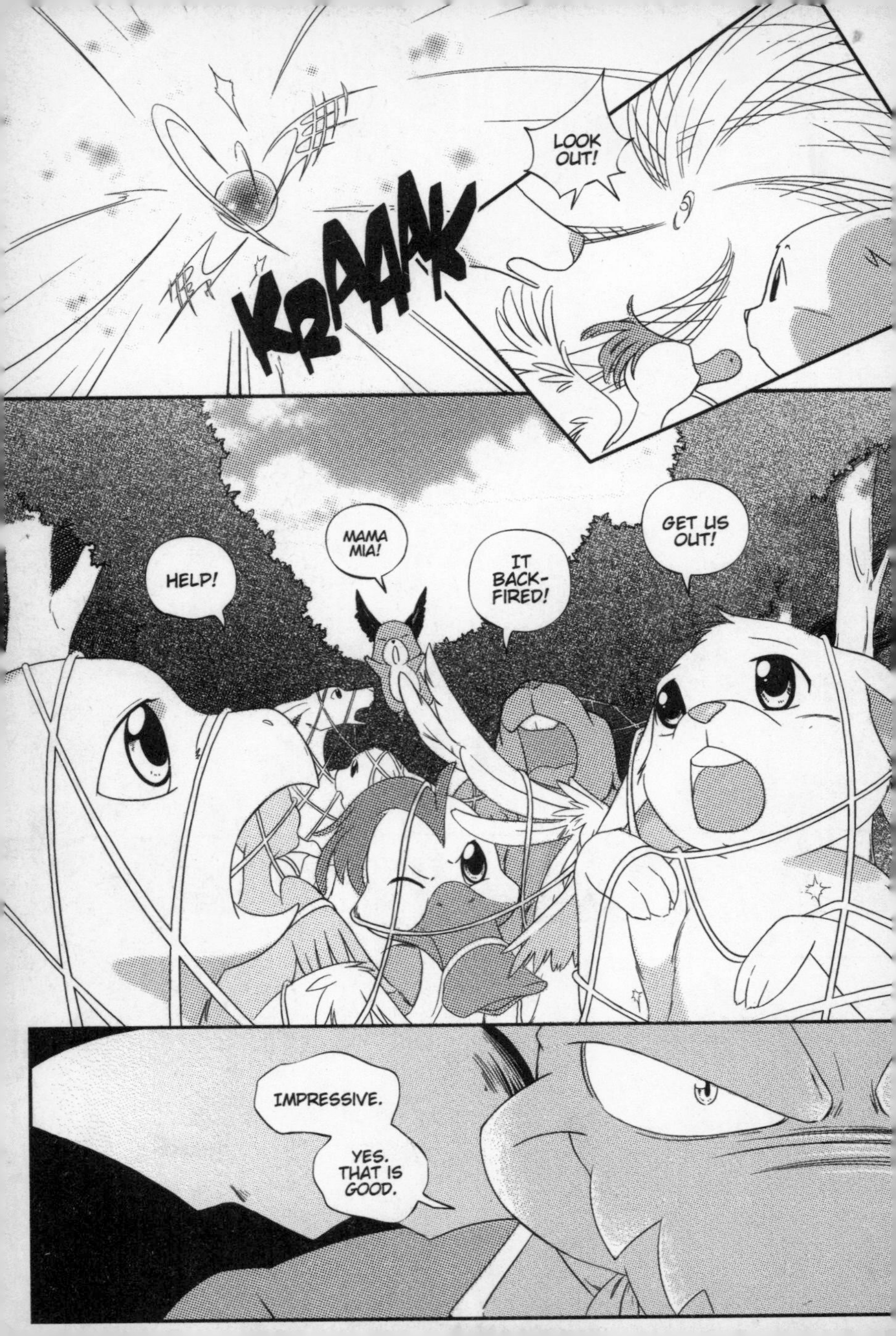
KRAAAK
LOOK OUT!
HELP!
MAMA MIA!
IT BACK-FIRED!
GET US OUT!
IMPRESSIVE.
YES. THAT IS GOOD.

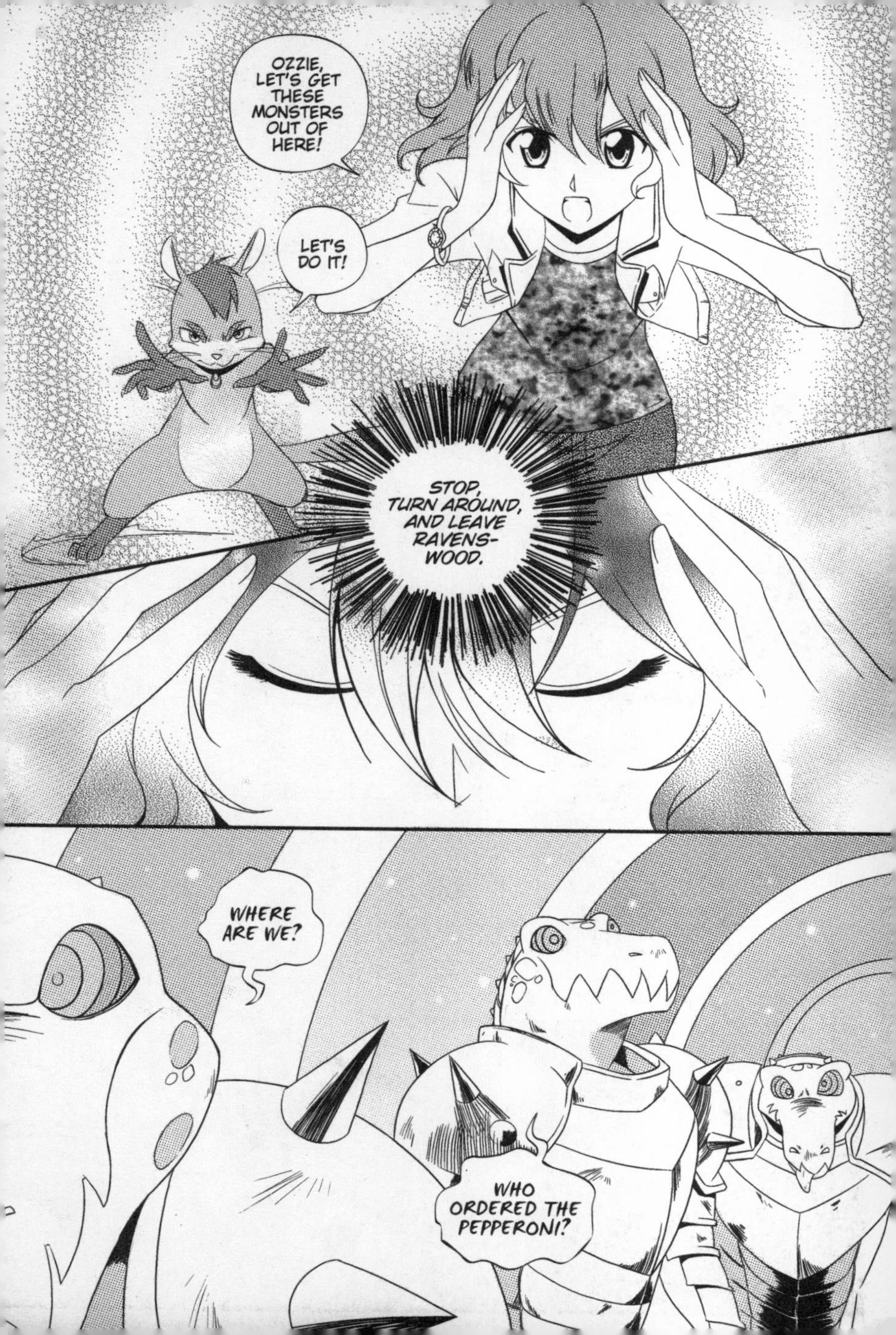
OZZIE, LET'S GET THESE MONSTERS OUT OF HERE!
LET'S DO IT!
STOP, TURN AROUND, AND LEAVE RAVENS-WOOD.
WHERE ARE WE?
WHO ORDERED THE PEPPERONI?

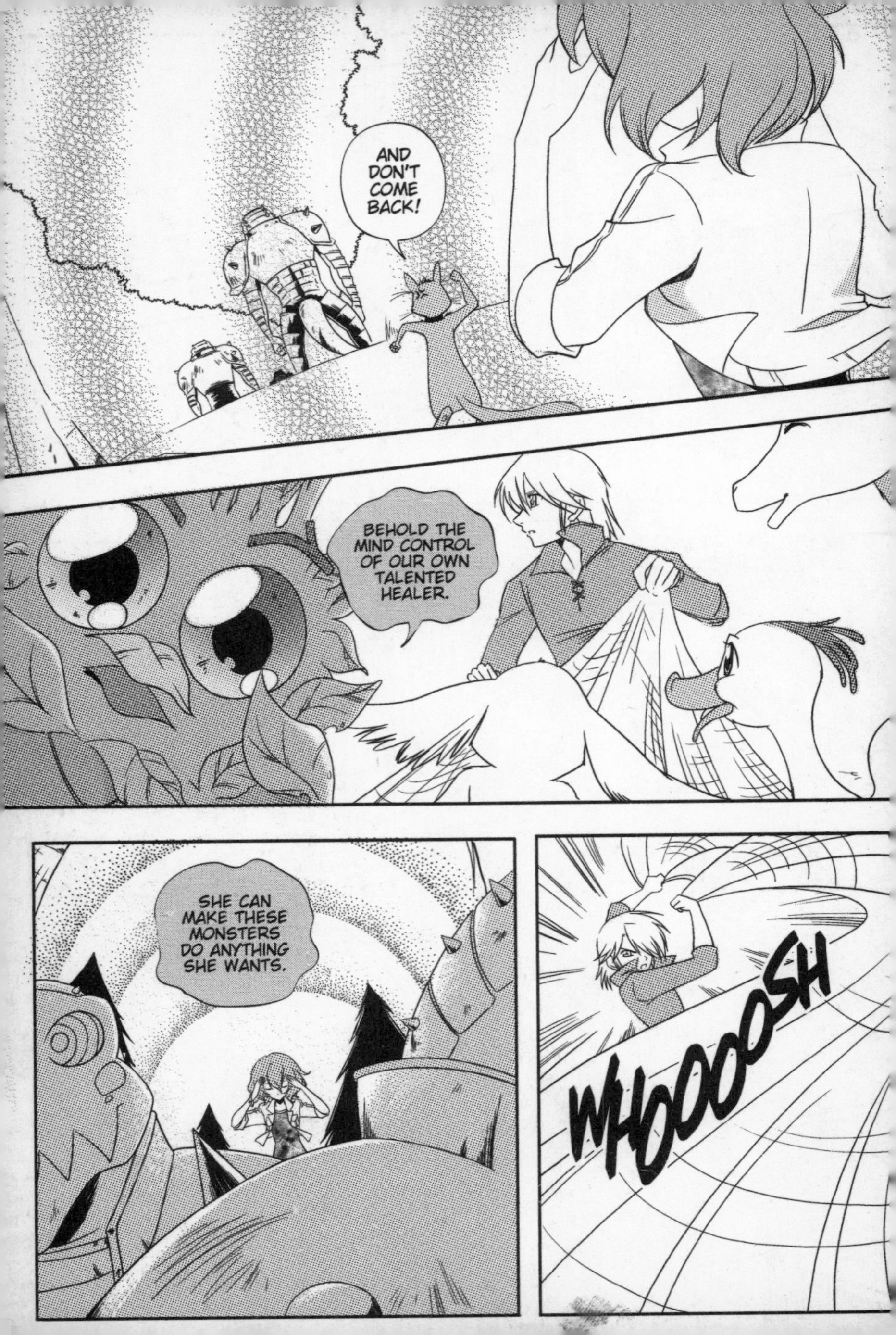
AND DON'T COME BACK!
BEHOLD THE MIND CONTROL OF OUR OWN TALENTED HEALER.
SHE CAN MAKE THESE MONSTERS DO ANYTHING SHE WANTS.
WHOOOOSH

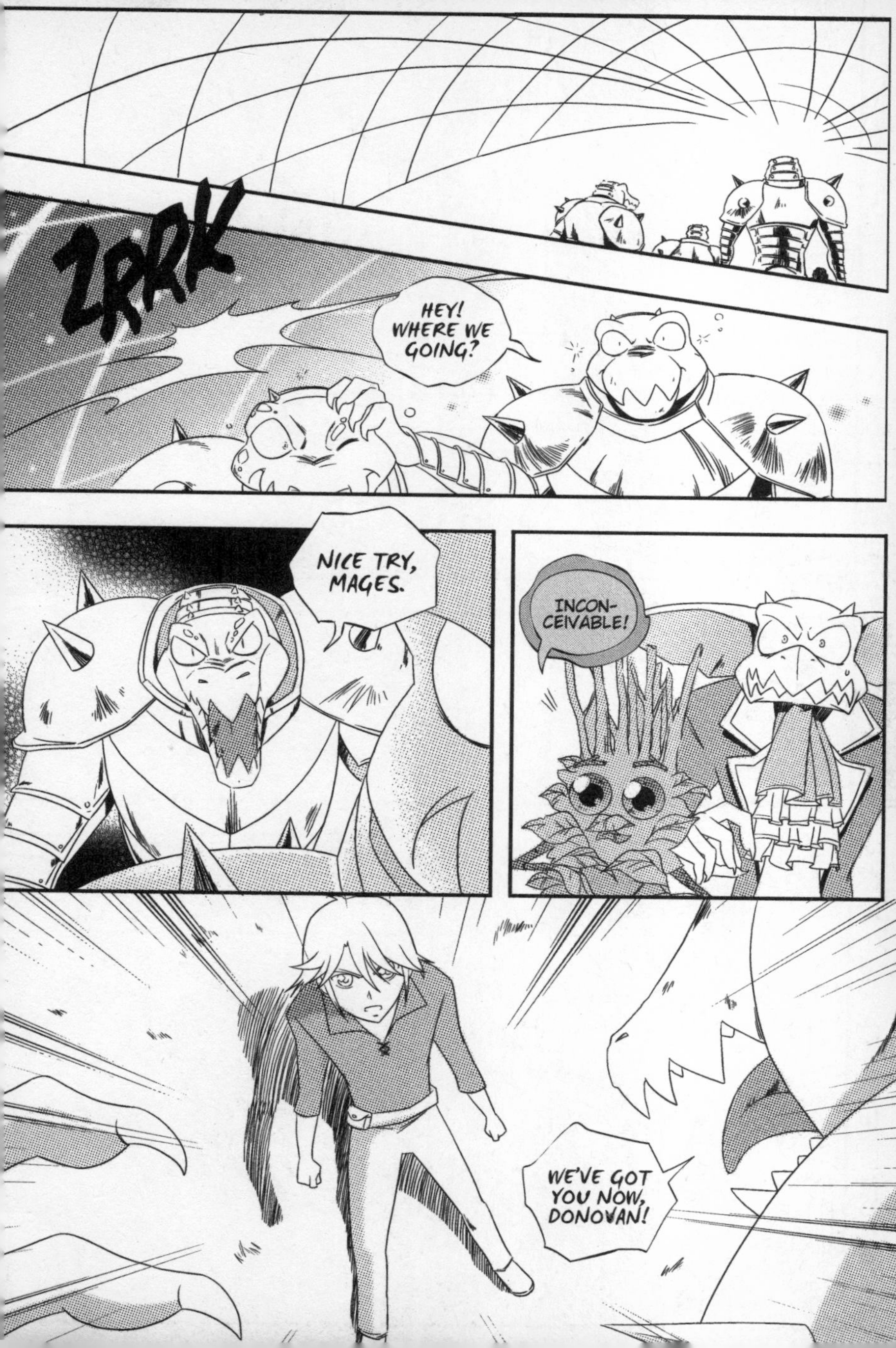
ZRRK
HEY! WHERE WE GOING?
NICE TRY, MAGES.
INCON-CEIVABLE!
WE'VE GOT YOU NOW, DONOVAN!

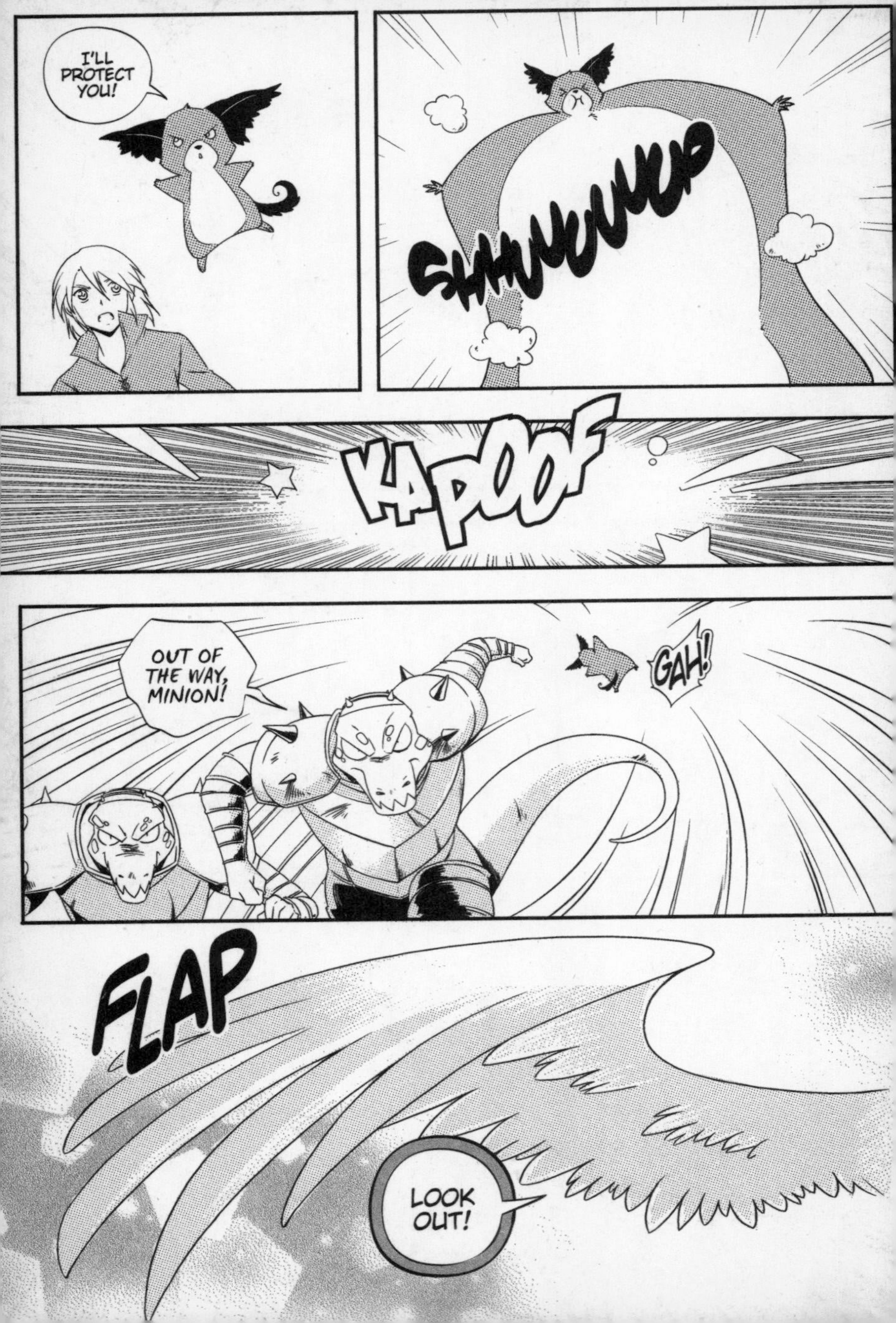
I'LL PROTECT YOU!
SHWUUUUP
KAPOOF
OUT OF THE WAY, MINION!
GAH!
FLAP
LOOK OUT!

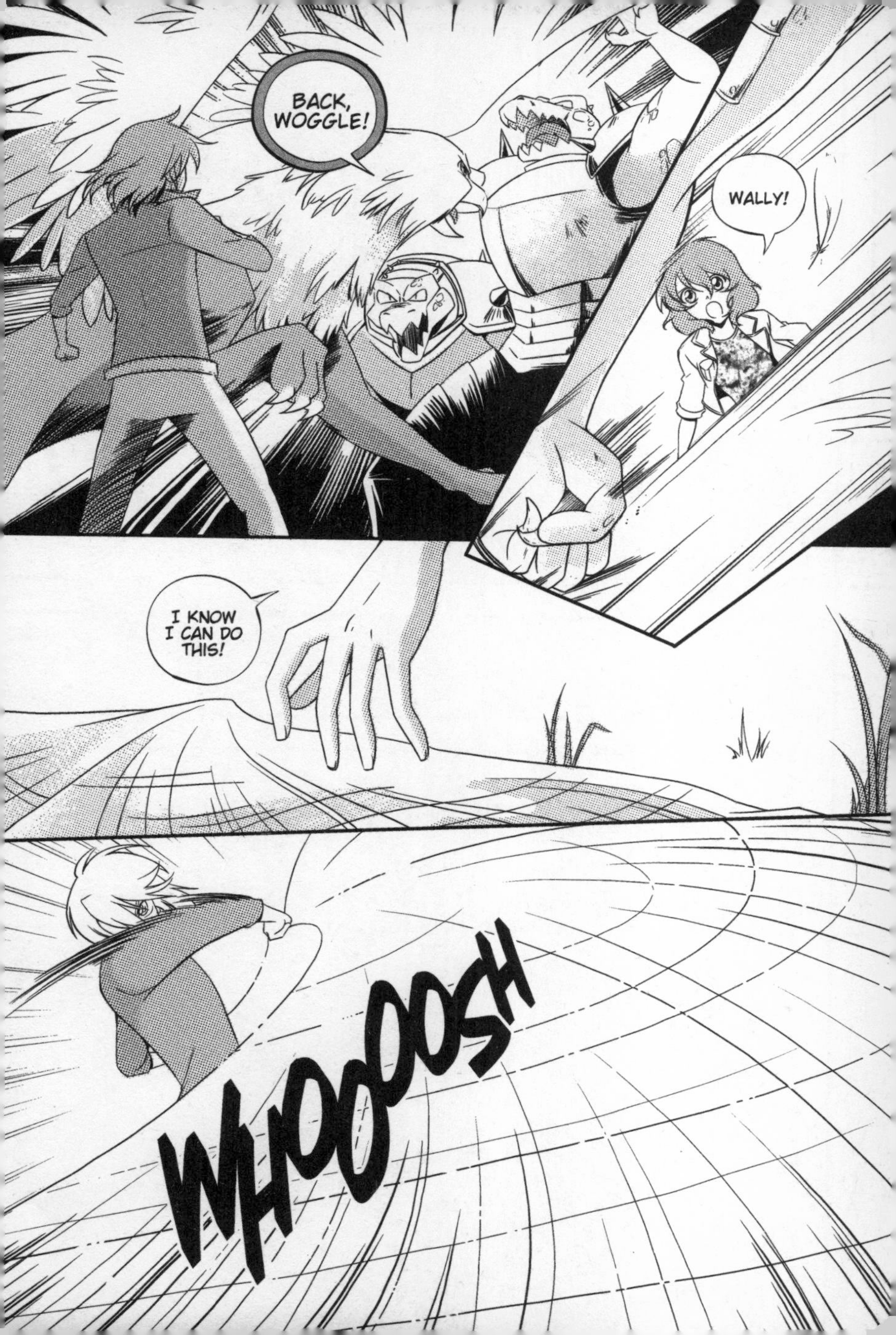
BACK, WOGGLE!
WALLY!
I KNOW I CAN DO THIS!
WHOOOOSH

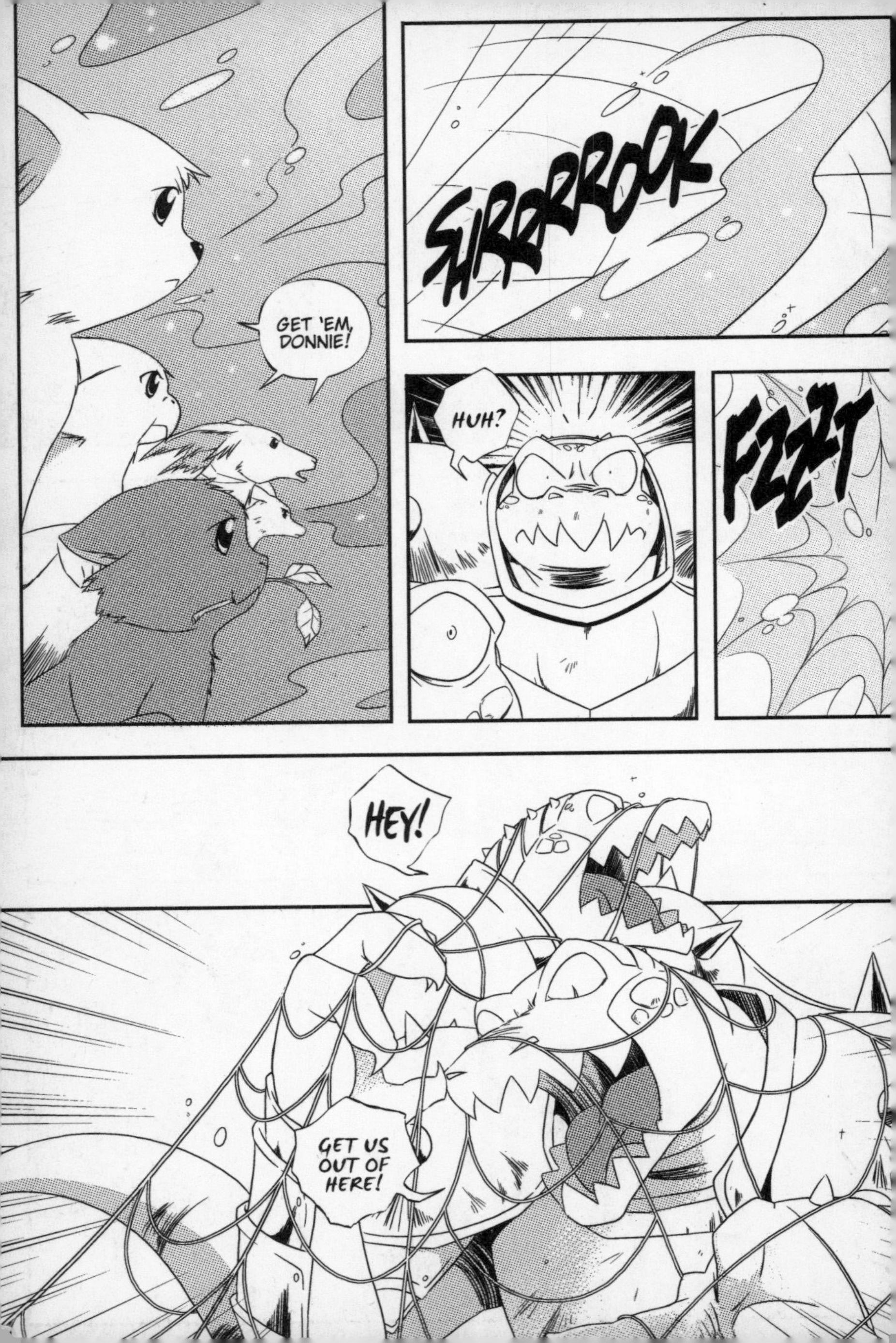
GET 'EM, DONNIE!
SHRRRROOK
HUH?
FZZZT
HEY!
GET US OUT OF HERE!

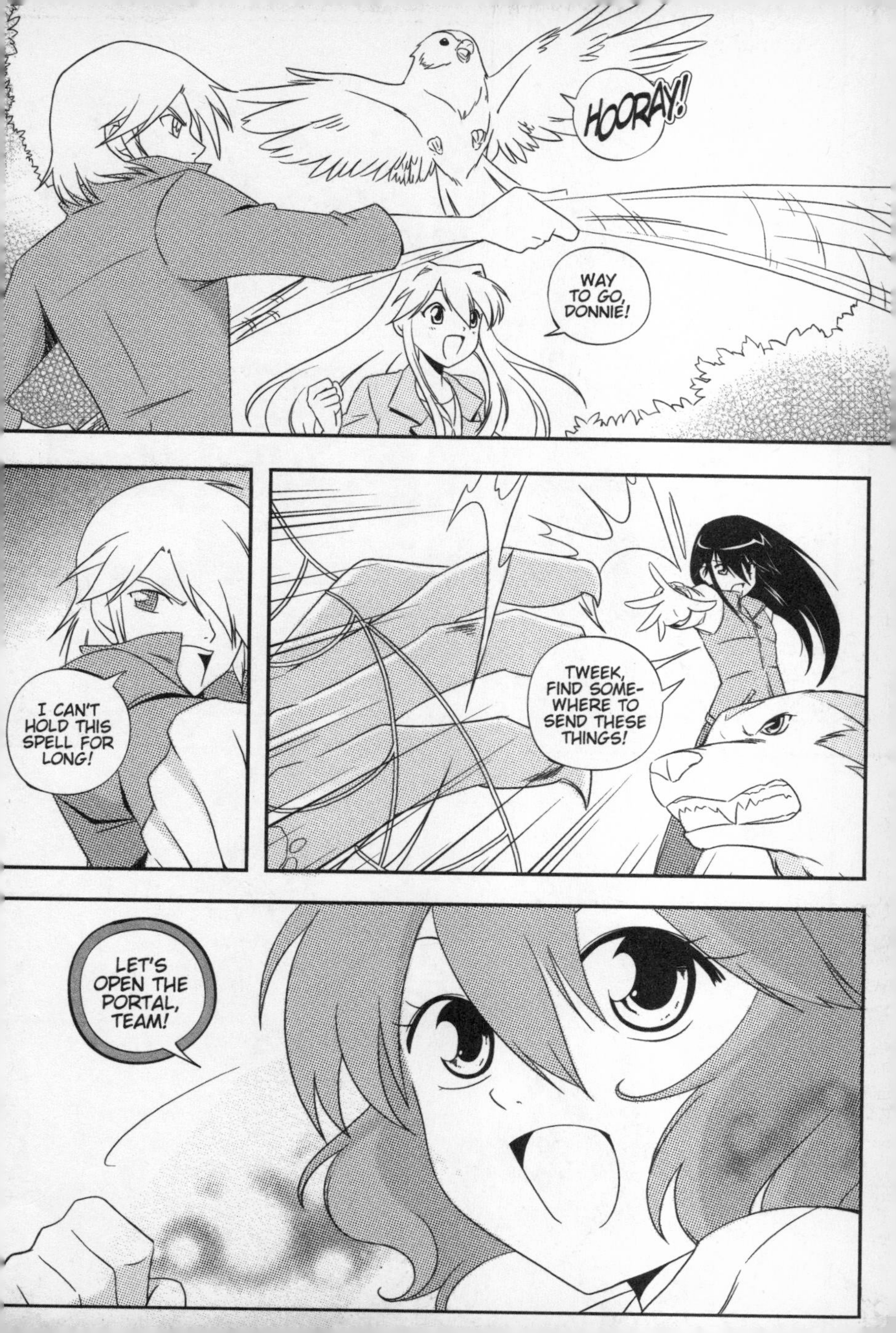
HOORAY!
WAY TO GO, DONNIE!
I CAN'T HOLD THIS SPELL FOR LONG!
TWEEK, FIND SOME-WHERE TO SEND THESE THINGS!
LET'S OPEN THE PORTAL, TEAM!

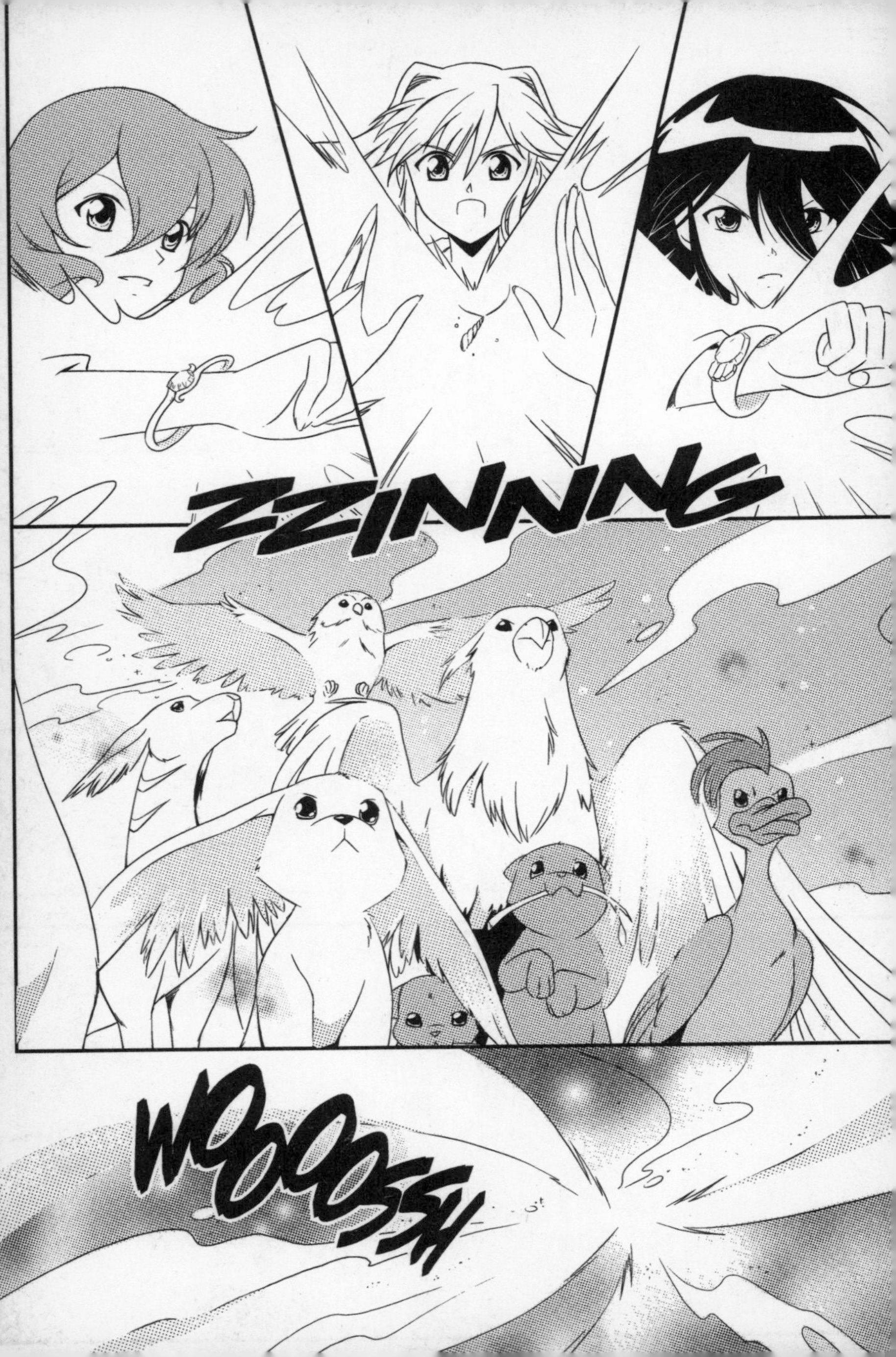
ZZINNNG
WOOOOSH

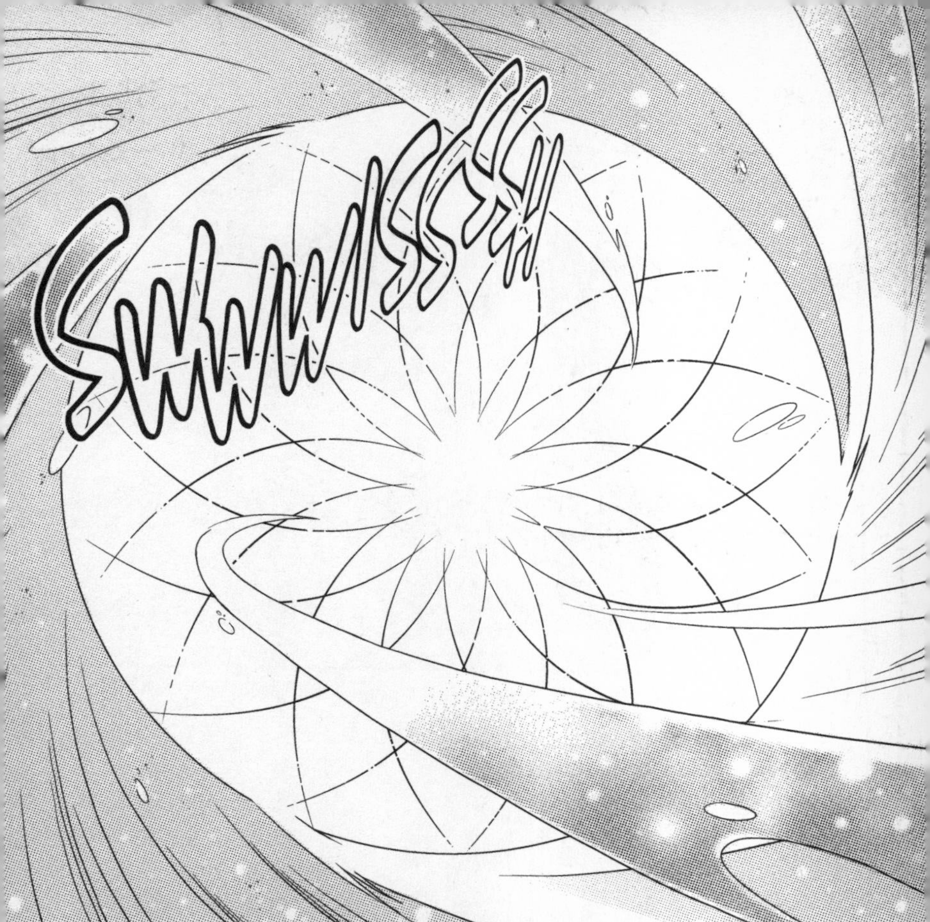
SWHWISSSSH

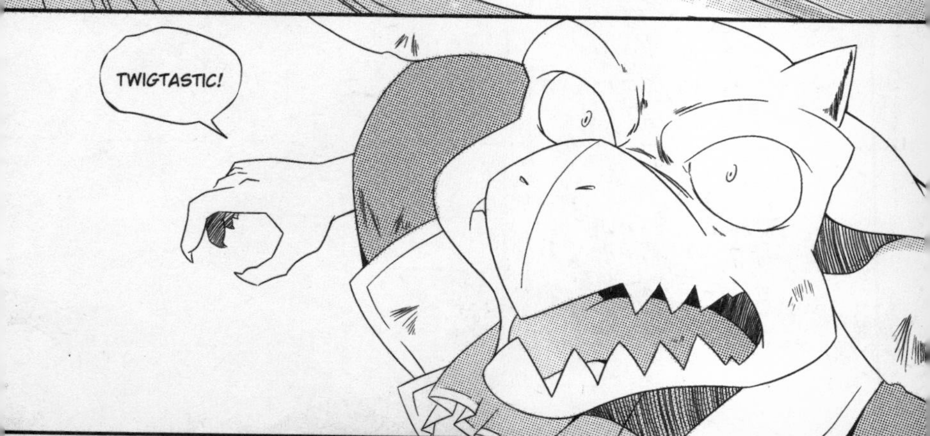
TWIGTASTIC!

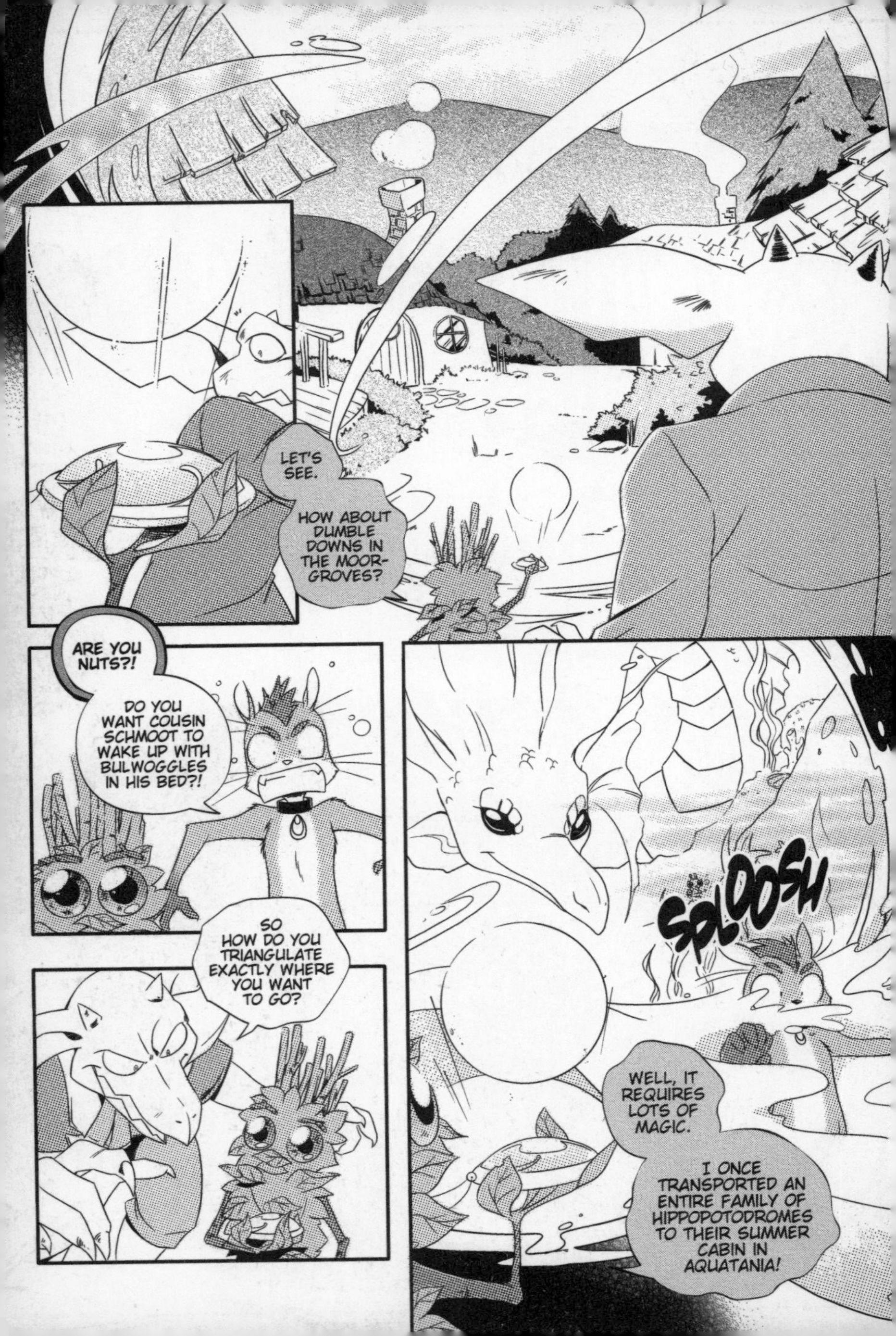
LET'S SEE.
HOW ABOUT DUMBLE DOWNS IN THE MOOR-GROVES?
ARE YOU NUTS?!
DO YOU WANT COUSIN SCHMOOT TO WAKE UP WITH BULWOGGLES IN HIS BED?!
SO HOW DO YOU TRIANGULATE EXACTLY WHERE YOU WANT TO GO?
SPLOOSH
WELL, IT REQUIRES LOTS OF MAGIC.
I ONCE TRANSPORTED AN ENTIRE FAMILY OF HIPPOPOTODROMES TO THEIR SUMMER CABIN IN AQUATANIA!

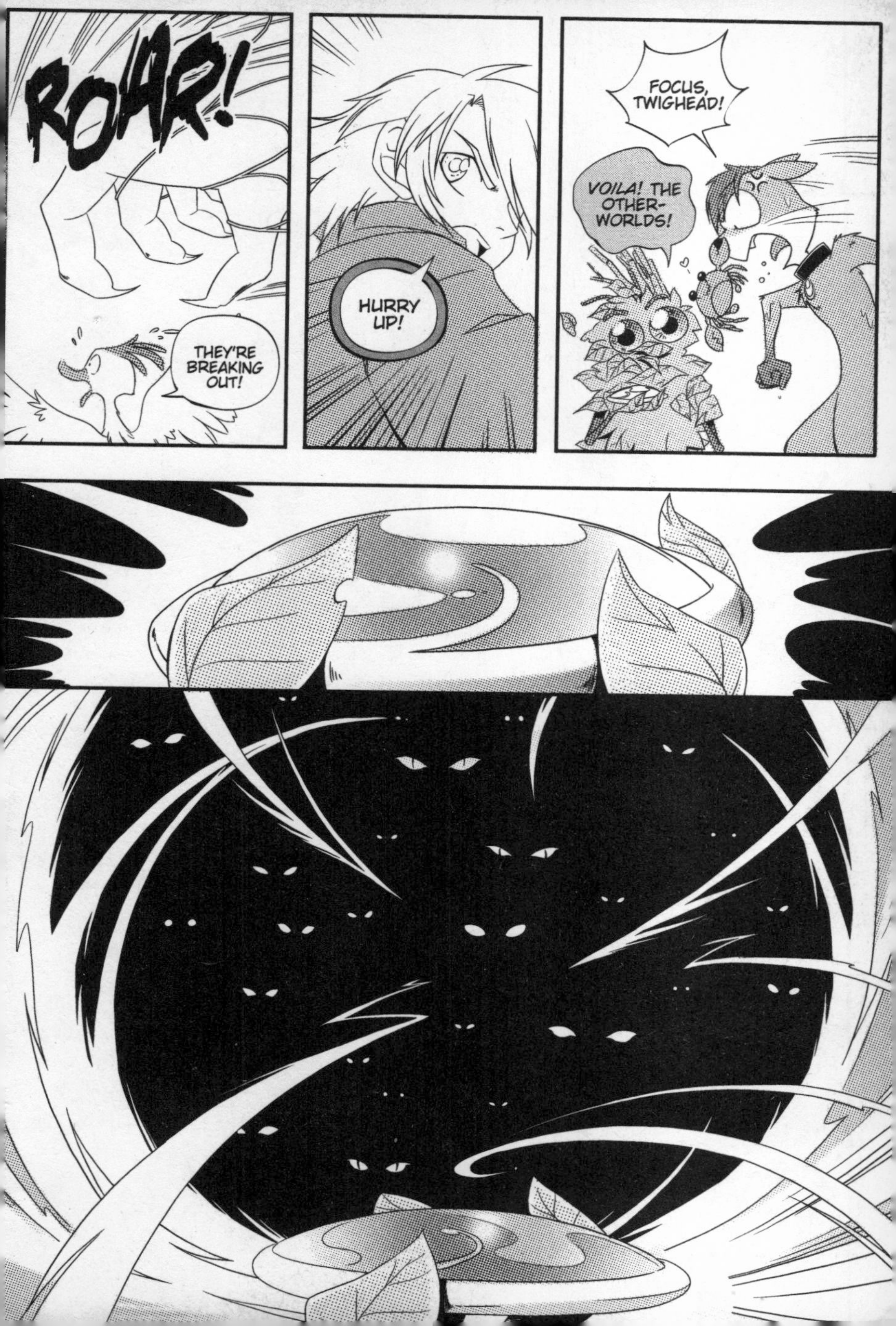
ROAR!
THEY'RE BREAKING OUT!
HURRY UP!
FOCUS, TWIGHEAD!
VOILA! THE OTHER-WORLDS!

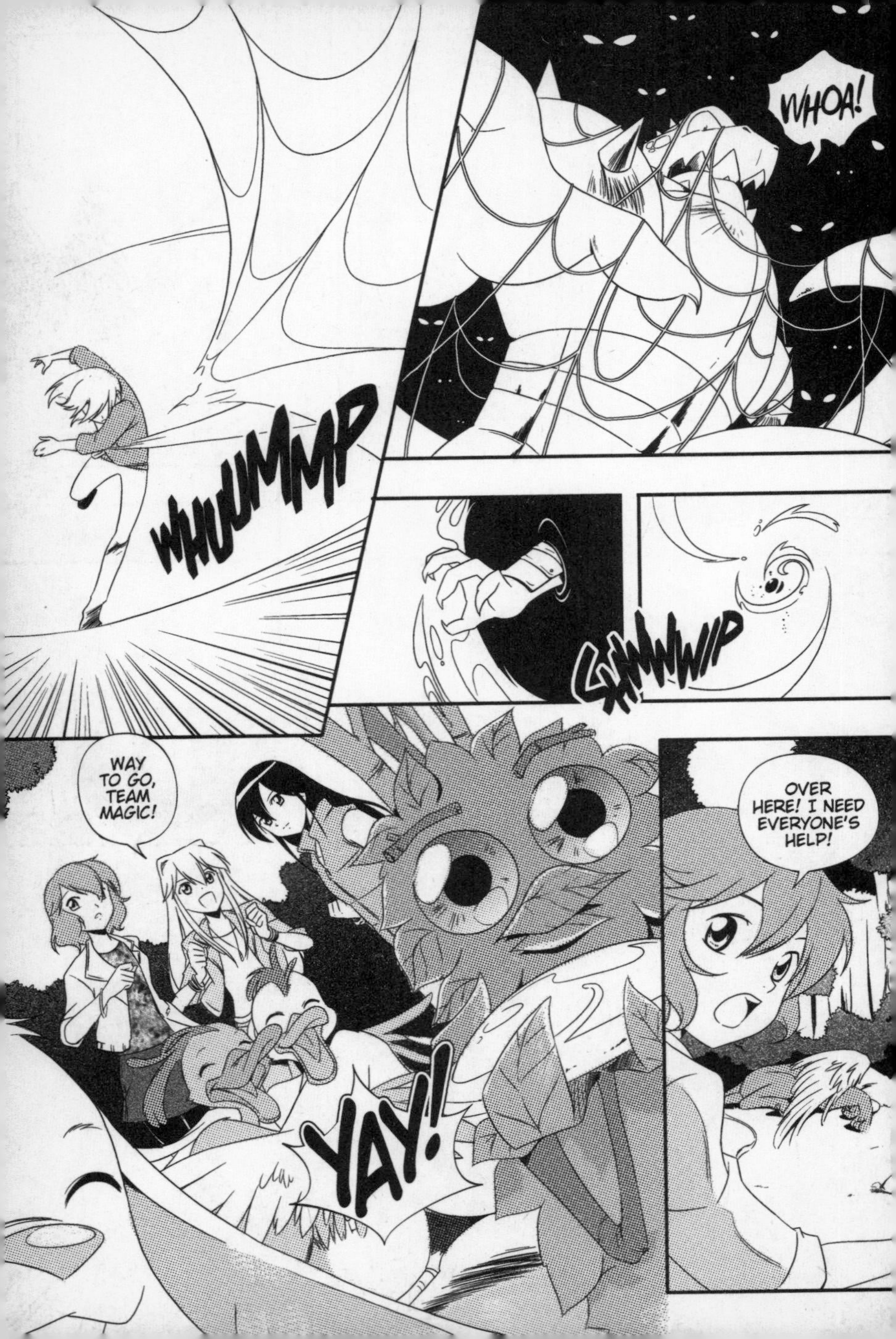
WHUUMMP
WHOA!
GWWWIP
WAY TO GO, TEAM MAGIC!
YAY!
OVER HERE! I NEED EVERYONE'S HELP!

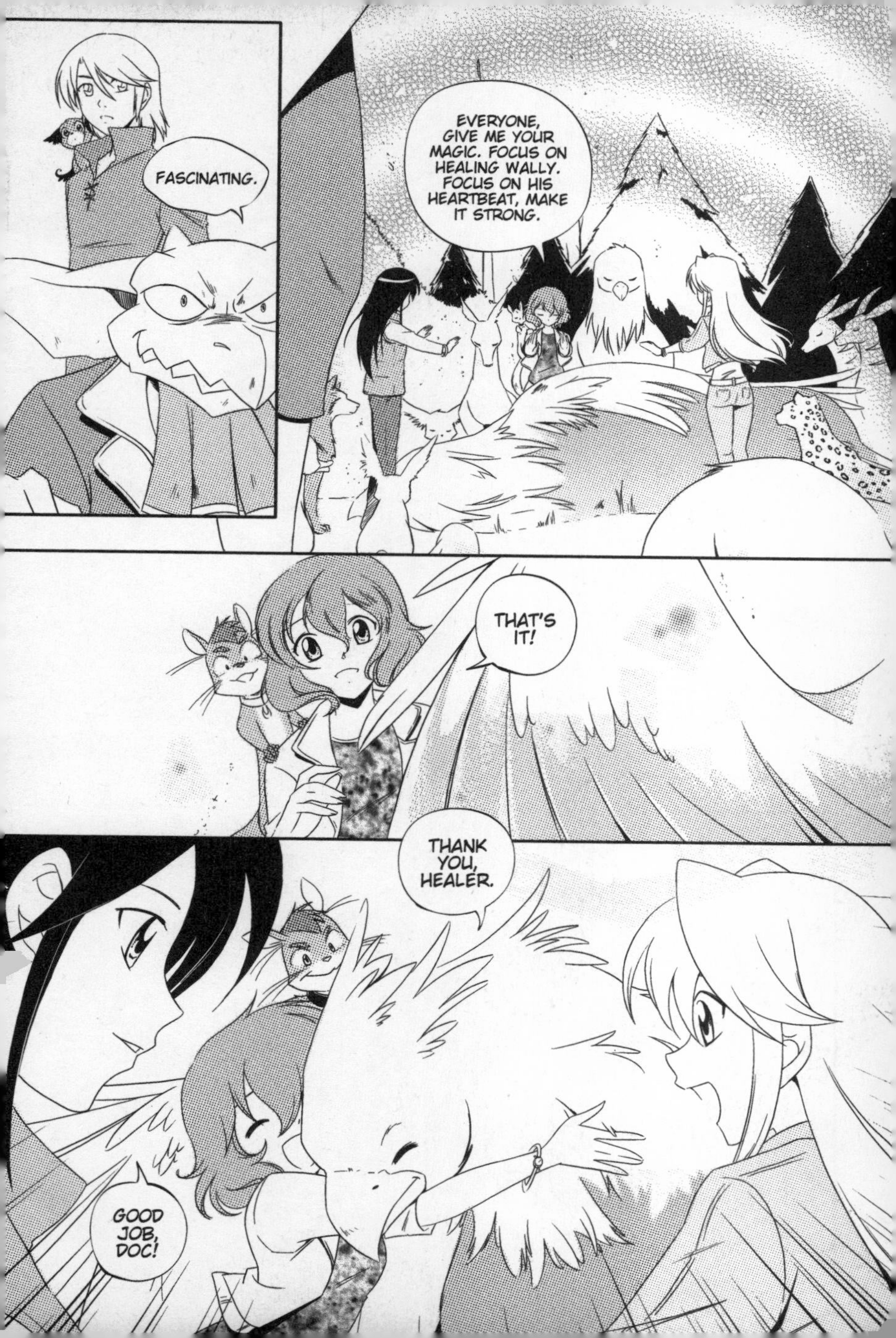
FASCINATING.
EVERYONE, GIVE ME YOUR MAGIC. FOCUS ON HEALING WALLY. FOCUS ON HIS HEARTBEAT, MAKE IT STRONG.
THAT'S IT!
THANK YOU, HEALER.
GOOD JOB, DOC!

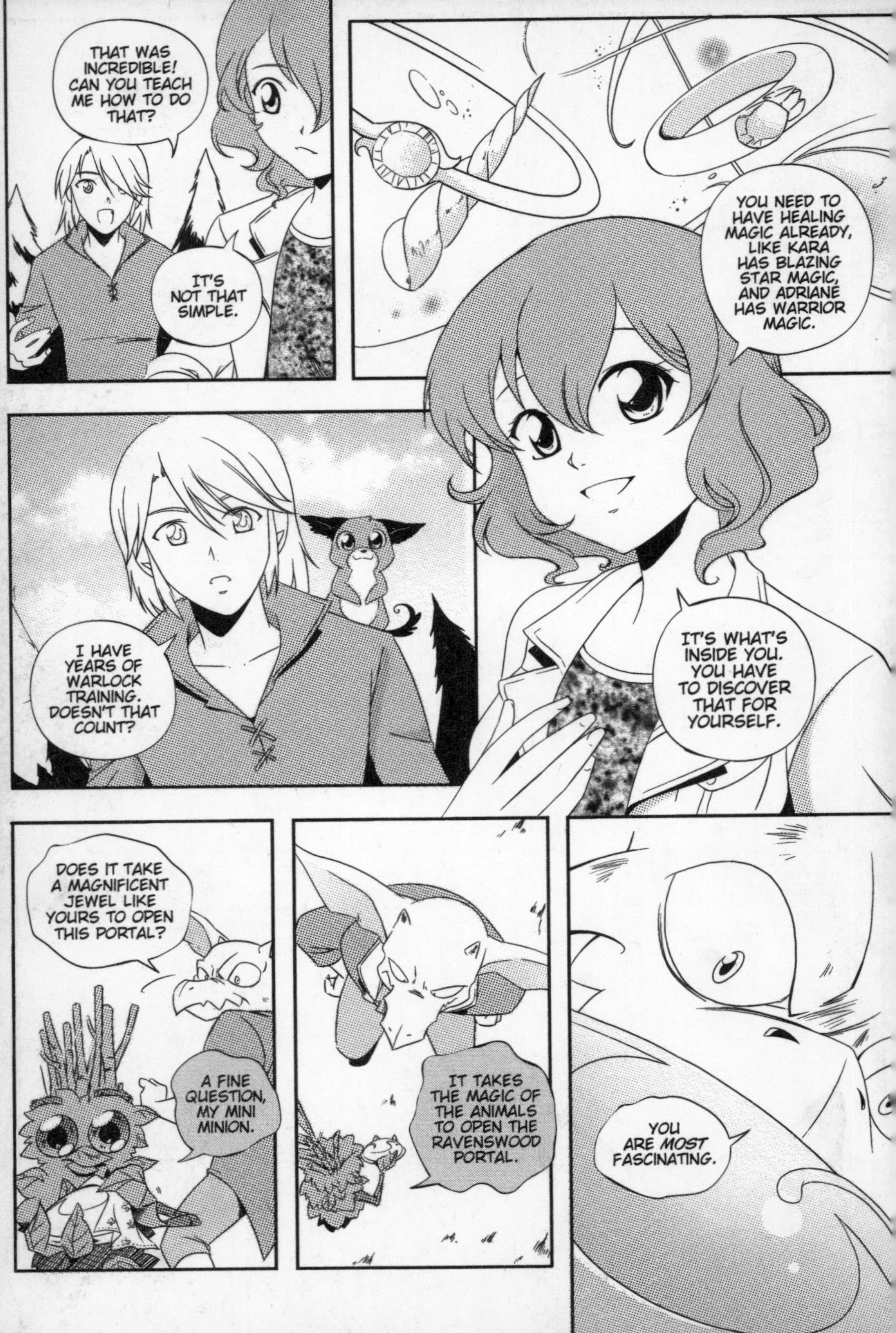
THAT WAS INCREDIBLE! CAN YOU TEACH ME HOW TO DO THAT?
IT'S NOT THAT SIMPLE.
YOU NEED TO HAVE HEALING MAGIC ALREADY, LIKE KARA HAS BLAZING STAR MAGIC, AND ADRIANE HAS WARRIOR MAGIC.
I HAVE YEARS OF WARLOCK TRAINING. DOESN'T THAT COUNT?
IT'S WHAT'S INSIDE YOU. YOU HAVE TO DISCOVER THAT FOR YOURSELF.
DOES IT TAKE A MAGNIFICENT JEWEL LIKE YOURS TO OPEN THIS PORTAL?
A FINE QUESTION, MY MINI MINION.
IT TAKES THE MAGIC OF THE ANIMALS TO OPEN THE RAVENSWOOD PORTAL.
YOU ARE *MOST* FASCINATING.

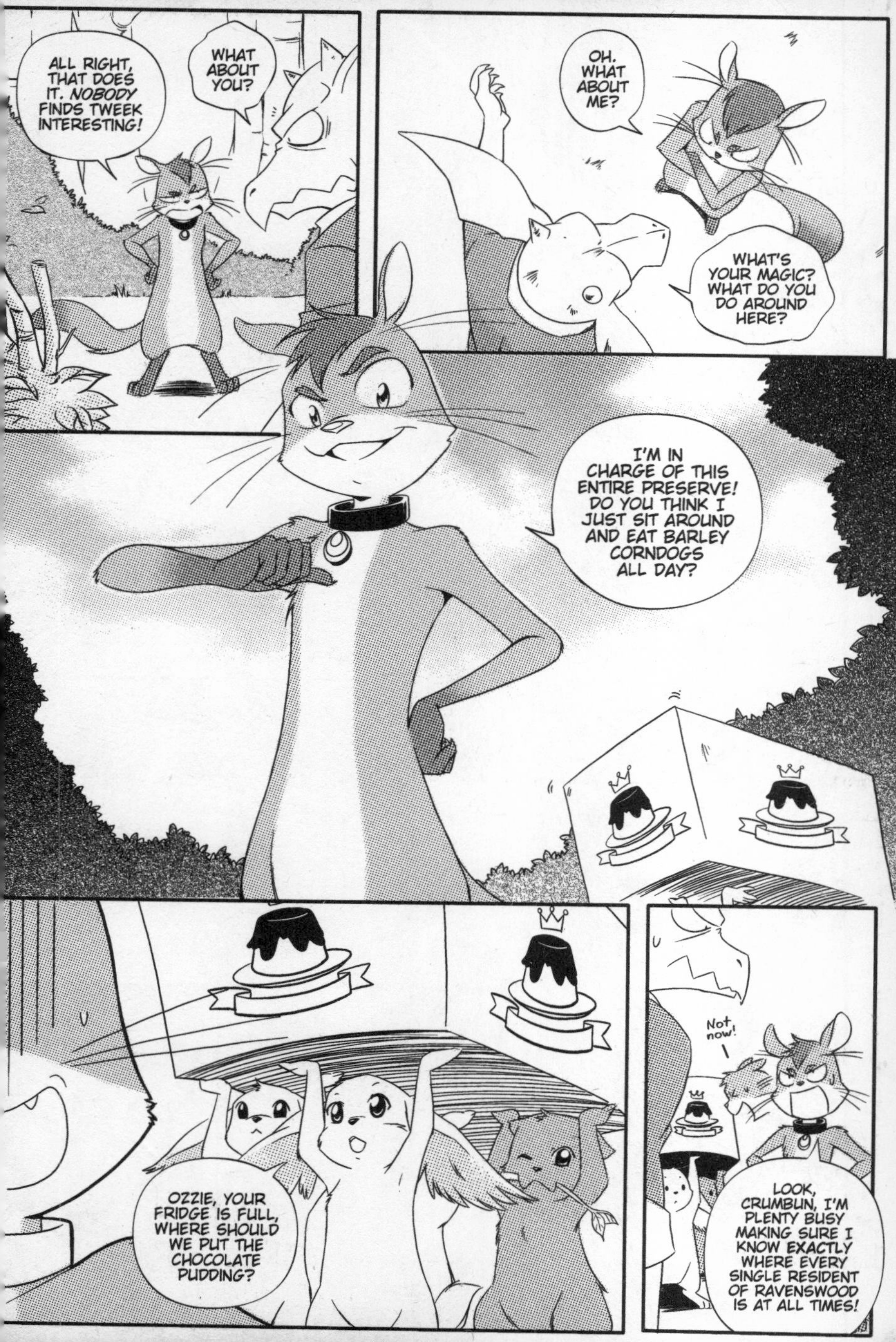
ALL RIGHT, THAT DOES IT. *NOBODY* FINDS TWEEK INTERESTING!
WHAT ABOUT YOU?
OH. WHAT ABOUT ME?
WHAT'S YOUR MAGIC? WHAT DO YOU DO AROUND HERE?
I'M IN CHARGE OF THIS ENTIRE PRESERVE! DO YOU THINK I JUST SIT AROUND AND EAT BARLEY CORNDOGS ALL DAY?
OZZIE, YOUR FRIDGE IS FULL, WHERE SHOULD WE PUT THE CHOCOLATE PUDDING?
Not now!
LOOK, CRUMBUN, I'M PLENTY BUSY MAKING SURE I KNOW EXACTLY WHERE EVERY SINGLE RESIDENT OF RAVENSWOOD IS AT ALL TIMES!

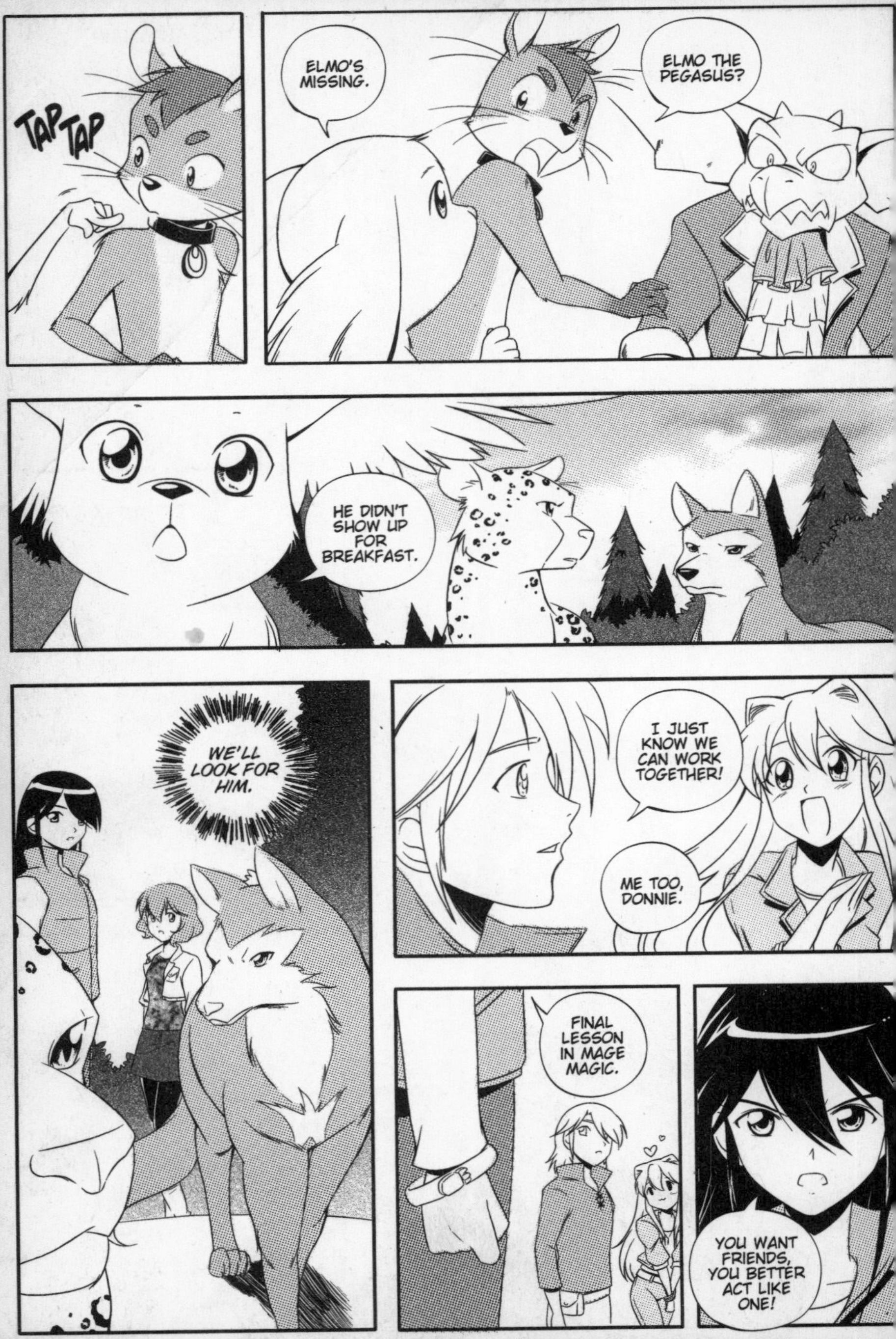
TAP TAP
ELMO'S MISSING.
ELMO THE PEGASUS?
HE DIDN'T SHOW UP FOR BREAKFAST.
WE'LL LOOK FOR HIM.
I JUST KNOW WE CAN WORK TOGETHER!
ME TOO, DONNIE.
FINAL LESSON IN MAGE MAGIC.
YOU WANT FRIENDS, YOU BETTER ACT LIKE ONE!

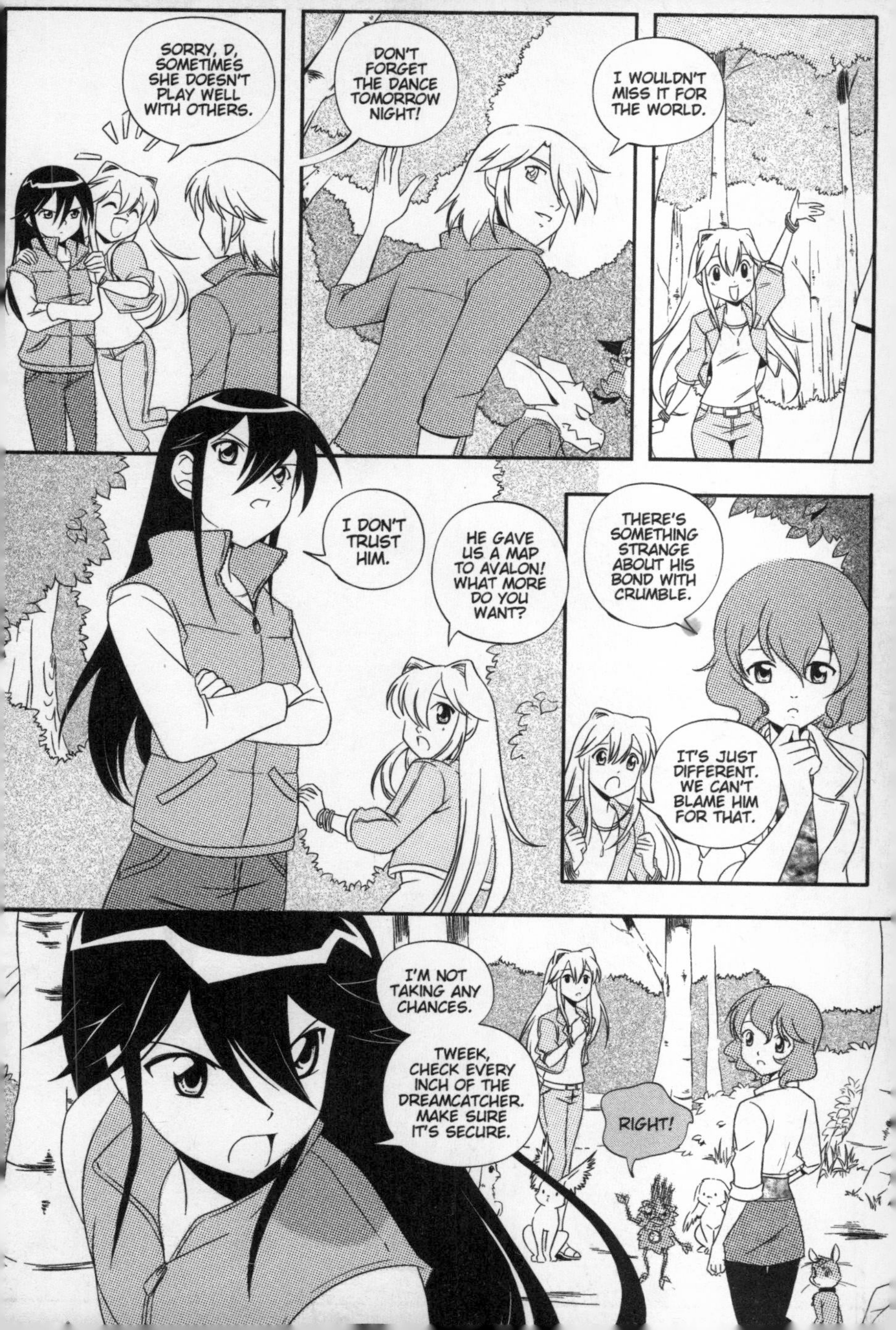
SORRY, D, SOMETIMES SHE DOESN'T PLAY WELL WITH OTHERS.
DON'T FORGET THE DANCE TOMORROW NIGHT!
I WOULDN'T MISS IT FOR THE WORLD.
I DON'T TRUST HIM.
HE GAVE US A MAP TO AVALON! WHAT MORE DO YOU WANT?
THERE'S SOMETHING STRANGE ABOUT HIS BOND WITH CRUMBLE.
IT'S JUST DIFFERENT. WE CAN'T BLAME HIM FOR THAT.
I'M NOT TAKING ANY CHANCES.
TWEEK, CHECK EVERY INCH OF THE DREAMCATCHER. MAKE SURE IT'S SECURE.
RIGHT!

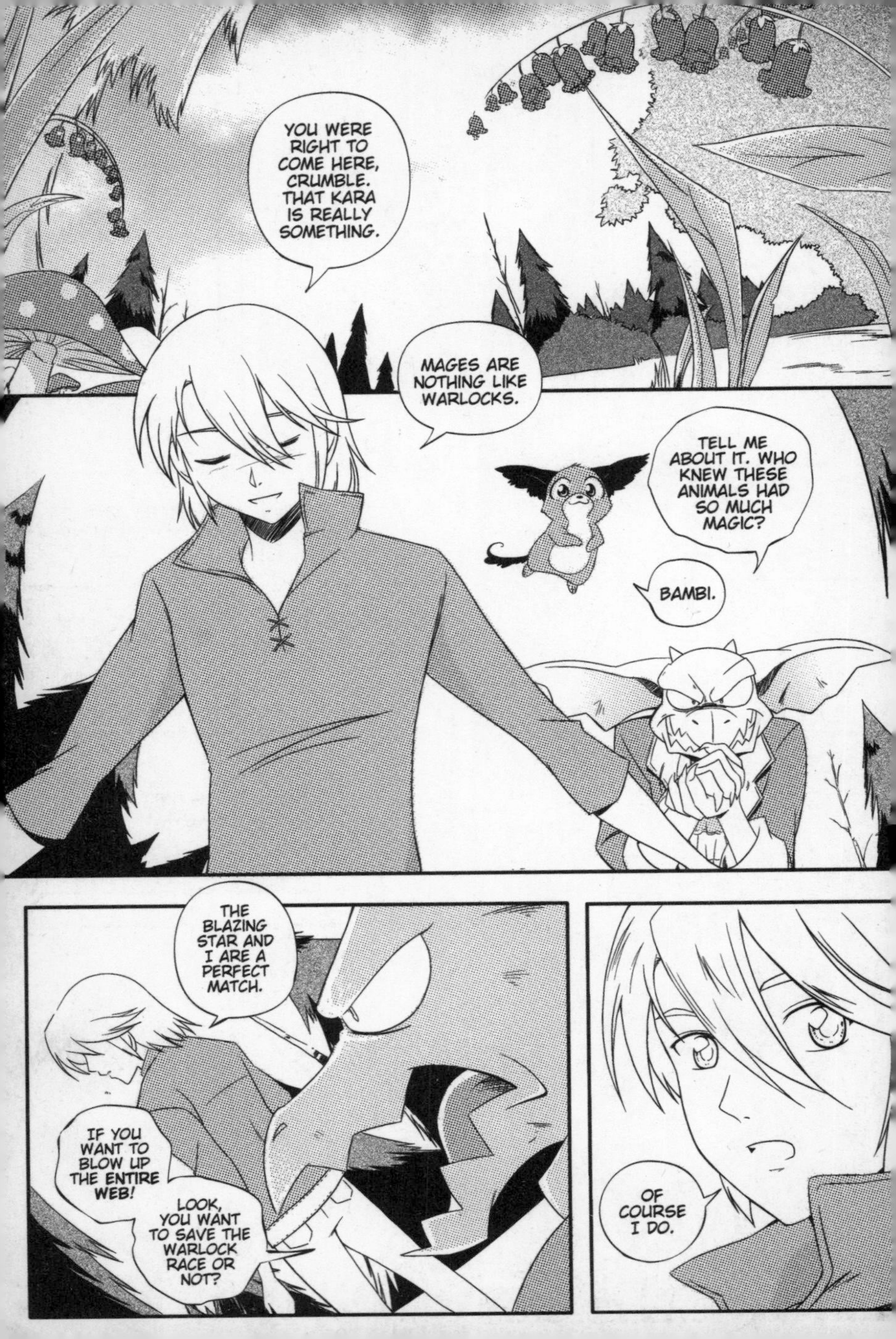
YOU WERE RIGHT TO COME HERE, CRUMBLE. THAT KARA IS REALLY SOMETHING.
MAGES ARE NOTHING LIKE WARLOCKS.
TELL ME ABOUT IT. WHO KNEW THESE ANIMALS HAD SO MUCH MAGIC?
BAMBI.
THE BLAZING STAR AND I ARE A PERFECT MATCH.
IF YOU WANT TO BLOW UP THE ENTIRE WEB!
LOOK, YOU WANT TO SAVE THE WARLOCK RACE OR NOT?
OF COURSE I DO.

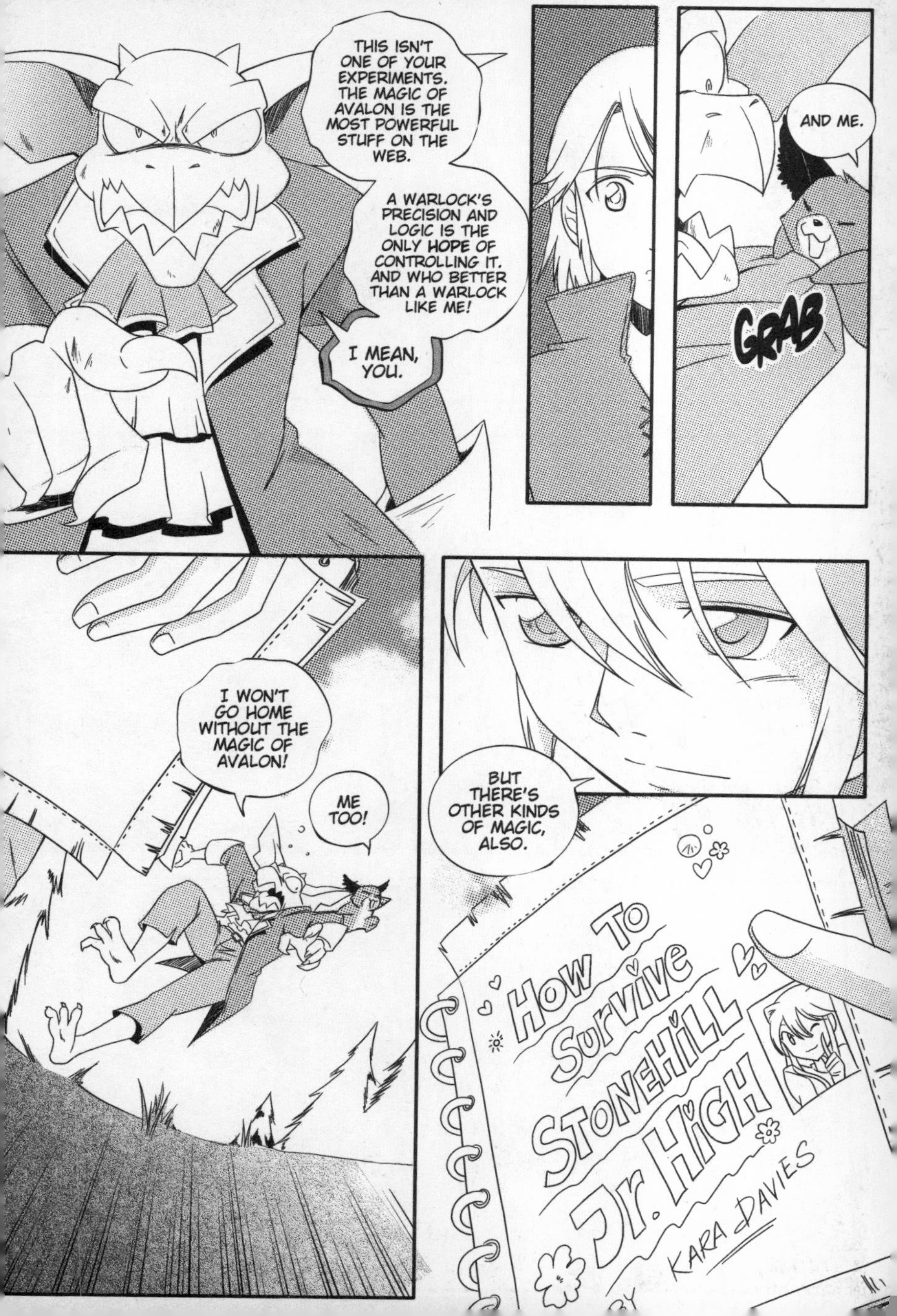
THIS ISN'T ONE OF YOUR EXPERIMENTS. THE MAGIC OF AVALON IS THE MOST POWERFUL STUFF ON THE WEB.
A WARLOCK'S PRECISION AND LOGIC IS THE ONLY HOPE OF CONTROLLING IT. AND WHO BETTER THAN A WARLOCK LIKE ME!
I MEAN, YOU.
AND ME.
GRAB
I WON'T GO HOME WITHOUT THE MAGIC OF AVALON!
ME TOO!
BUT THERE'S OTHER KINDS OF MAGIC, ALSO.
How To Survive StoneHill Jr. High
BY KARA DAVIES

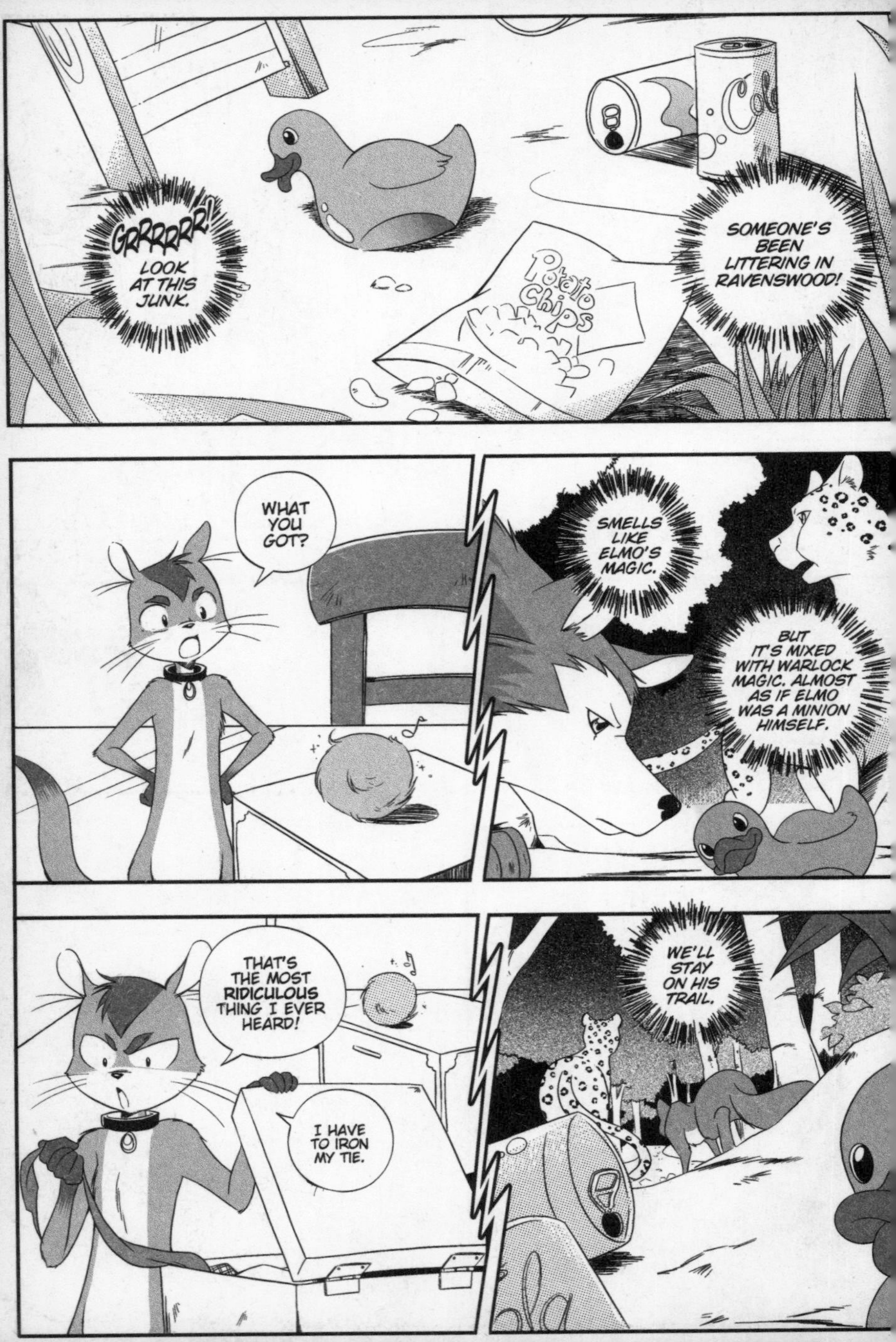
GRRRRRR! LOOK AT THIS JUNK.
SOMEONE'S BEEN LITTERING IN RAVENSWOOD!
Potato Chips
WHAT YOU GOT?
SMELLS LIKE ELMO'S MAGIC.
BUT IT'S MIXED WITH WARLOCK MAGIC. ALMOST AS IF ELMO WAS A MINION HIMSELF.
THAT'S THE MOST RIDICULOUS THING I EVER HEARD!
I HAVE TO IRON MY TIE.
WE'LL STAY ON HIS TRAIL.

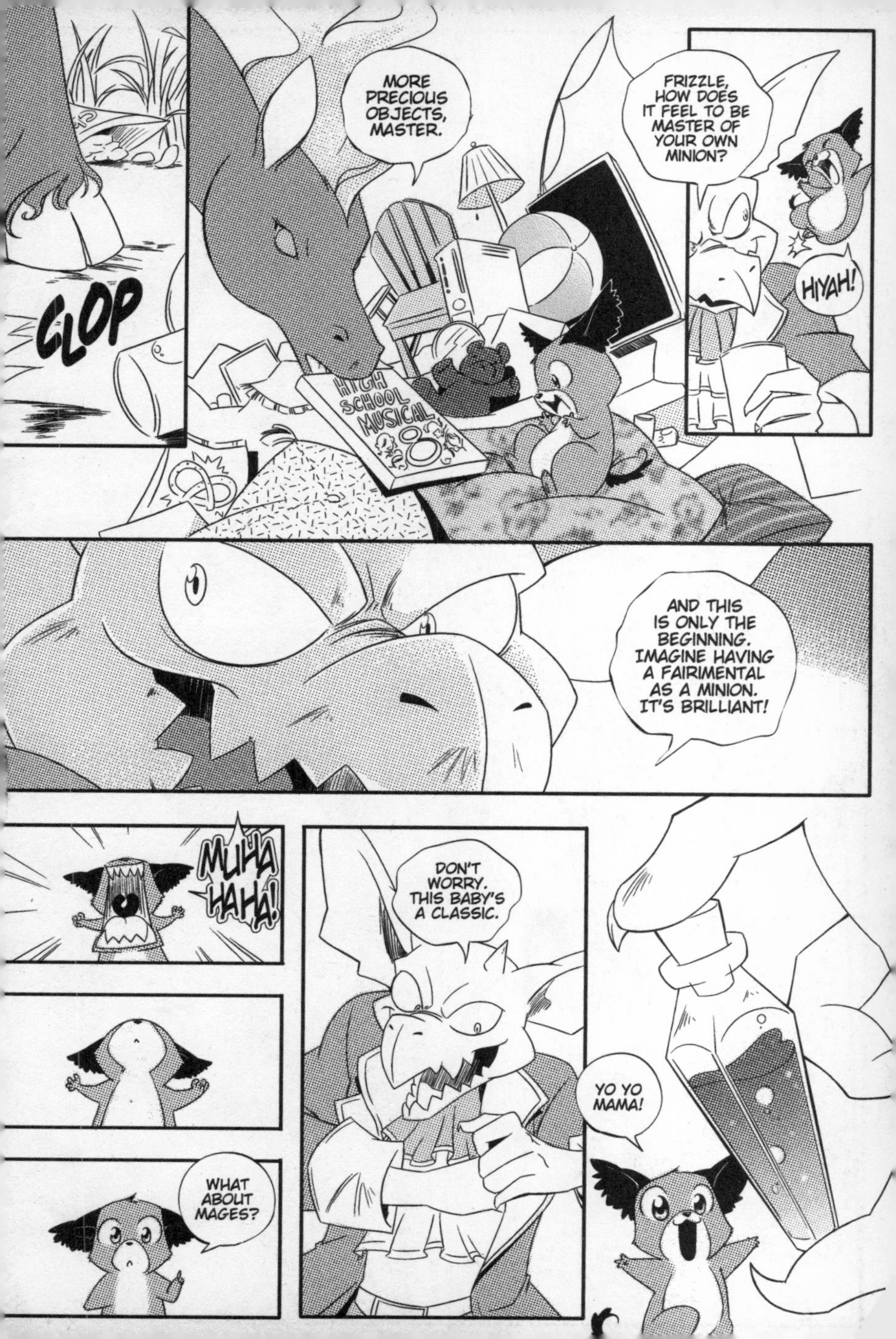
CLOP
HIGH SCHOOL MUSICAL 8
MORE PRECIOUS OBJECTS, MASTER.
FRIZZLE, HOW DOES IT FEEL TO BE MASTER OF YOUR OWN MINION?
HIYAH!
AND THIS IS ONLY THE BEGINNING. IMAGINE HAVING A FAIRIMENTAL AS A MINION. IT'S BRILLIANT!
MUHA HAHA!
WHAT ABOUT MAGES?
DON'T WORRY. THIS BABY'S A CLASSIC.
YO YO MAMA!

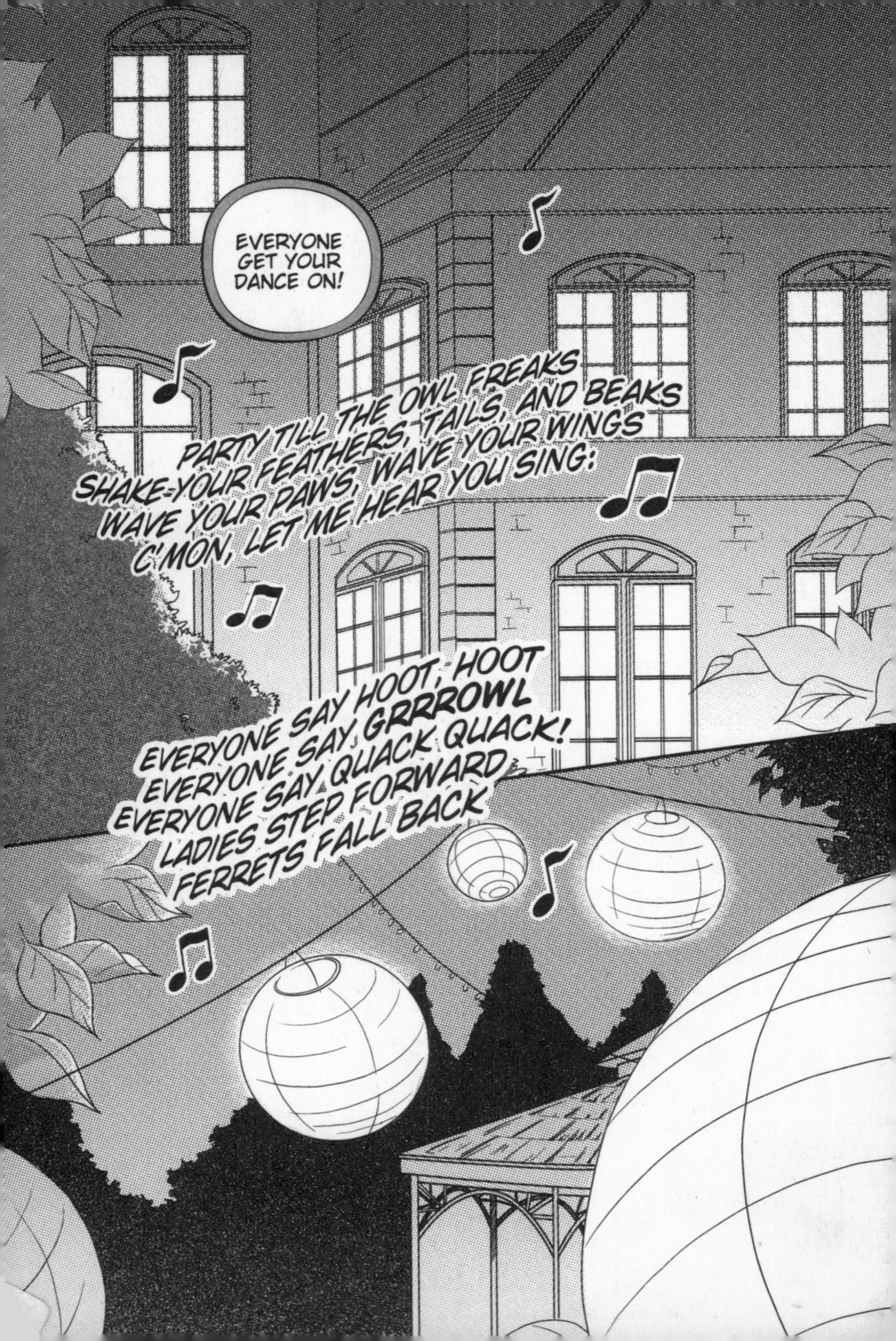
EVERYONE GET YOUR DANCE ON!
PARTY TILL THE OWL FREAKS
SHAKE YOUR FEATHERS, TAILS, AND BEAKS
WAVE YOUR PAWS, WAVE YOUR WINGS
C'MON, LET ME HEAR YOU SING:
EVERYONE SAY HOOT, HOOT
EVERYONE SAY GRRROWL
EVERYONE SAY QUACK QUACK!
LADIES STEP FORWARD
FERRETS FALL BACK

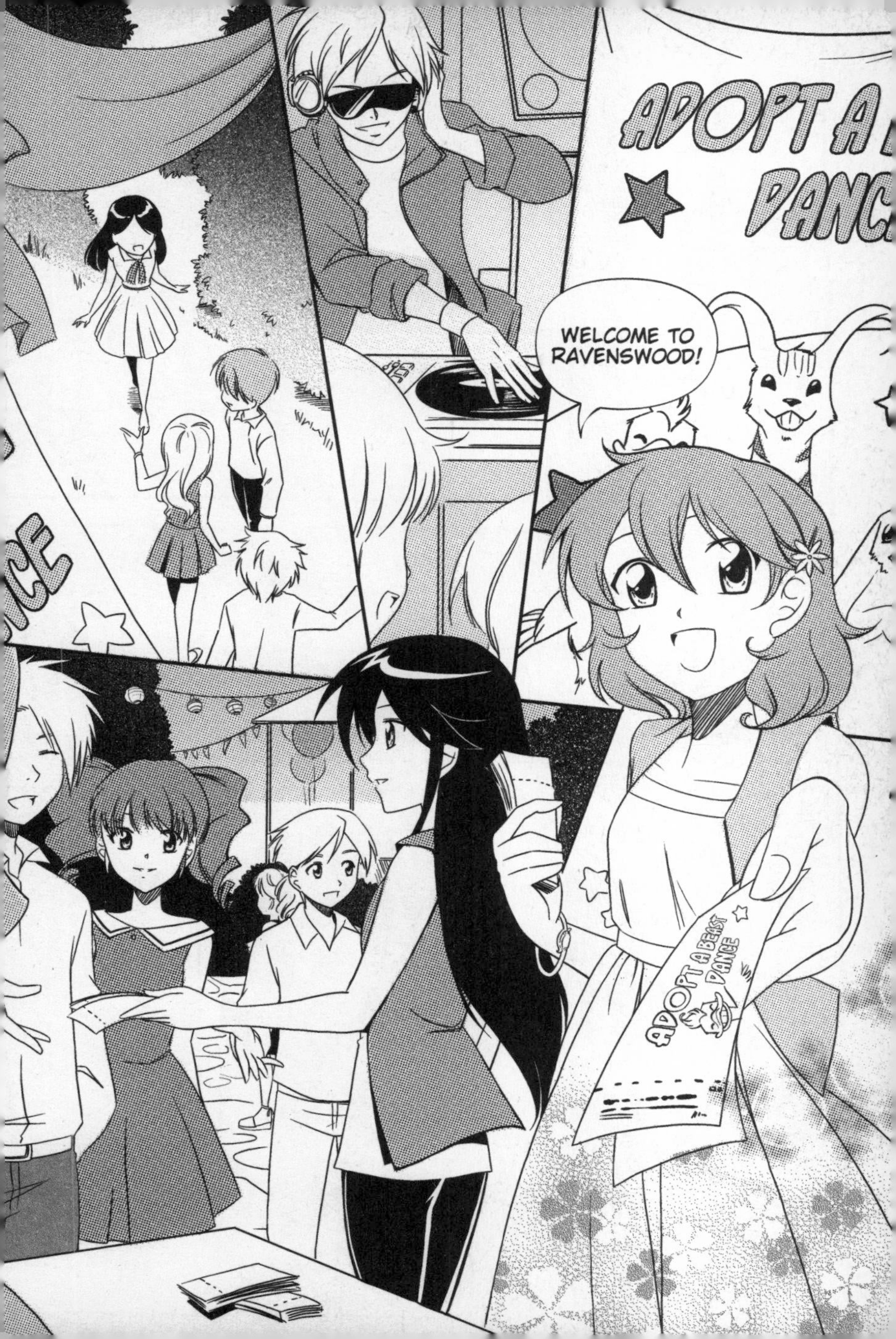
ADOPT A
WELCOME TO RAVENSWOOD!
ADOPT A BEAST DANCE

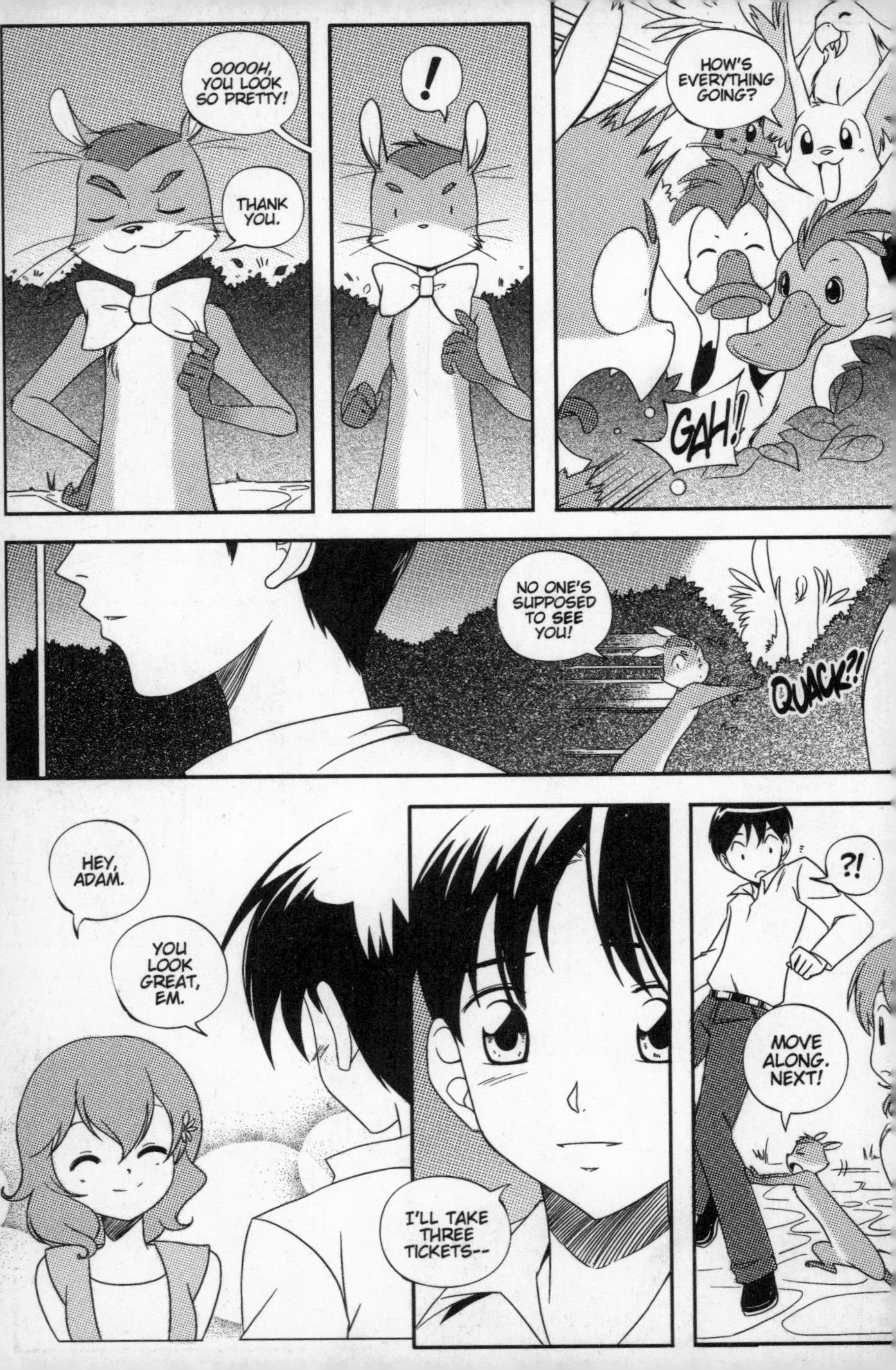
OOOOH, YOU LOOK SO PRETTY!
THANK YOU.
!
HOW'S EVERYTHING GOING?
GAH!!
NO ONE'S SUPPOSED TO SEE YOU!
QUACK?!
HEY, ADAM.
YOU LOOK GREAT, EM.
I'LL TAKE THREE TICKETS--
?!
MOVE ALONG. NEXT!

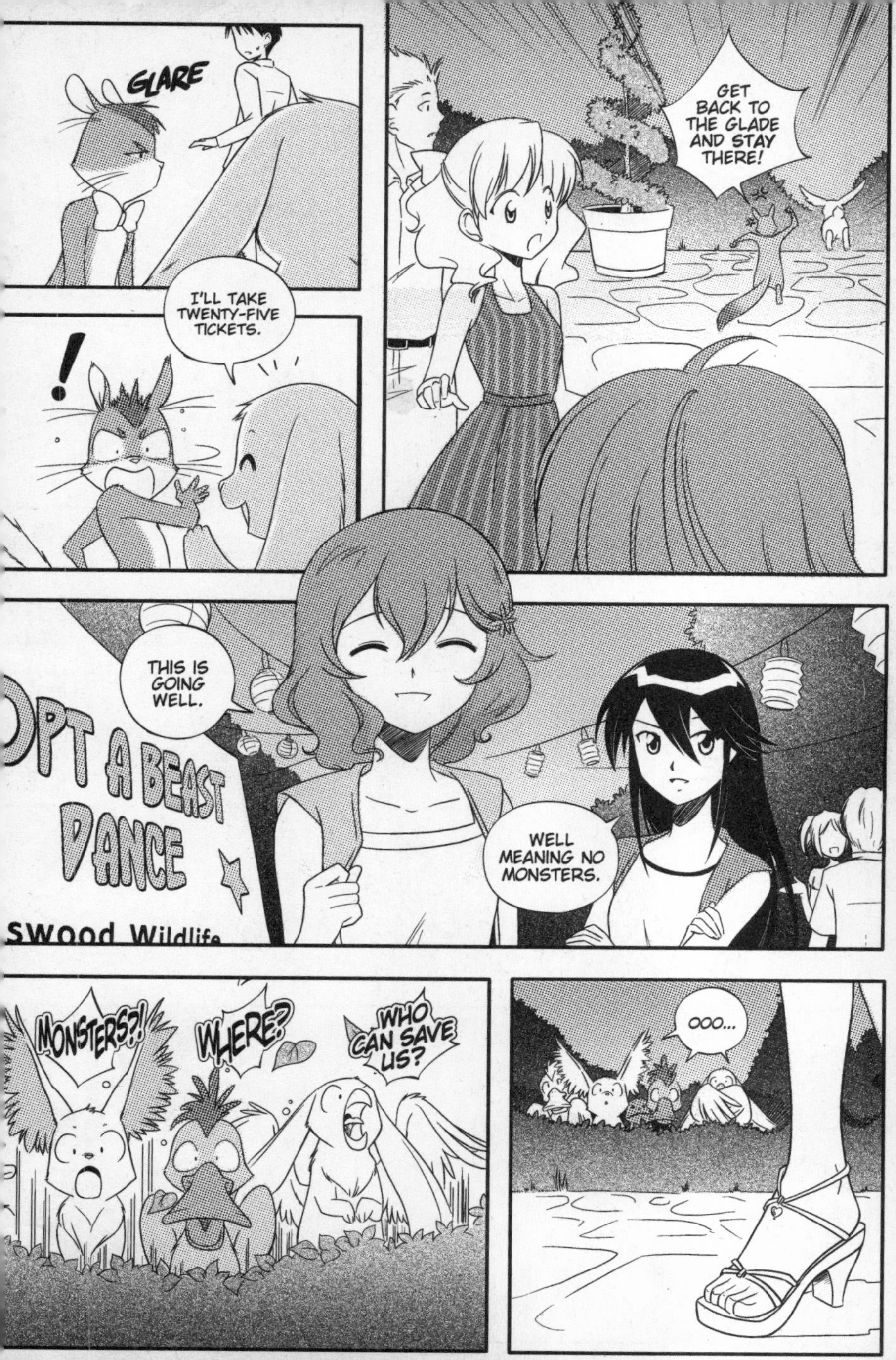
GLARE
I'LL TAKE TWENTY-FIVE TICKETS.
!
GET BACK TO THE GLADE AND STAY THERE!
THIS IS GOING WELL.
OPT A BEAST DANCE
SWOOD Wildlife
WELL MEANING NO MONSTERS.
MONSTERS?!
WHERE?
WHO CAN SAVE US?
OOO...

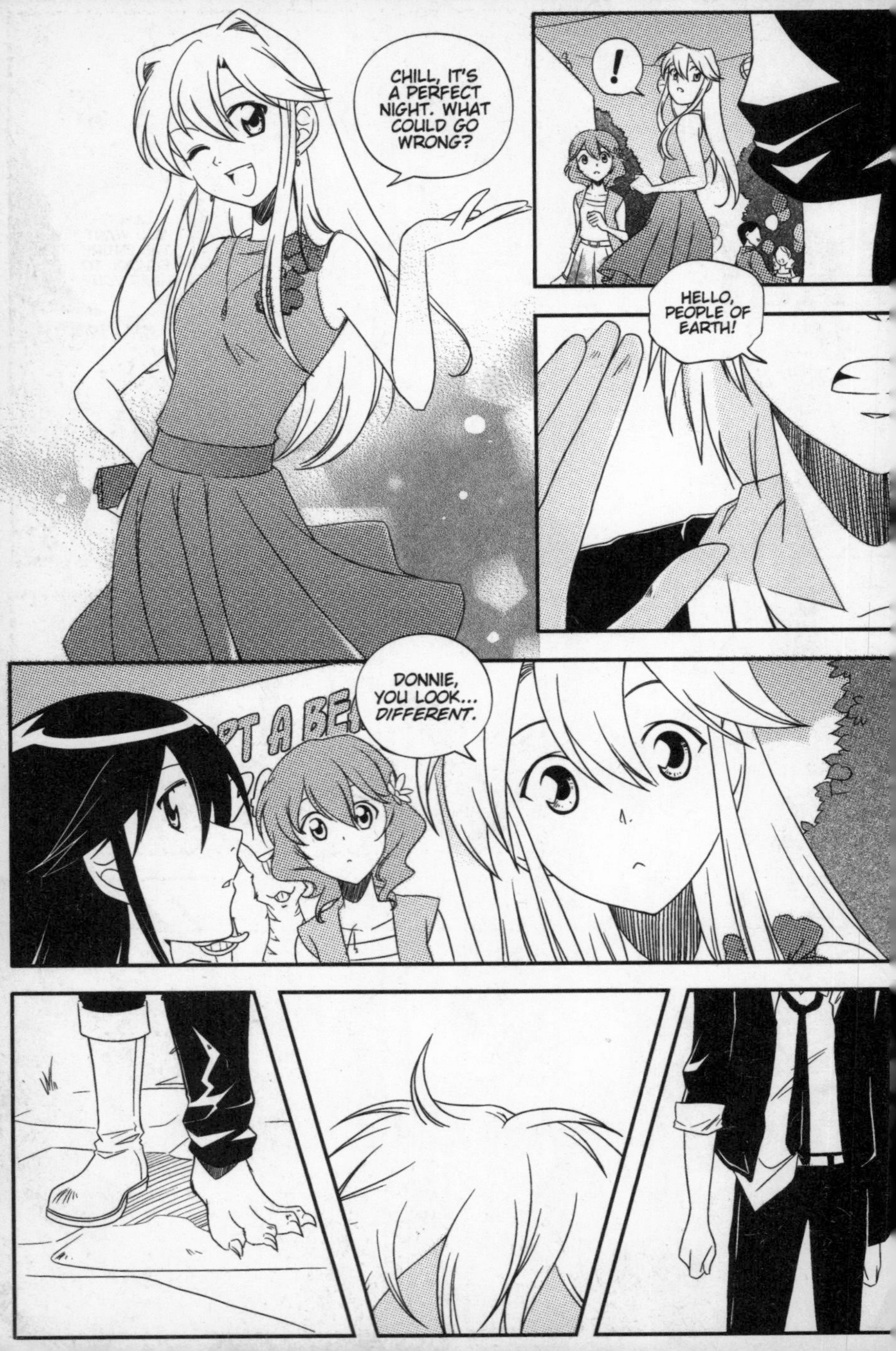
CHILL, IT'S A PERFECT NIGHT. WHAT COULD GO WRONG?
!
HELLO, PEOPLE OF EARTH!
DONNIE, YOU LOOK... DIFFERENT.

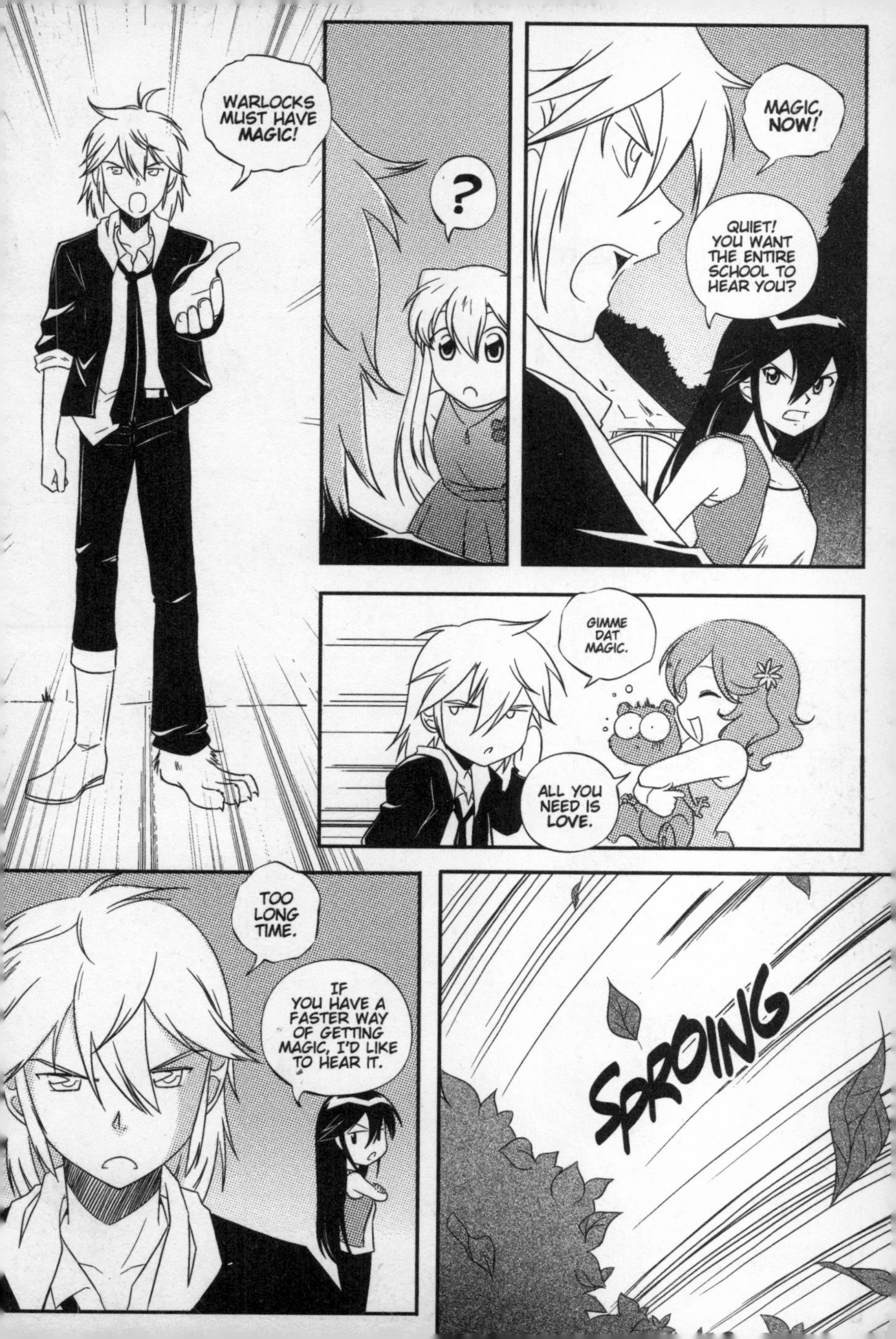
WARLOCKS MUST HAVE MAGIC!
?
MAGIC, NOW!
QUIET! YOU WANT THE ENTIRE SCHOOL TO HEAR YOU?
GIMME DAT MAGIC.
ALL YOU NEED IS LOVE.
TOO LONG TIME.
IF YOU HAVE A FASTER WAY OF GETTING MAGIC, I'D LIKE TO HEAR IT.
SPROING

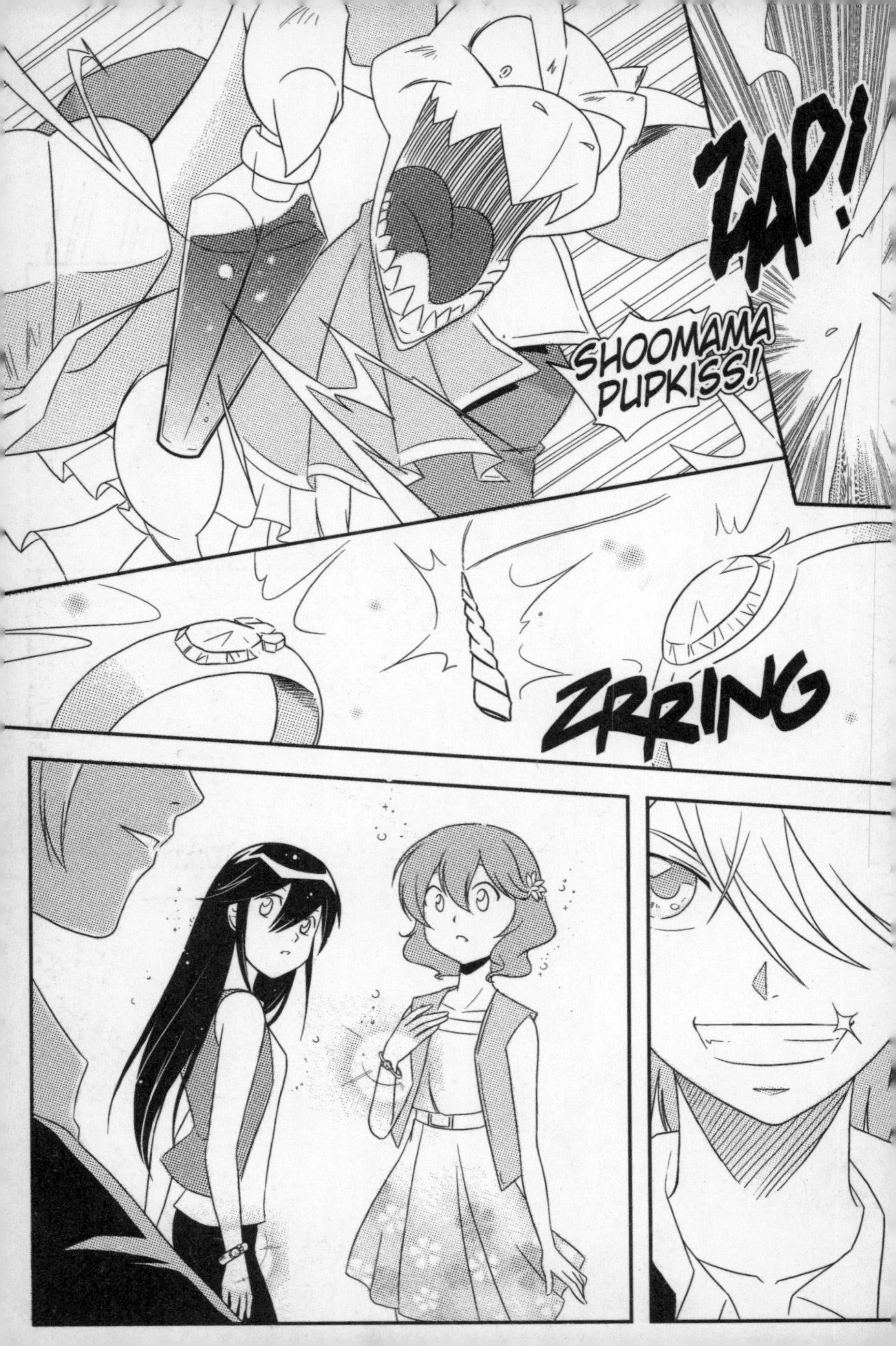
ZAP!
SHOOMAMA PUPKISS!
ZRRING

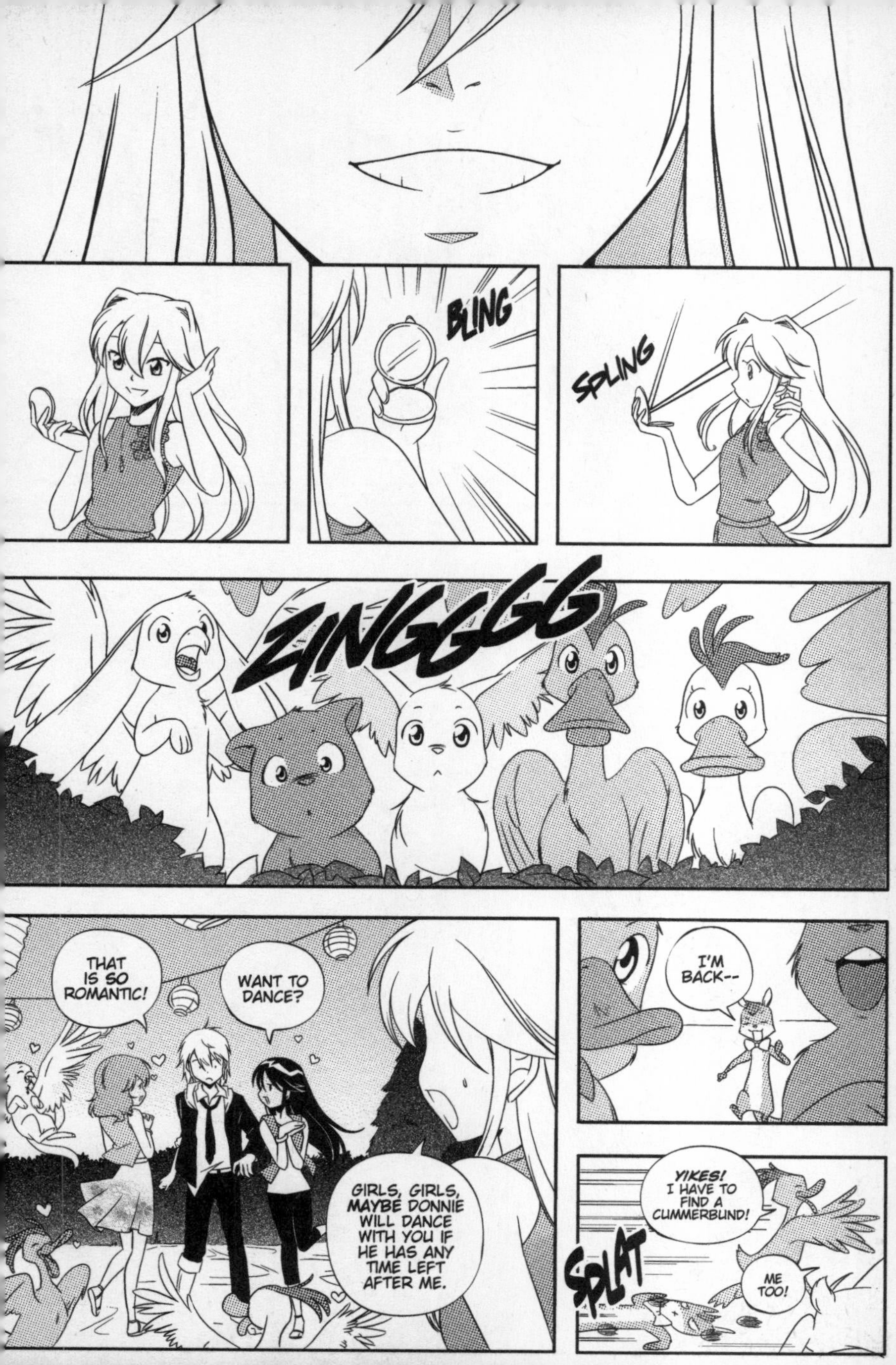
BLING
SPLING
ZINGGGG
THAT IS SO ROMANTIC!
WANT TO DANCE?
GIRLS, GIRLS, MAYBE DONNIE WILL DANCE WITH YOU IF HE HAS ANY TIME LEFT AFTER ME.
I'M BACK--
YIKES! I HAVE TO FIND A CUMMERBUND!
SPLAT
ME TOO!

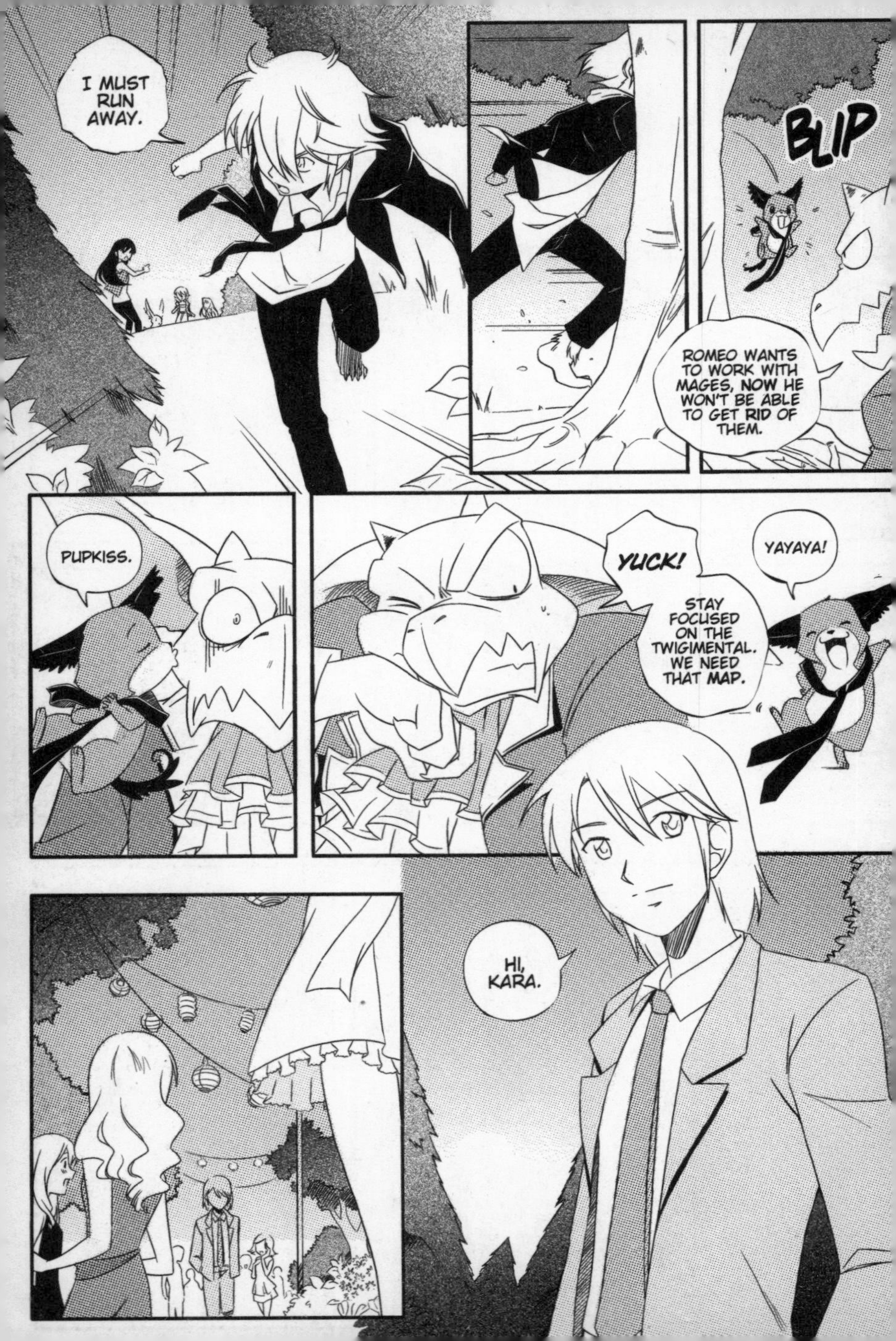
I MUST RUN AWAY.
BLIP
ROMEO WANTS TO WORK WITH MAGES, NOW HE WON'T BE ABLE TO GET RID OF THEM.
PUPKISS.
YUCK!
YAYAYA!
STAY FOCUSED ON THE TWIGIMENTAL. WE NEED THAT MAP.
HI, KARA.

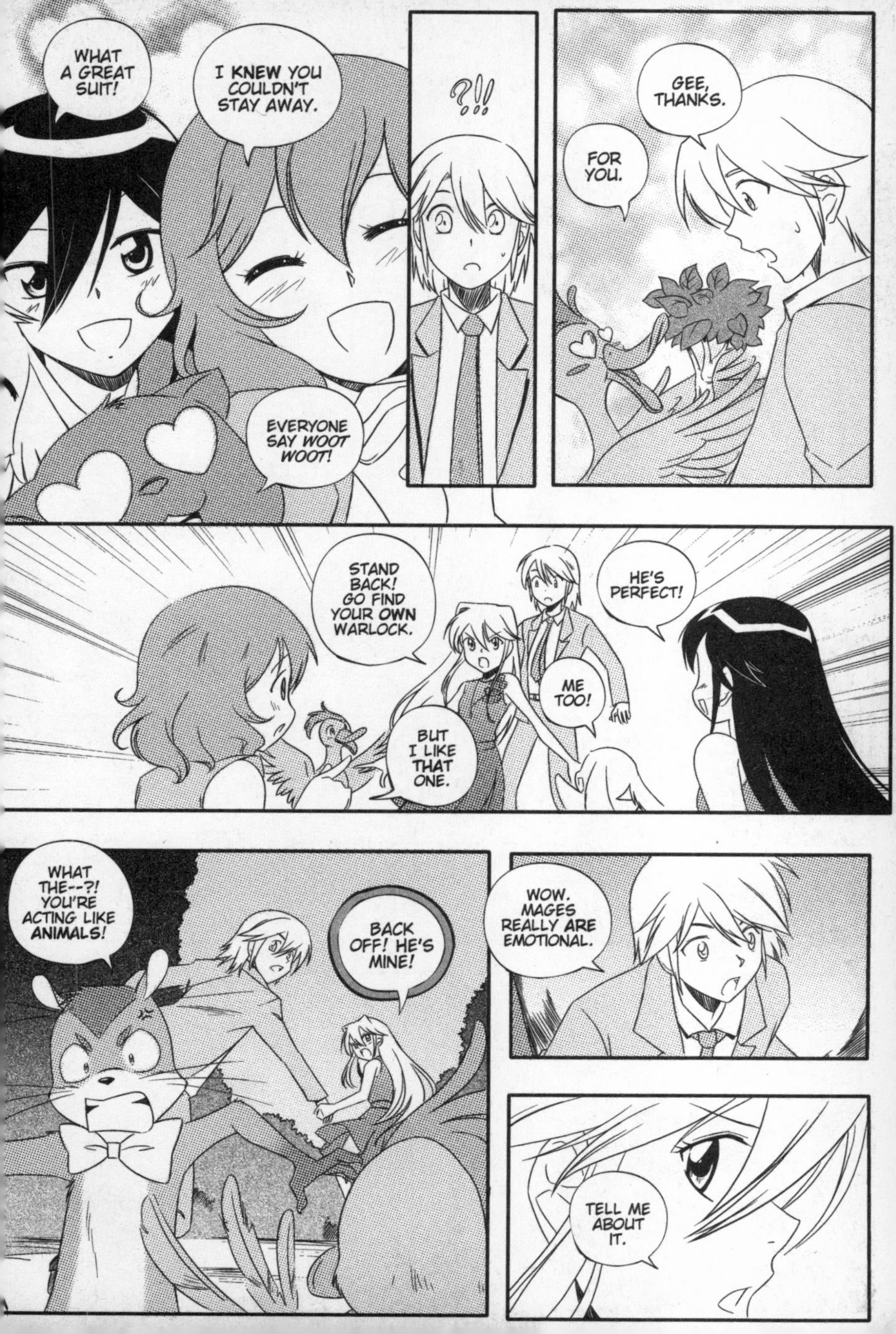
WHAT A GREAT SUIT!
I KNEW YOU COULDN'T STAY AWAY.
EVERYONE SAY WOOT WOOT!
?!!
GEE, THANKS.
FOR YOU.
STAND BACK! GO FIND YOUR OWN WARLOCK.
BUT I LIKE THAT ONE.
ME TOO!
HE'S PERFECT!
WHAT THE--?! YOU'RE ACTING LIKE ANIMALS!
BACK OFF! HE'S MINE!
WOW. MAGES REALLY ARE EMOTIONAL.
TELL ME ABOUT IT.

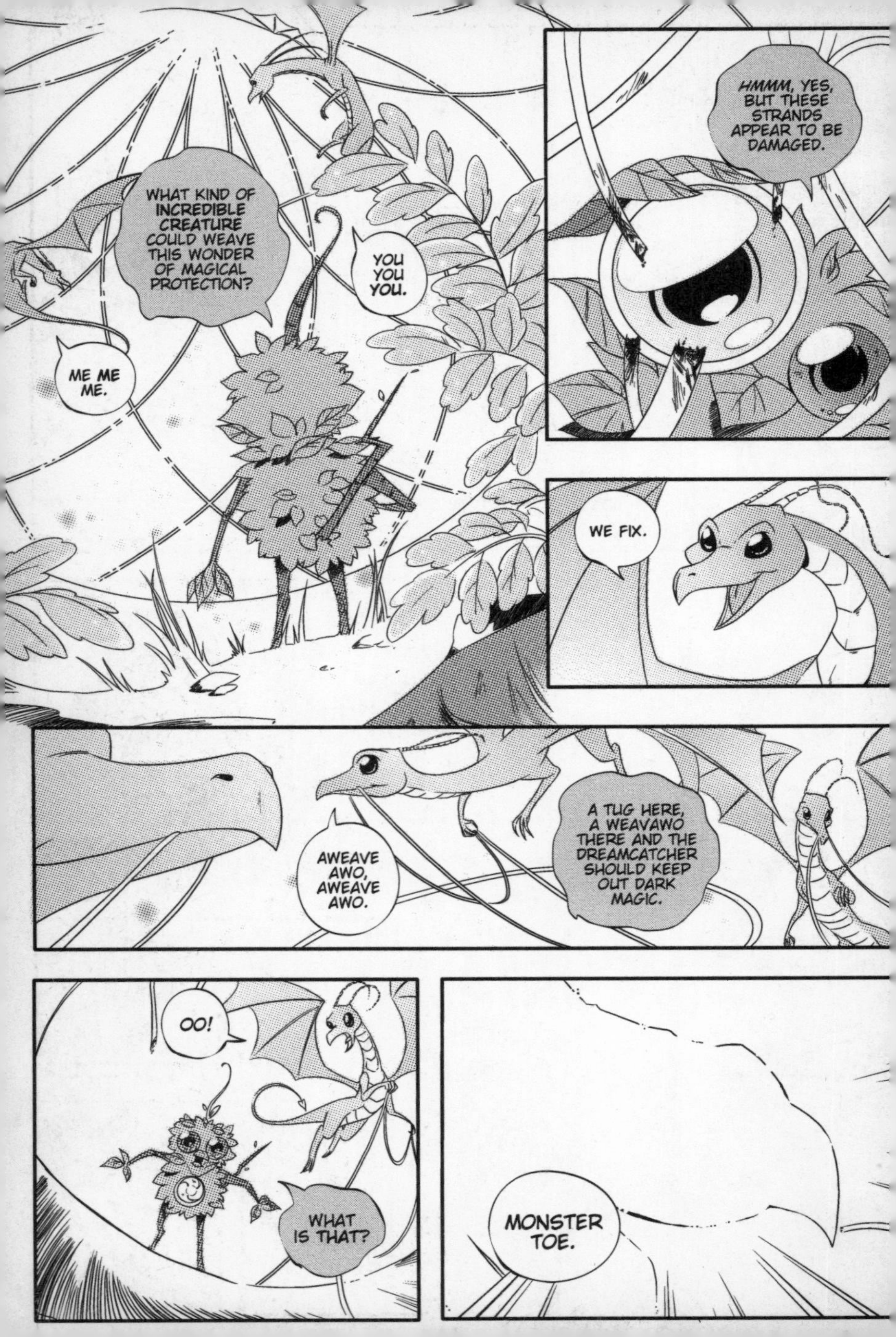
WHAT KIND OF INCREDIBLE CREATURE COULD WEAVE THIS WONDER OF MAGICAL PROTECTION?
YOU YOU YOU.
ME ME ME.
HMMM, YES, BUT THESE STRANDS APPEAR TO BE DAMAGED.
WE FIX.
AWEAVE AWO, AWEAVE AWO.
A TUG HERE, A WEAVAWO THERE AND THE DREAMCATCHER SHOULD KEEP OUT DARK MAGIC.
OO!
WHAT IS THAT?
MONSTER TOE.

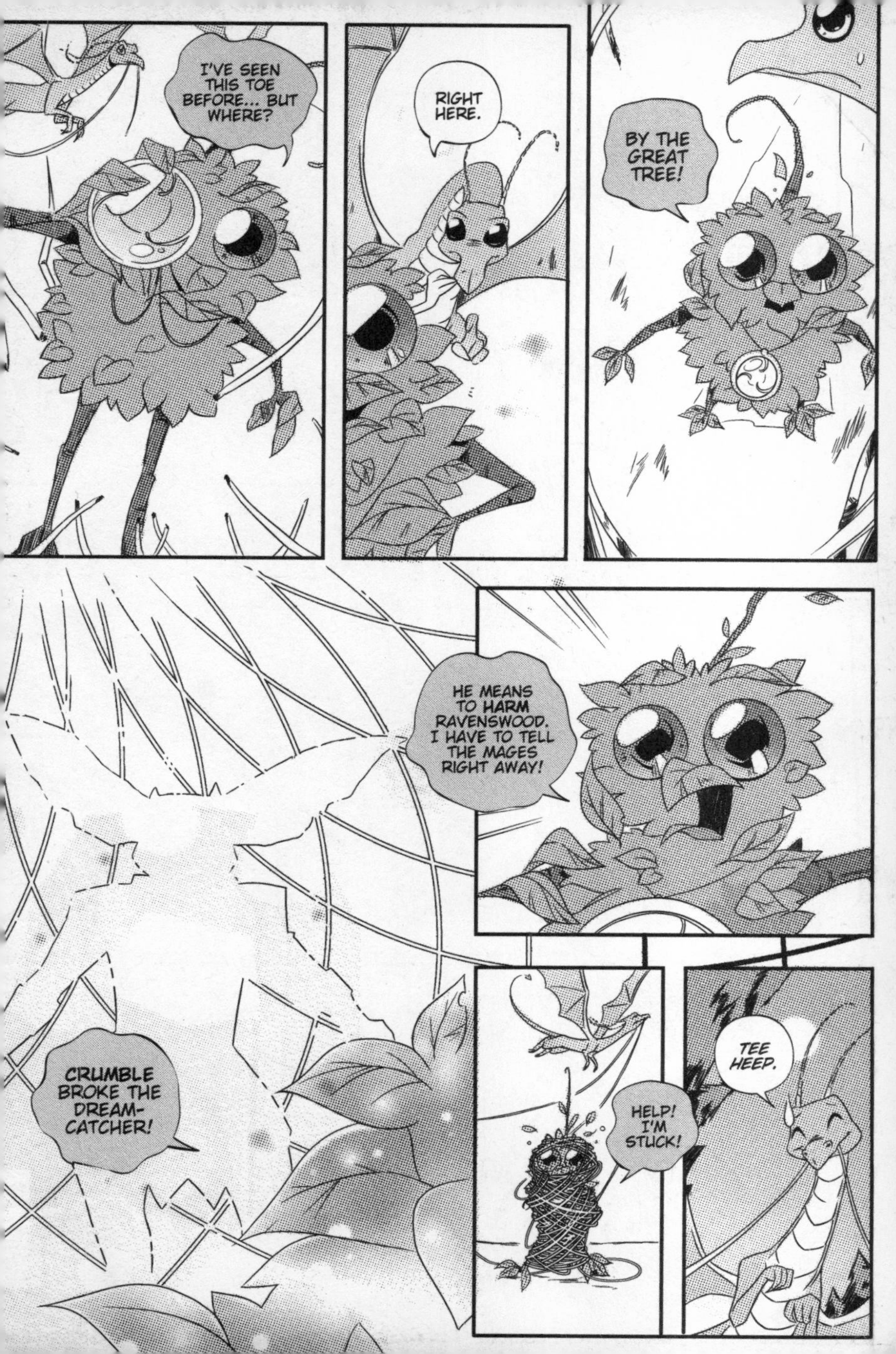
I'VE SEEN THIS TOE BEFORE... BUT WHERE?
RIGHT HERE.
BY THE GREAT TREE!
HE MEANS TO HARM RAVENSWOOD. I HAVE TO TELL THE MAGES RIGHT AWAY!
CRUMBLE BROKE THE DREAM-CATCHER!
HELP! I'M STUCK!
TEE HEEP.

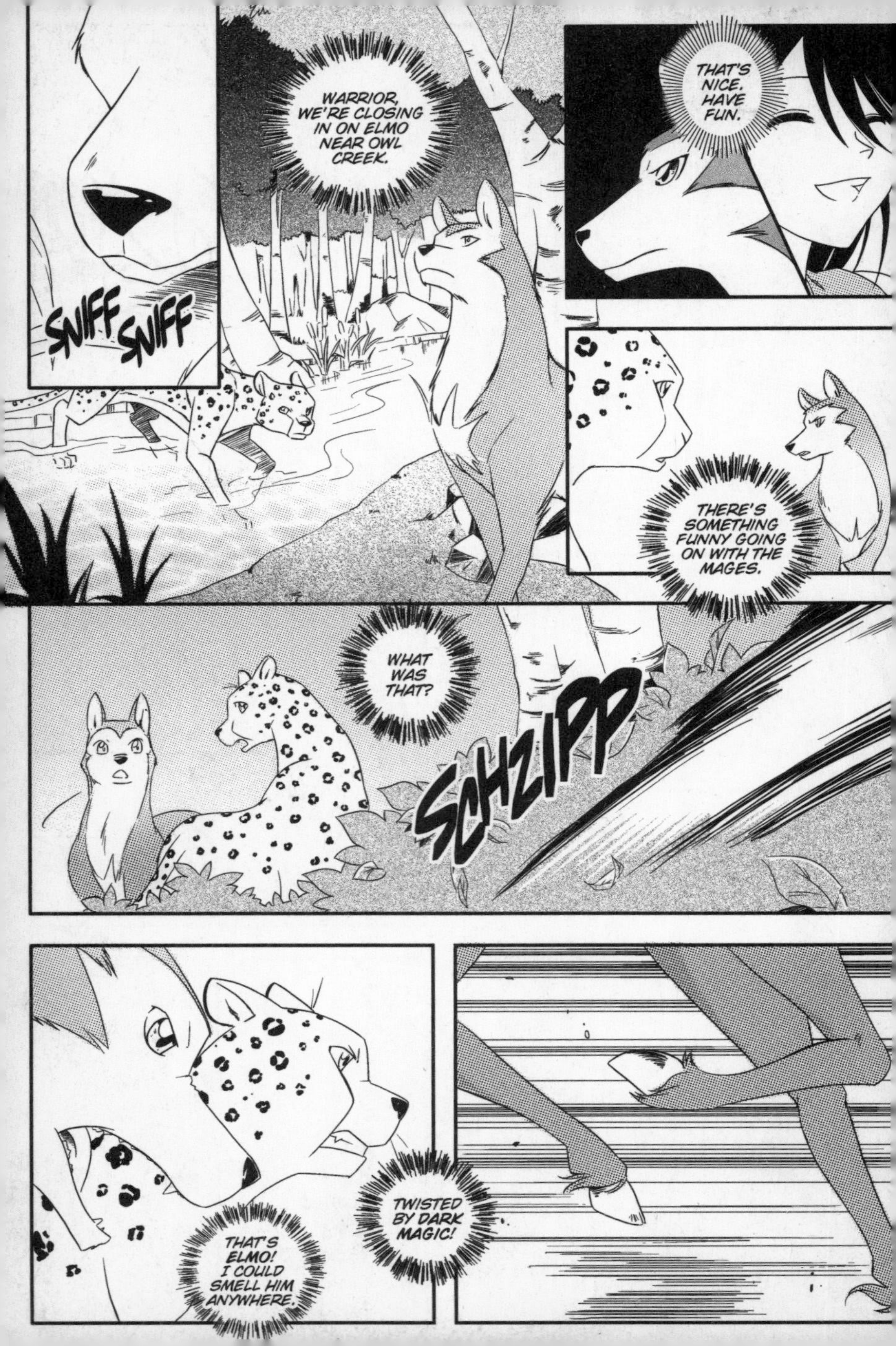
SNIFF SNIFF
WARRIOR, WE'RE CLOSING IN ON ELMO NEAR OWL CREEK.
THAT'S NICE. HAVE FUN.
THERE'S SOMETHING FUNNY GOING ON WITH THE MAGES.
WHAT WAS THAT?
SCHZIPP
THAT'S ELMO! I COULD SMELL HIM ANYWHERE.
TWISTED BY DARK MAGIC!

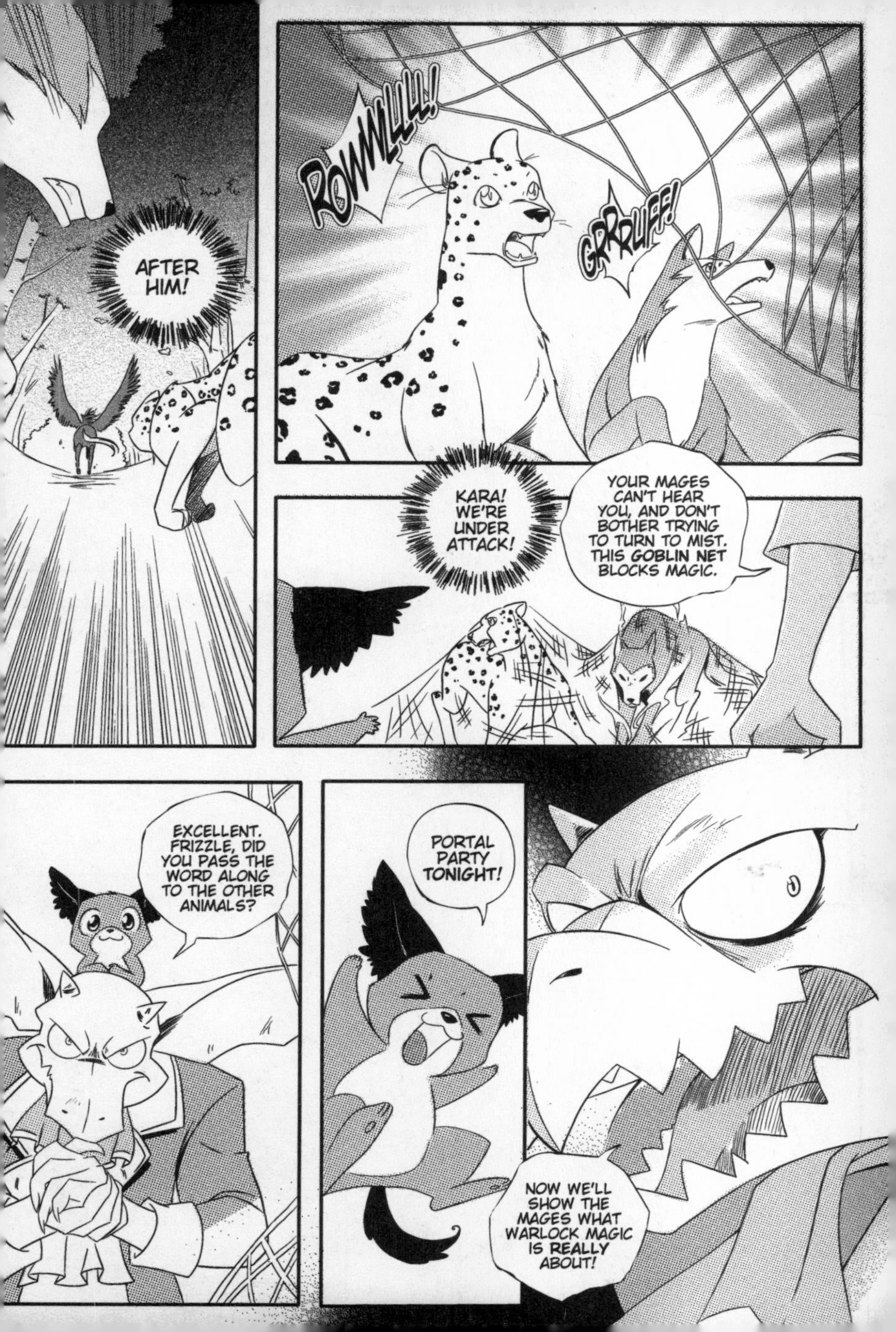
AFTER HIM!
ROWWLLLL!
GRRRUFF!
KARA! WE'RE UNDER ATTACK!
YOUR MAGES CAN'T HEAR YOU, AND DON'T BOTHER TRYING TO TURN TO MIST. THIS GOBLIN NET BLOCKS MAGIC.
EXCELLENT. FRIZZLE, DID YOU PASS THE WORD ALONG TO THE OTHER ANIMALS?
PORTAL PARTY TONIGHT!
NOW WE'LL SHOW THE MAGES WHAT WARLOCK MAGIC IS REALLY ABOUT!

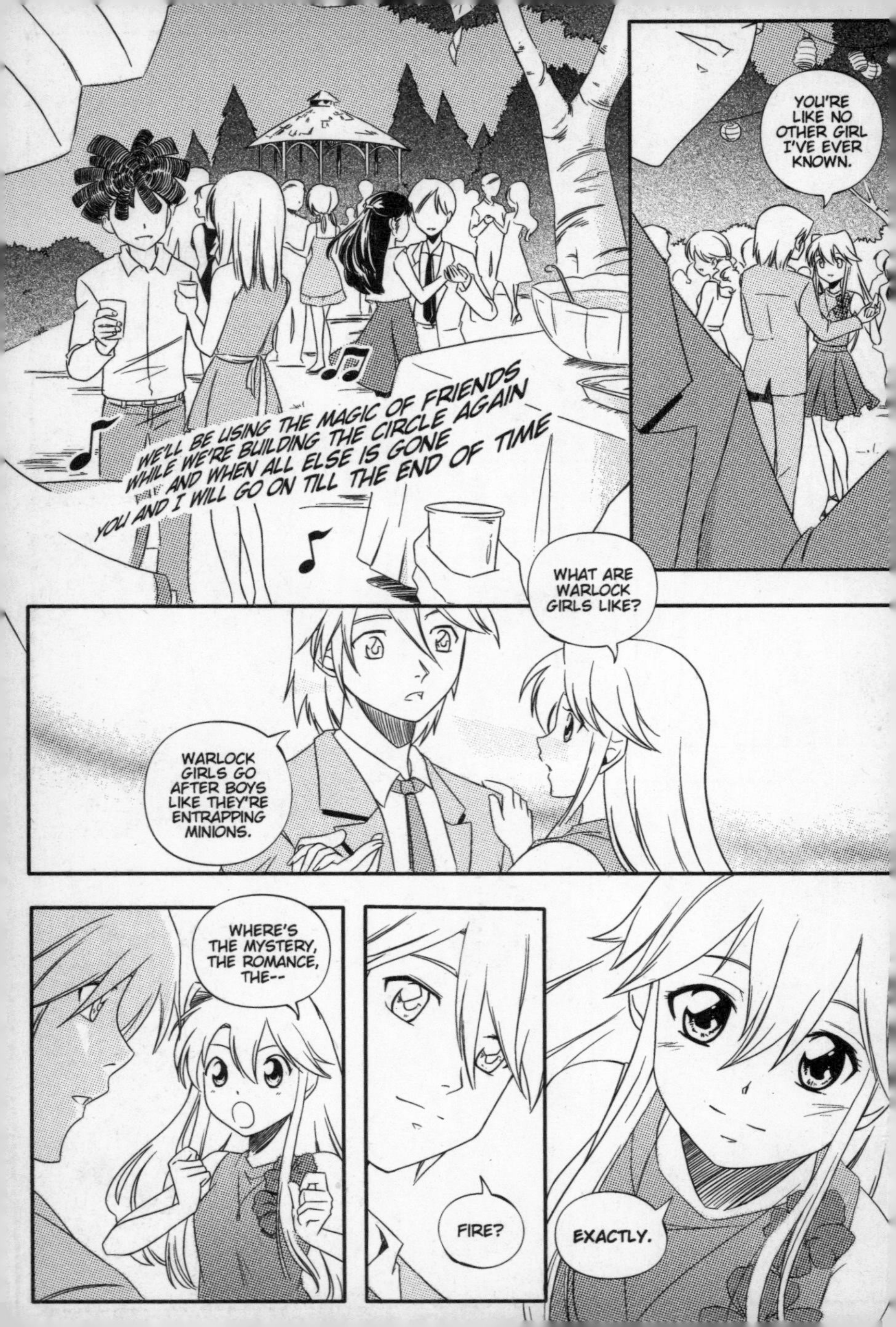
WE'LL BE USING THE MAGIC OF FRIENDS
WHILE WE'RE BUILDING THE CIRCLE AGAIN
AND WHEN ALL ELSE IS GONE
YOU AND I WILL GO ON TILL THE END OF TIME
YOU'RE LIKE NO OTHER GIRL I'VE EVER KNOWN.
WHAT ARE WARLOCK GIRLS LIKE?
WARLOCK GIRLS GO AFTER BOYS LIKE THEY'RE ENTRAPPING MINIONS.
WHERE'S THE MYSTERY, THE ROMANCE, THE--
FIRE?
EXACTLY.

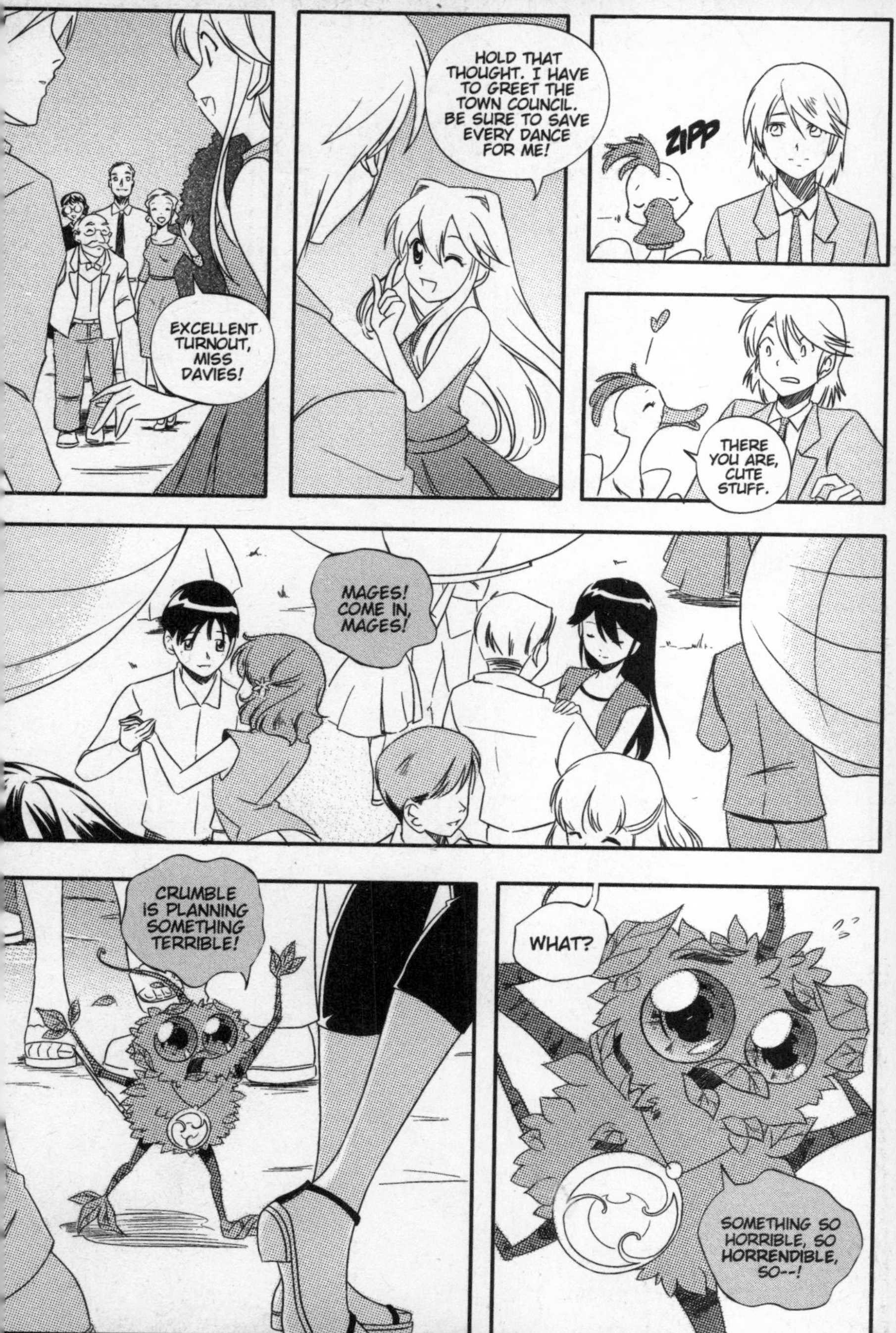
EXCELLENT TURNOUT, MISS DAVIES!
HOLD THAT THOUGHT. I HAVE TO GREET THE TOWN COUNCIL. BE SURE TO SAVE EVERY DANCE FOR ME!
ZIPP
THERE YOU ARE, CUTE STUFF.
MAGES! COME IN, MAGES!
CRUMBLE IS PLANNING SOMETHING TERRIBLE!
WHAT?
SOMETHING SO HORRIBLE, SO HORRENDIBLE, SO--!

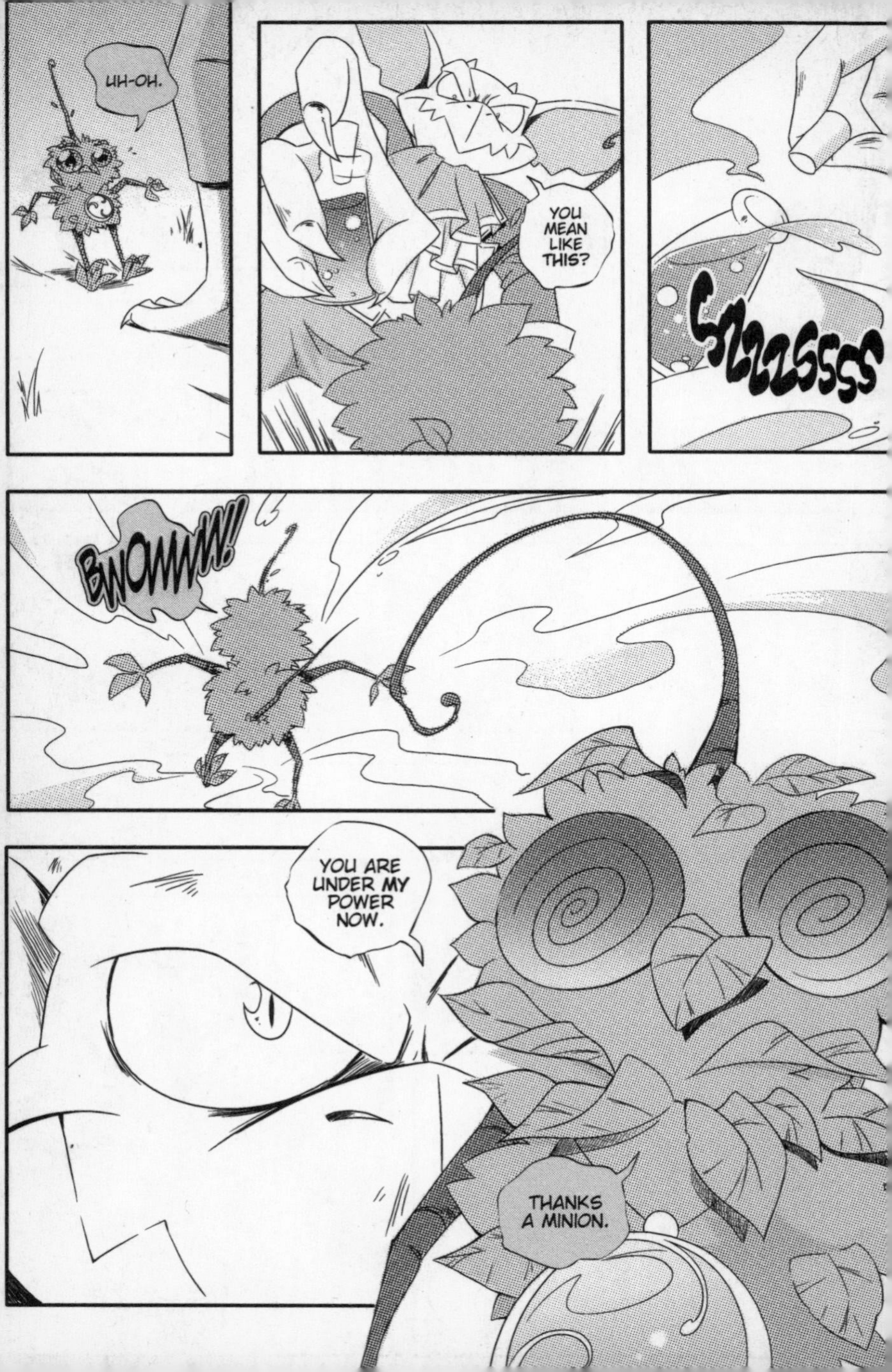
UH-OH.
YOU MEAN LIKE THIS?
SZZZSSSS
BWOWWW!
YOU ARE UNDER MY POWER NOW.
THANKS A MINION.

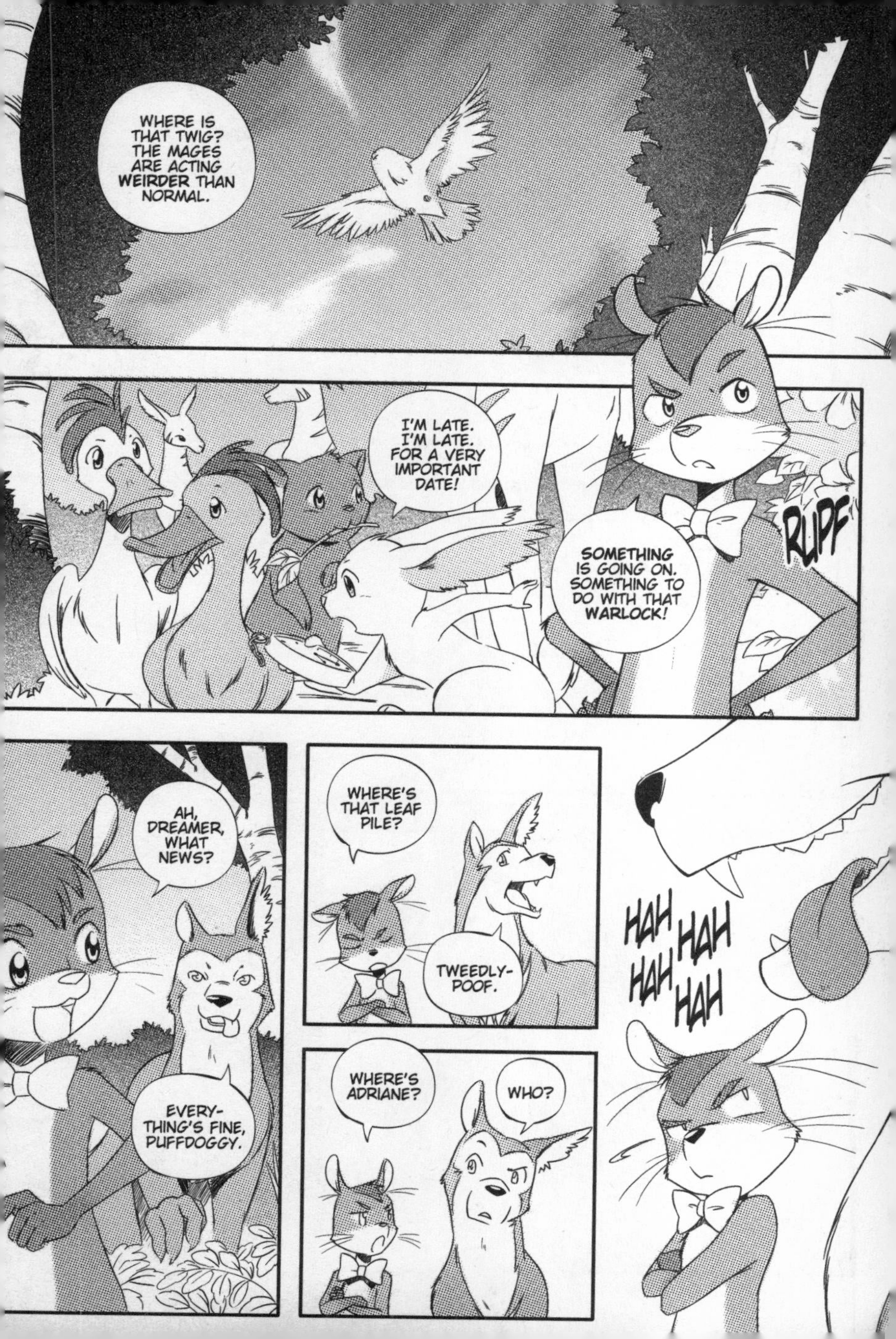
WHERE IS THAT TWIG? THE MAGES ARE ACTING WEIRDER THAN NORMAL.
I'M LATE. I'M LATE. FOR A VERY IMPORTANT DATE!
SOMETHING IS GOING ON. SOMETHING TO DO WITH THAT WARLOCK!
RUPF
AH, DREAMER, WHAT NEWS?
EVERY-THING'S FINE, PUFFDOGGY.
WHERE'S THAT LEAF PILE?
TWEEDLY-POOF.
WHERE'S ADRIANE?
WHO?
HAH HAH HAH HAH HAH

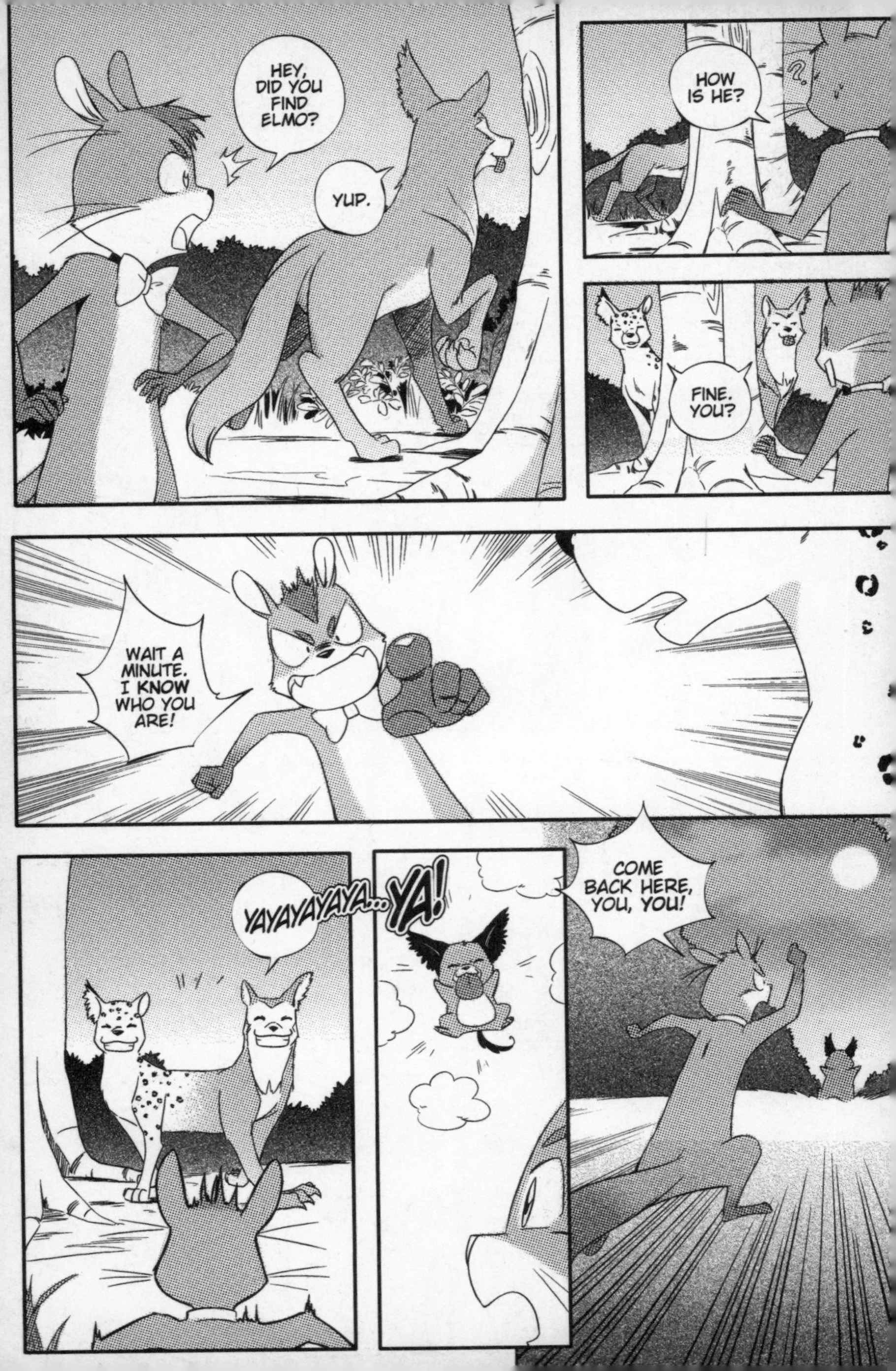
HEY, DID YOU FIND ELMO?
YUP.
HOW IS HE?
FINE. YOU?
WAIT A MINUTE. I KNOW WHO YOU ARE!
YAYAYAYAYA...YA!
COME BACK HERE, YOU, YOU!

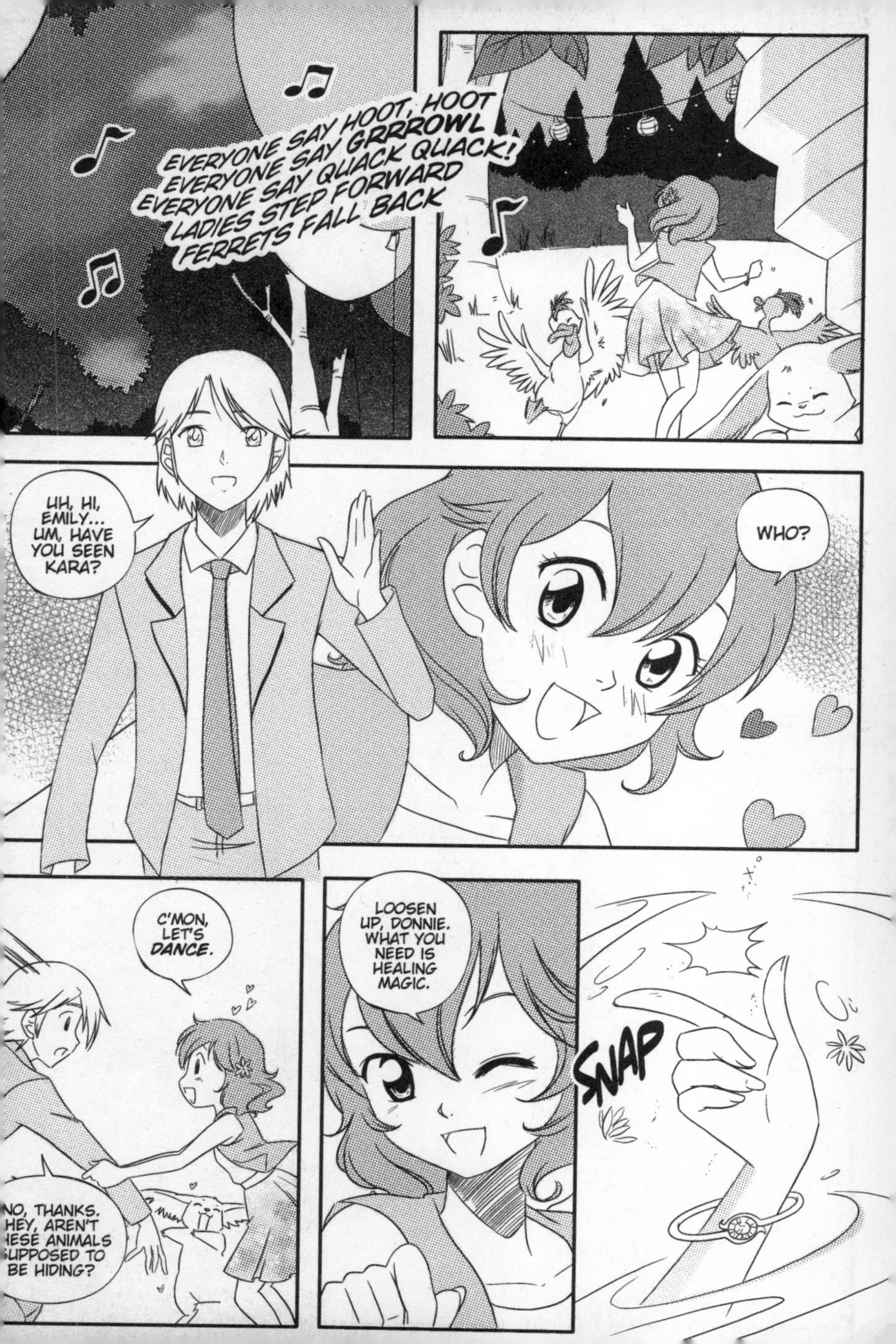
EVERYONE SAY HOOT, HOOT
EVERYONE SAY GRRROWL
EVERYONE SAY QUACK QUACK!
LADIES STEP FORWARD
FERRETS FALL BACK
UH, HI, EMILY... UM, HAVE YOU SEEN KARA?
WHO?
C'MON, LET'S DANCE.
NO, THANKS. HEY, AREN'T THESE ANIMALS SUPPOSED TO BE HIDING?
LOOSEN UP, DONNIE. WHAT YOU NEED IS HEALING MAGIC.
SNAP

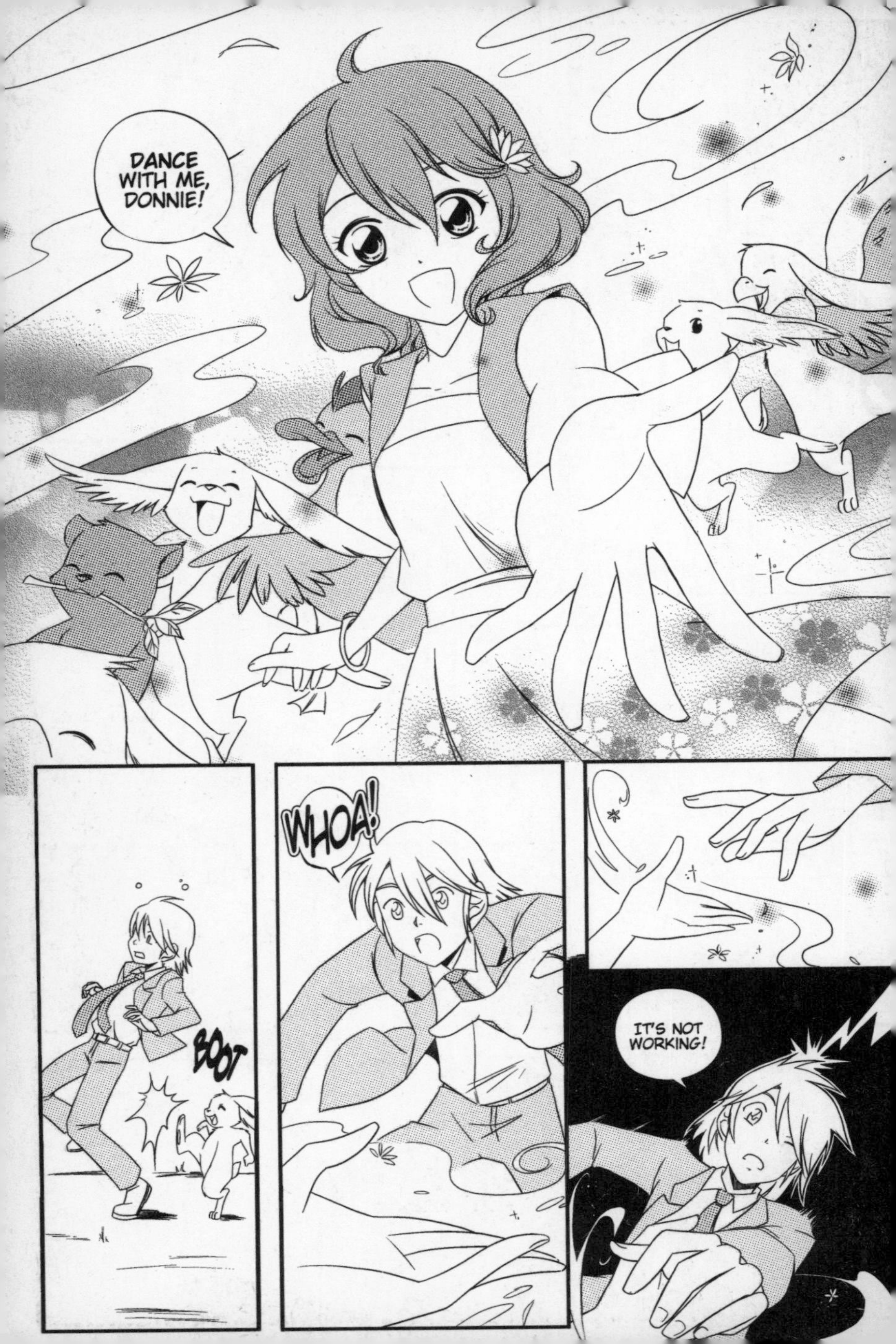
DANCE WITH ME, DONNIE!
BOOT
WHOA!
IT'S NOT WORKING!

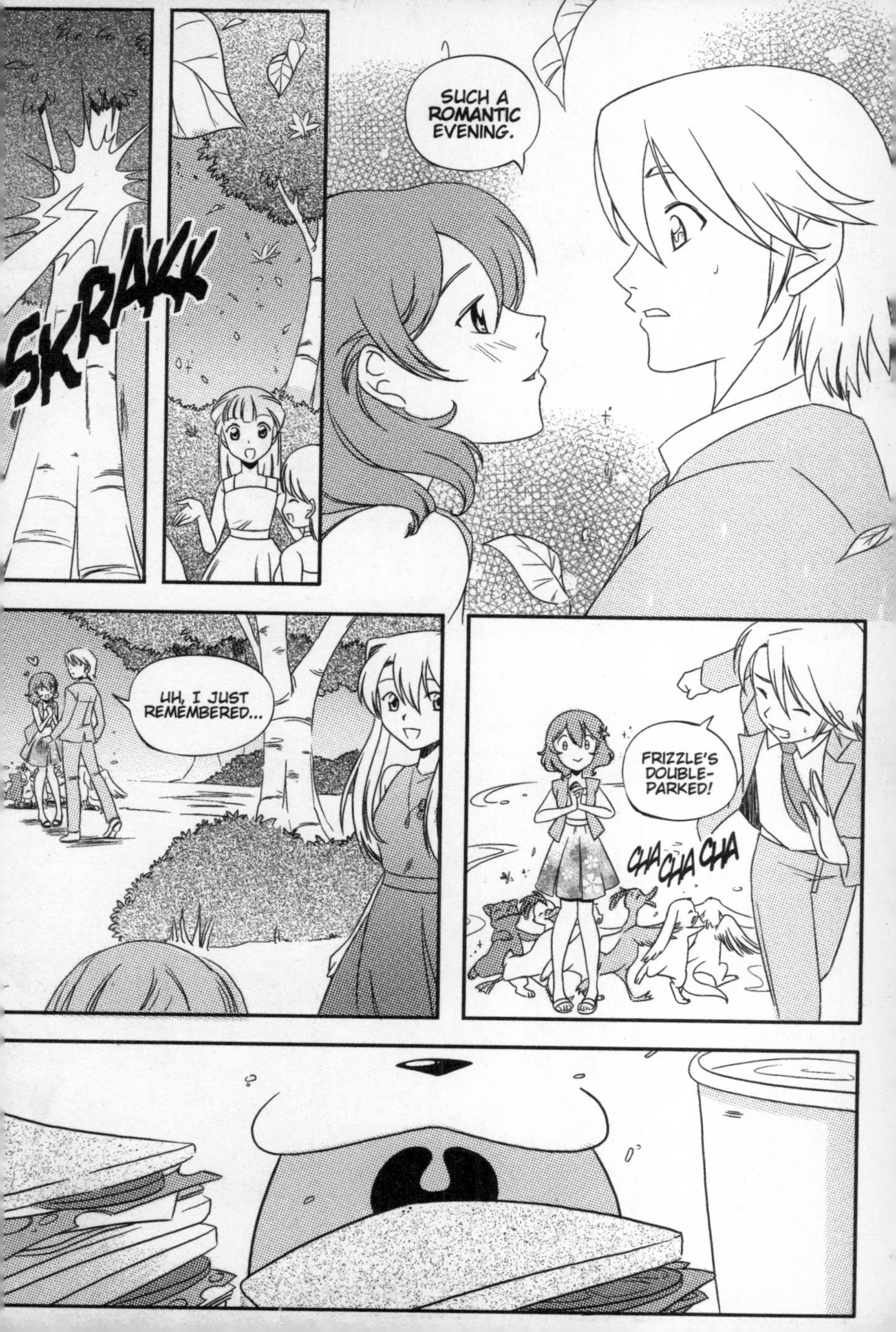
SKRAKK
SUCH A ROMANTIC EVENING.
UH, I JUST REMEMBERED...
FRIZZLE'S DOUBLE-PARKED!
CHA CHA CHA

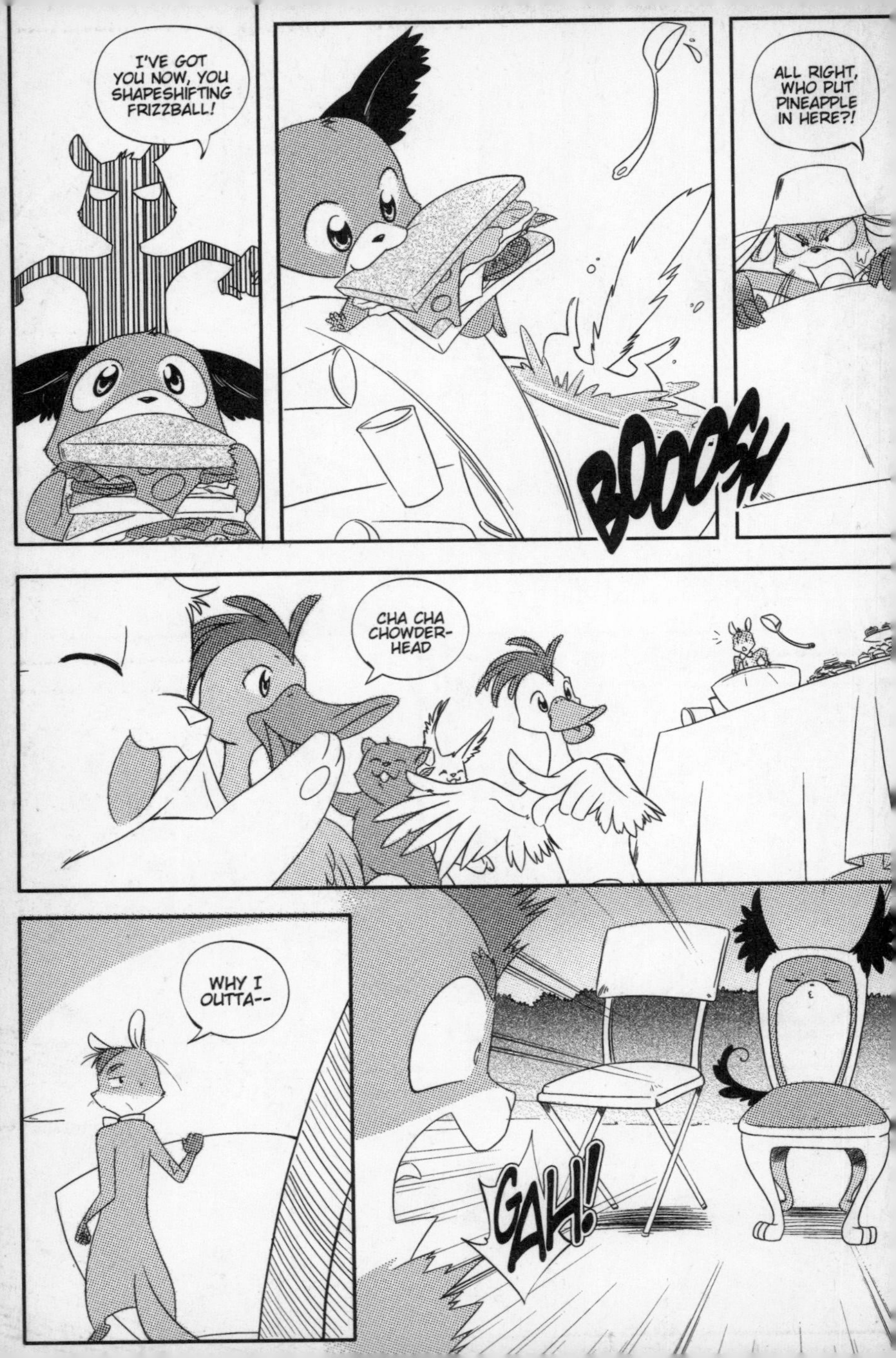
I'VE GOT YOU NOW, YOU SHAPESHIFTING FRIZZBALL!
ALL RIGHT, WHO PUT PINEAPPLE IN HERE?!
BOOOSH
CHA CHA CHOWDER-HEAD
WHY I OUTTA--
GAH!

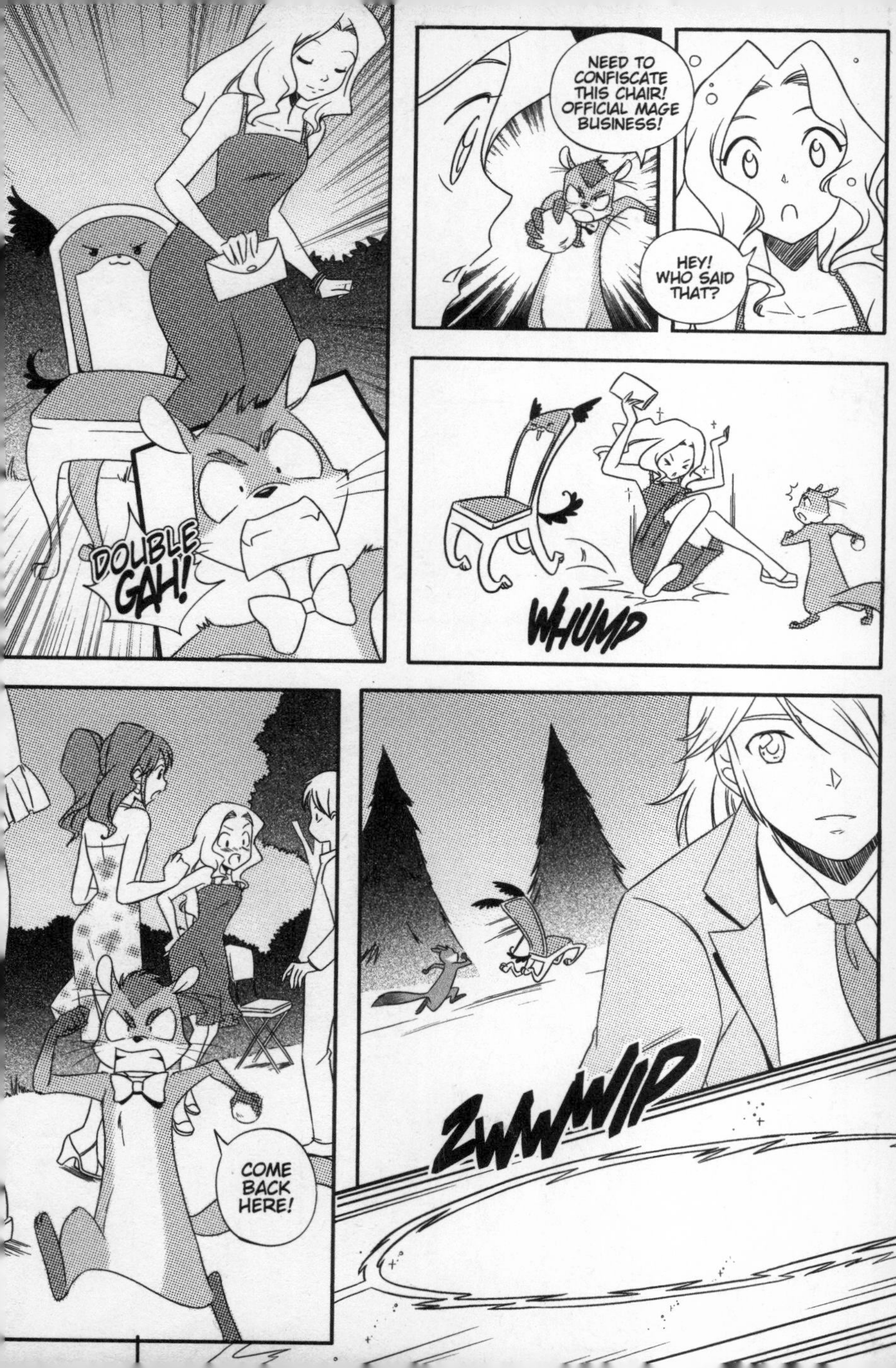
DOUBLE GAH!
NEED TO CONFISCATE THIS CHAIR! OFFICIAL MAGE BUSINESS!
HEY! WHO SAID THAT?
WHUMP
COME BACK HERE!
ZWWWIP

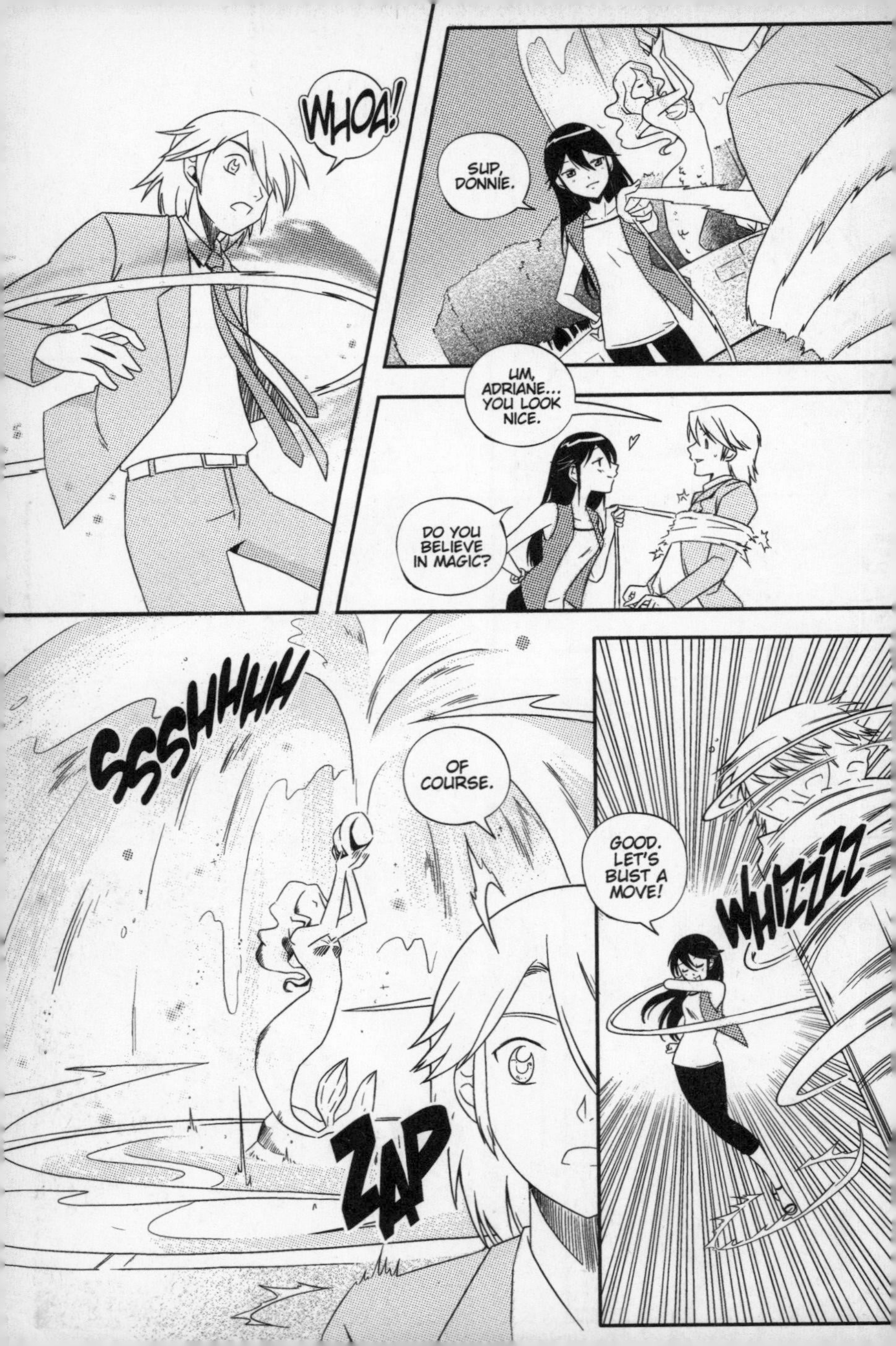
WHOA!
SUP, DONNIE.
UM, ADRIANE... YOU LOOK NICE.
DO YOU BELIEVE IN MAGIC?
SSSHHHH
OF COURSE.
ZAP
GOOD. LET'S BUST A MOVE!
WHIZZZZ

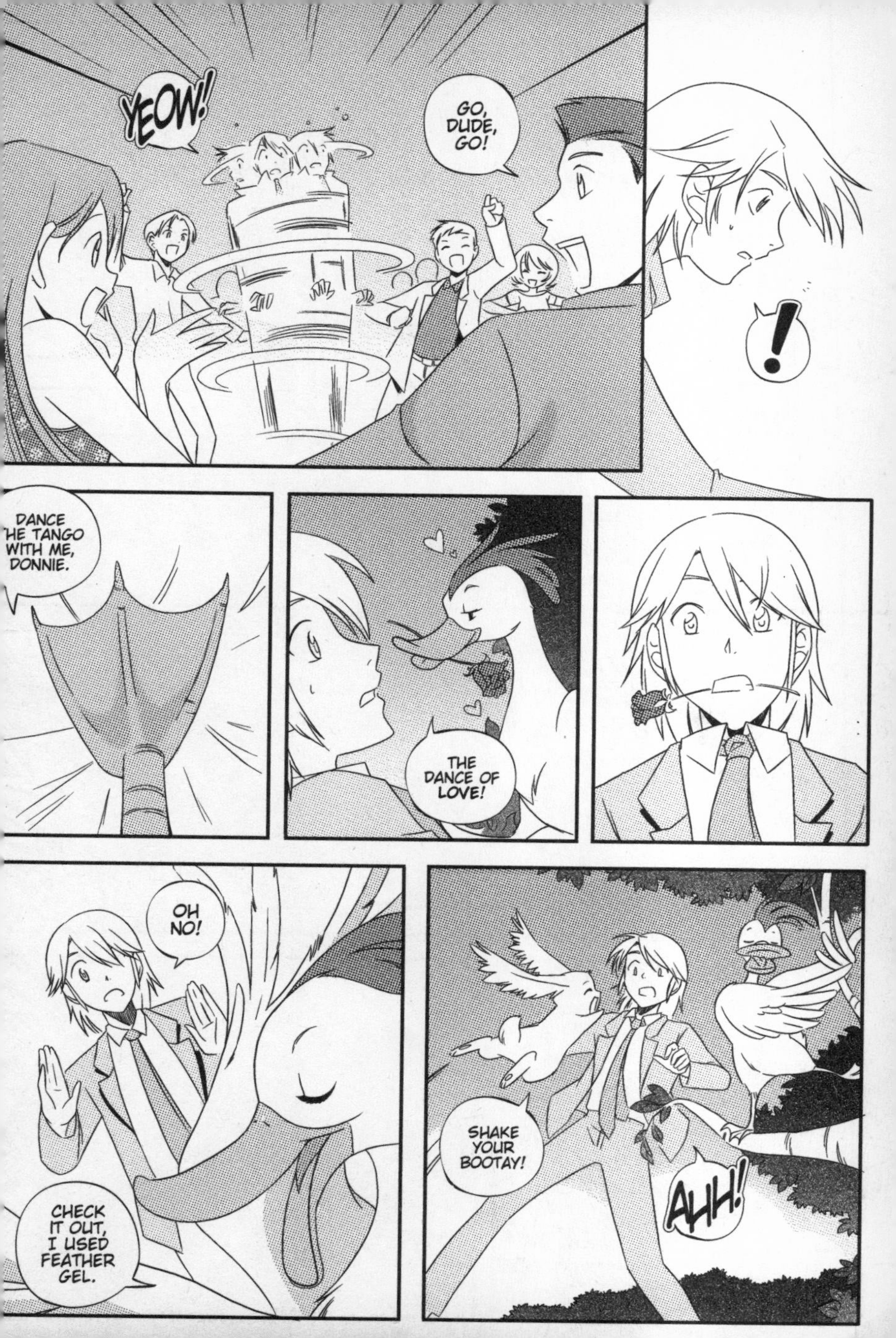

YEOW!
GO, DUDE, GO!
!
DANCE THE TANGO WITH ME, DONNIE.
THE DANCE OF LOVE!
OH NO!
CHECK IT OUT, I USED FEATHER GEL.
SHAKE YOUR BOOTAY!
AHH!

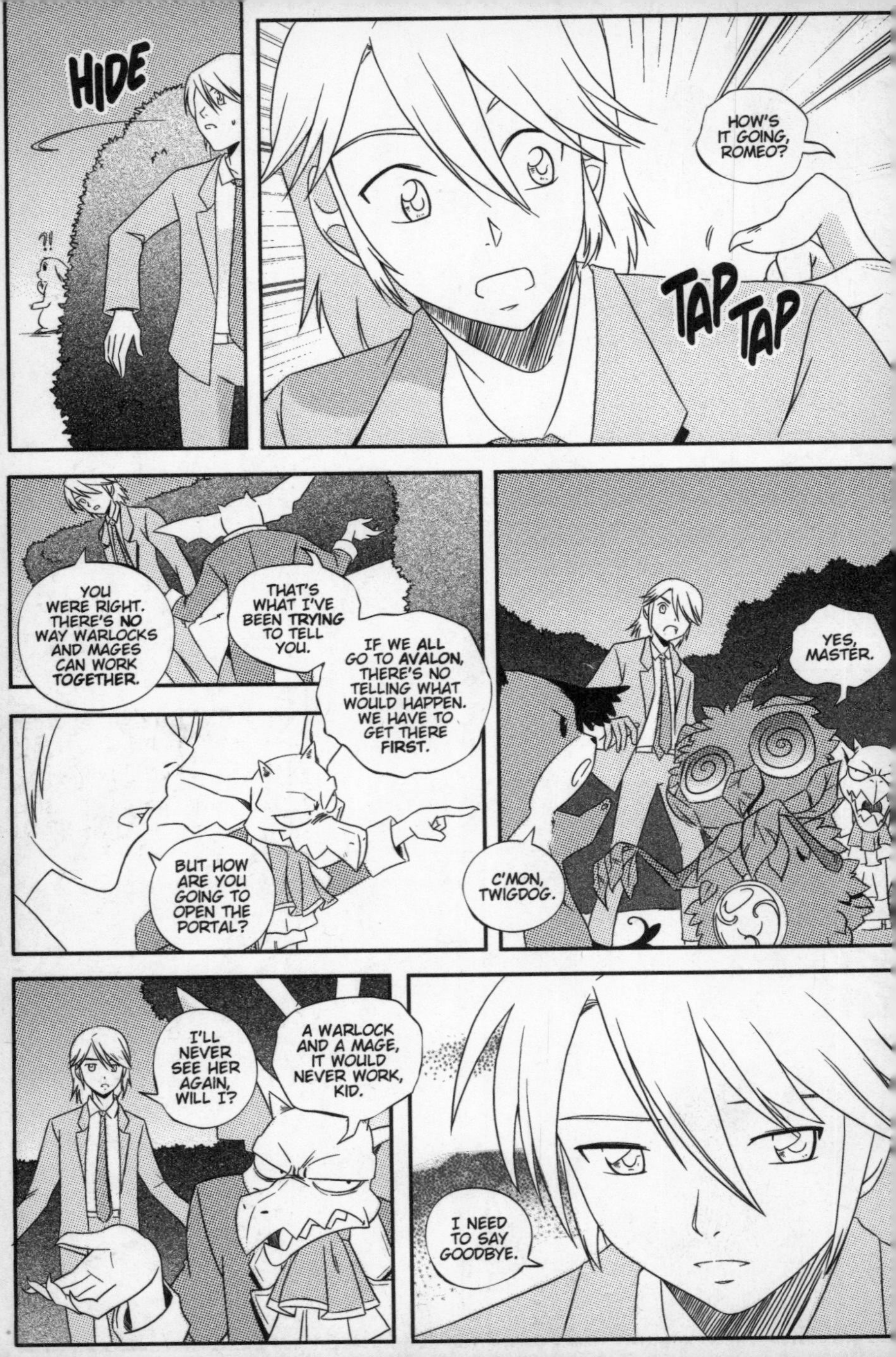
HIDE
?!
HOW'S IT GOING, ROMEO?
TAP TAP
YOU WERE RIGHT. THERE'S NO WAY WARLOCKS AND MAGES CAN WORK TOGETHER.
THAT'S WHAT I'VE BEEN TRYING TO TELL YOU.
IF WE ALL GO TO AVALON, THERE'S NO TELLING WHAT WOULD HAPPEN. WE HAVE TO GET THERE FIRST.
BUT HOW ARE YOU GOING TO OPEN THE PORTAL?
C'MON, TWIGDOG.
YES, MASTER.
I'LL NEVER SEE HER AGAIN, WILL I?
A WARLOCK AND A MAGE, IT WOULD NEVER WORK, KID.
I NEED TO SAY GOODBYE.

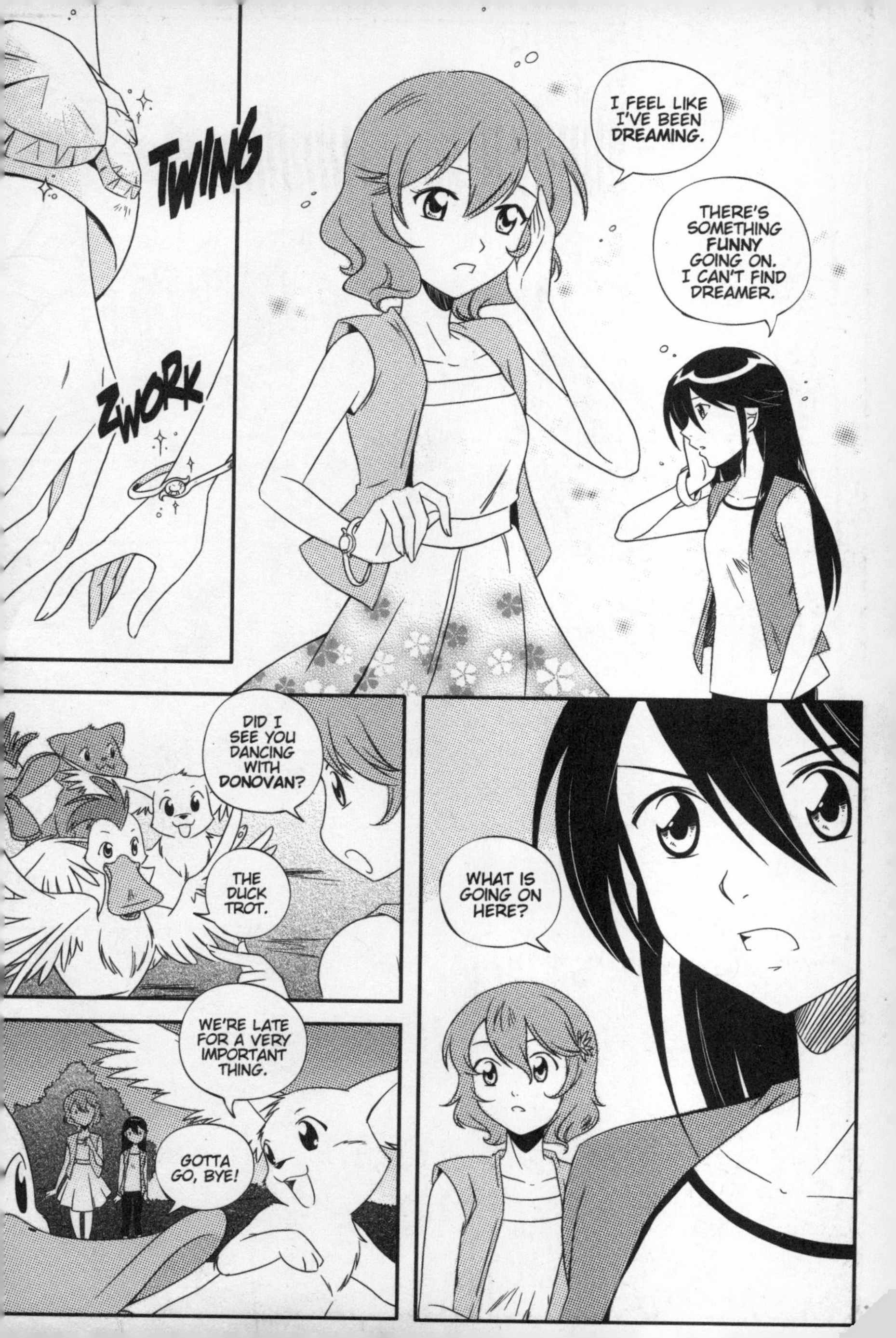
TWING
ZWORK
I FEEL LIKE I'VE BEEN DREAMING.
THERE'S SOMETHING FUNNY GOING ON. I CAN'T FIND DREAMER.
DID I SEE YOU DANCING WITH DONOVAN?
THE DUCK TROT.
WE'RE LATE FOR A VERY IMPORTANT THING.
GOTTA GO, BYE!
WHAT IS GOING ON HERE?

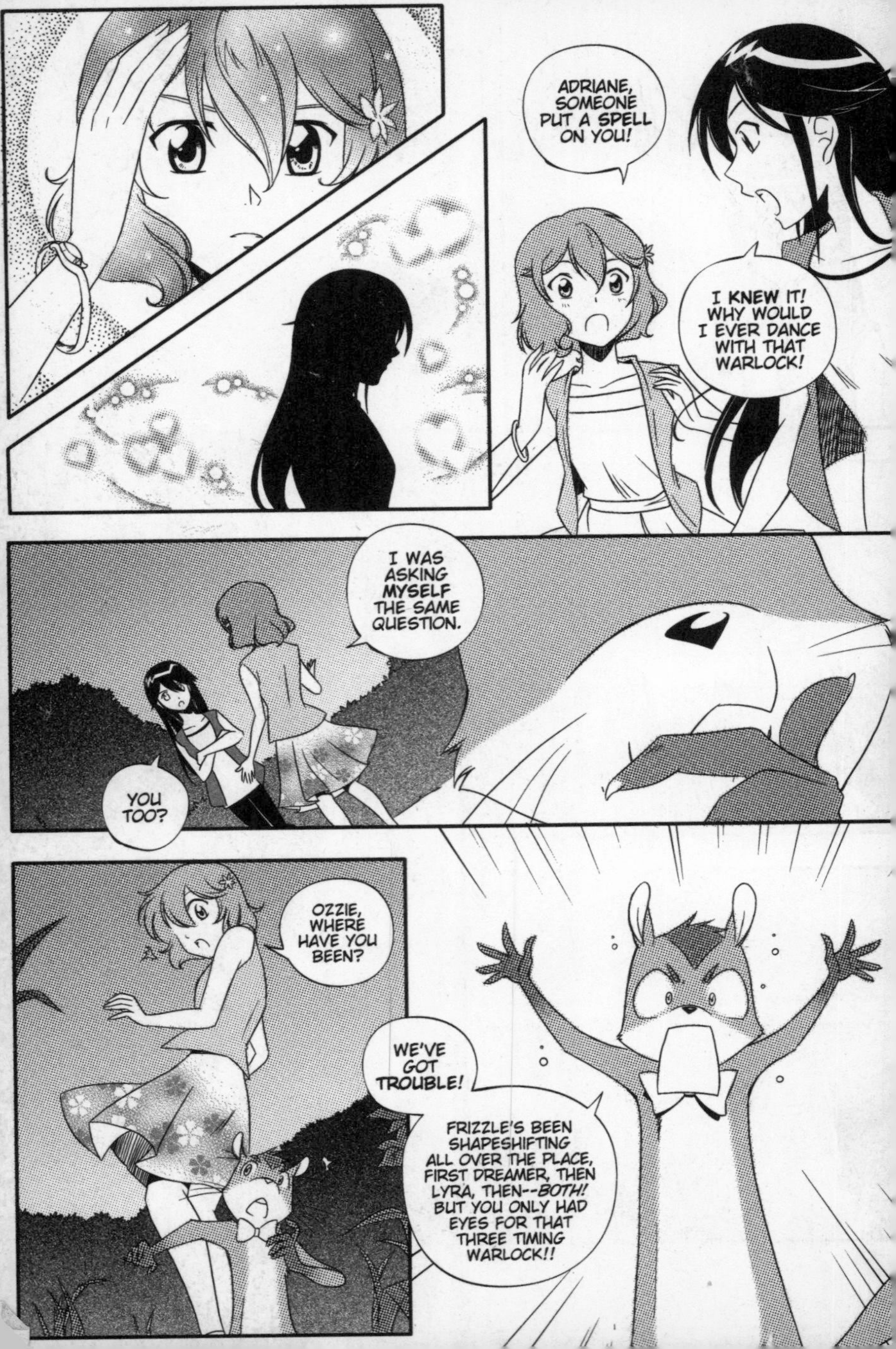
ADRIANE, SOMEONE PUT A SPELL ON YOU!
I KNEW IT! WHY WOULD I EVER DANCE WITH THAT WARLOCK!
I WAS ASKING MYSELF THE SAME QUESTION.
YOU TOO?
OZZIE, WHERE HAVE YOU BEEN?
WE'VE GOT TROUBLE!
FRIZZLE'S BEEN SHAPESHIFTING ALL OVER THE PLACE, FIRST DREAMER, THEN LYRA, THEN--BOTH! BUT YOU ONLY HAD EYES FOR THAT THREE TIMING WARLOCK!!

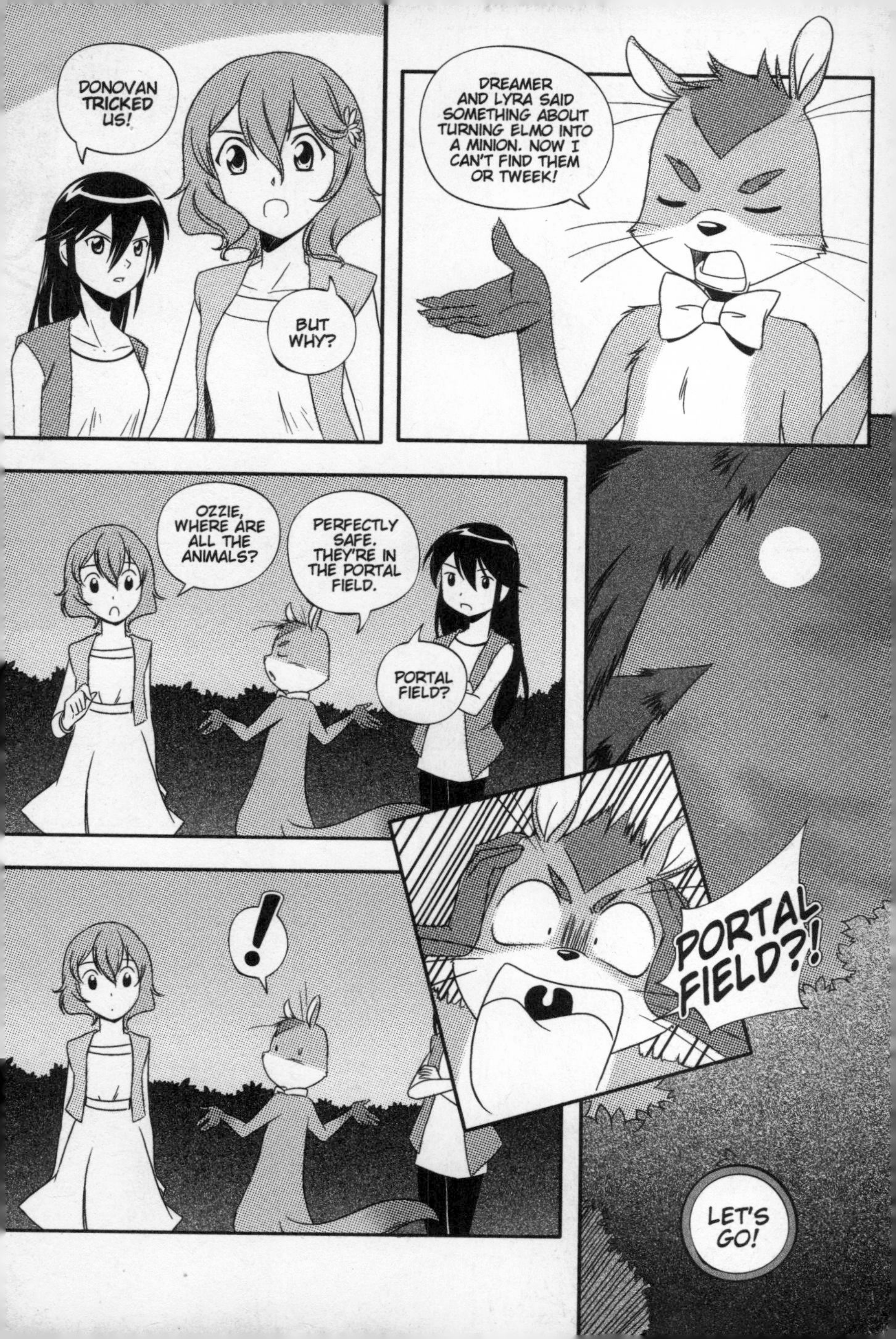
DONOVAN TRICKED US!
BUT WHY?
DREAMER AND LYRA SAID SOMETHING ABOUT TURNING ELMO INTO A MINION. NOW I CAN'T FIND THEM OR TWEEK!
OZZIE, WHERE ARE ALL THE ANIMALS?
PERFECTLY SAFE. THEY'RE IN THE PORTAL FIELD.
PORTAL FIELD?
!
PORTAL FIELD?!
LET'S GO!

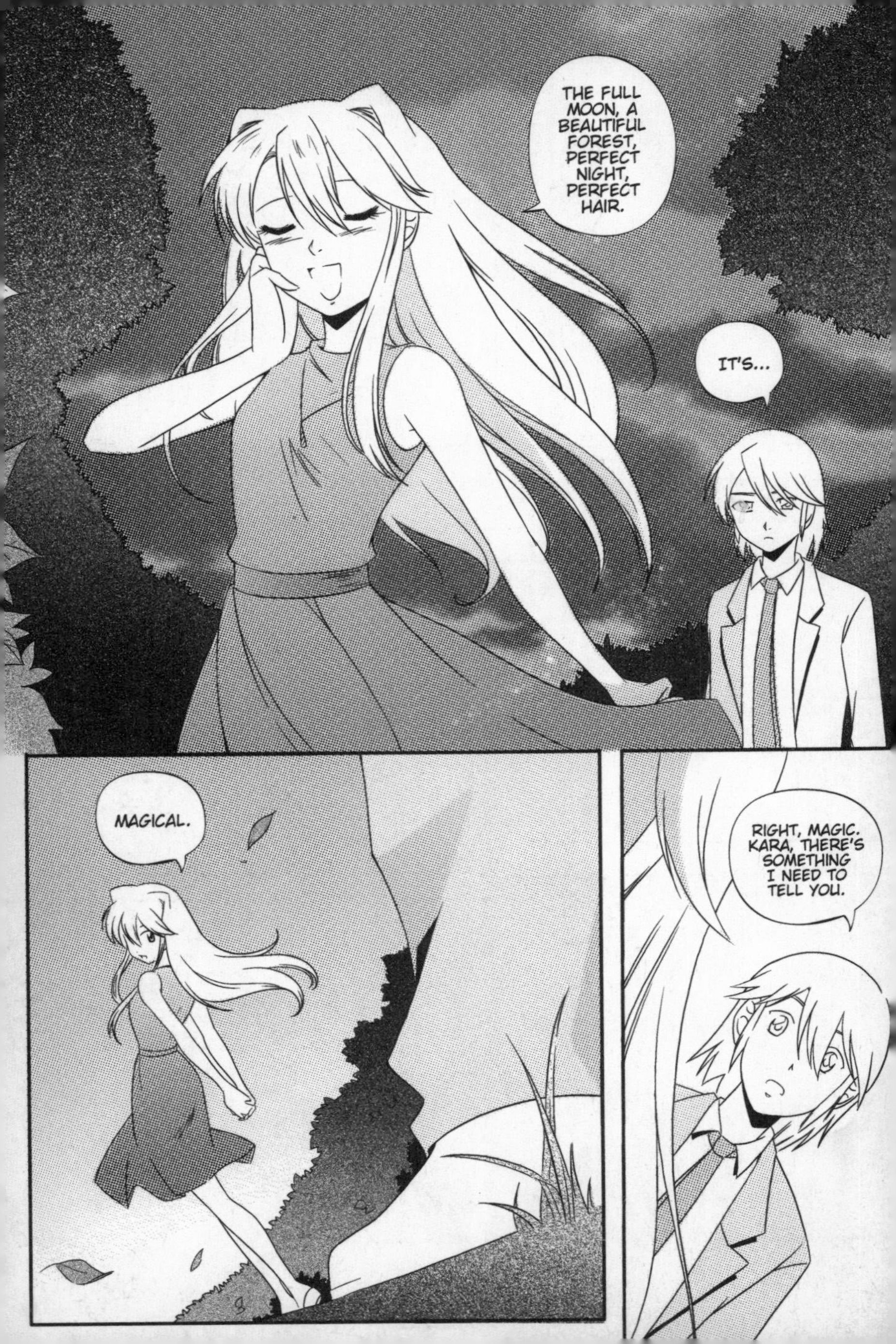
THE FULL MOON, A BEAUTIFUL FOREST, PERFECT NIGHT, PERFECT HAIR.
IT'S...
MAGICAL.
RIGHT, MAGIC. KARA, THERE'S SOMETHING I NEED TO TELL YOU.

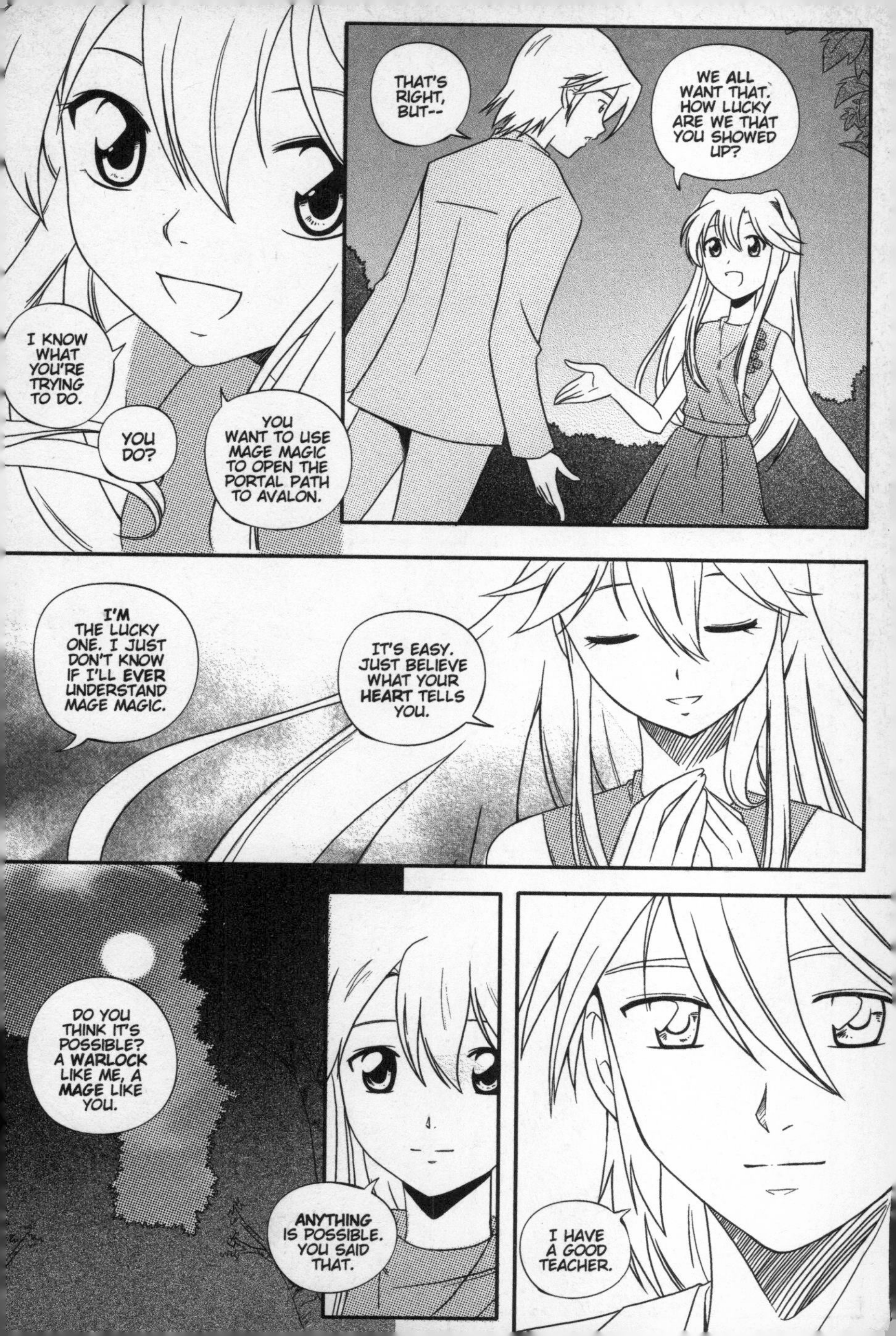
I KNOW WHAT YOU'RE TRYING TO DO.
YOU DO?
YOU WANT TO USE MAGE MAGIC TO OPEN THE PORTAL PATH TO AVALON.
THAT'S RIGHT, BUT--
WE ALL WANT THAT. HOW LUCKY ARE WE THAT YOU SHOWED UP?
I'M THE LUCKY ONE. I JUST DON'T KNOW IF I'LL EVER UNDERSTAND MAGE MAGIC.
IT'S EASY. JUST BELIEVE WHAT YOUR HEART TELLS YOU.
DO YOU THINK IT'S POSSIBLE? A WARLOCK LIKE ME, A MAGE LIKE YOU.
ANYTHING IS POSSIBLE. YOU SAID THAT.
I HAVE A GOOD TEACHER.

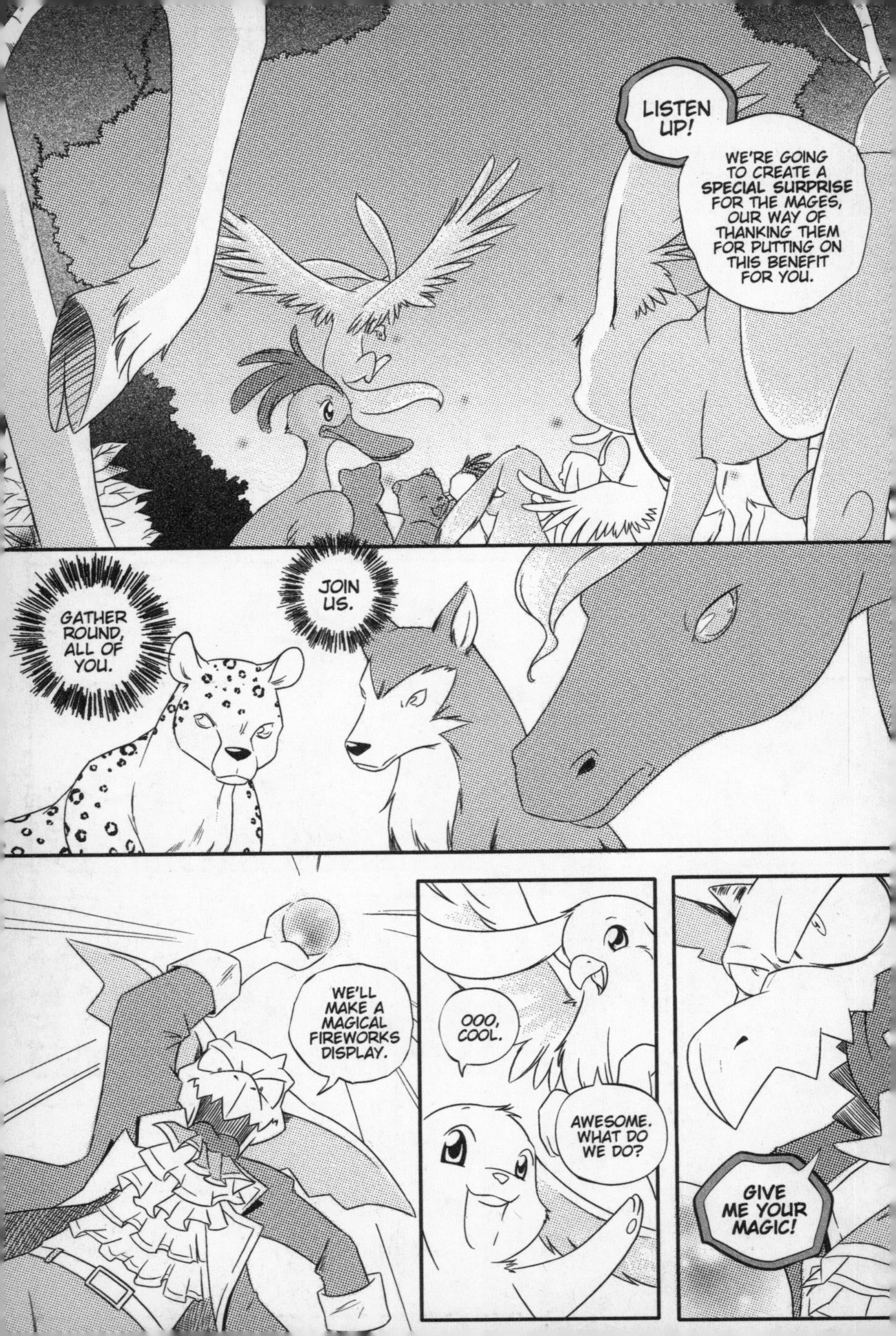
LISTEN UP!
WE'RE GOING TO CREATE A SPECIAL SURPRISE FOR THE MAGES, OUR WAY OF THANKING THEM FOR PUTTING ON THIS BENEFIT FOR YOU.
GATHER ROUND, ALL OF YOU.
JOIN US.
WE'LL MAKE A MAGICAL FIREWORKS DISPLAY.
OOO, COOL.
AWESOME. WHAT DO WE DO?
GIVE ME YOUR MAGIC!

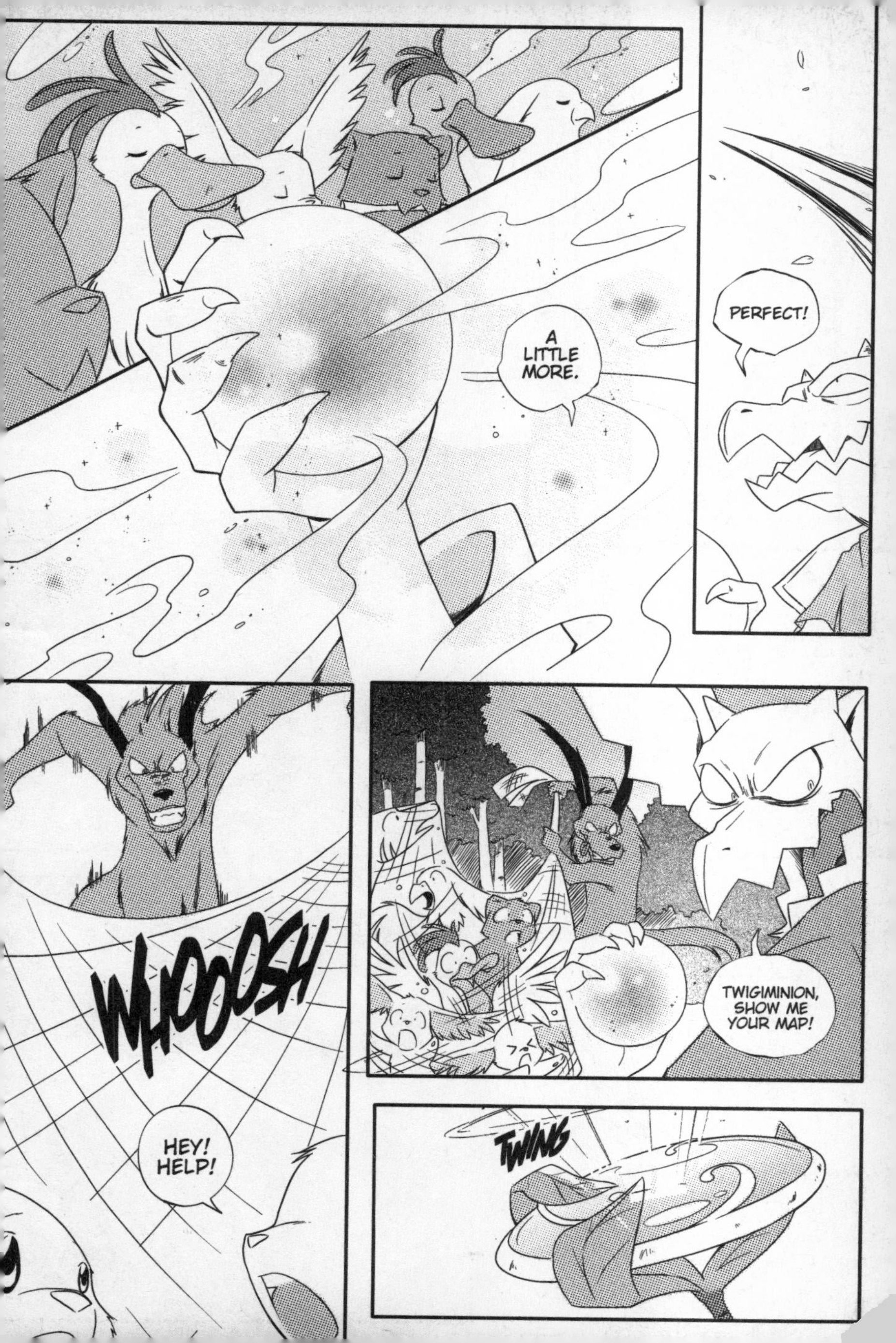
A LITTLE MORE.
PERFECT!
WHOOOSH
HEY! HELP!
TWIGIMINION, SHOW ME YOUR MAP!
TWING

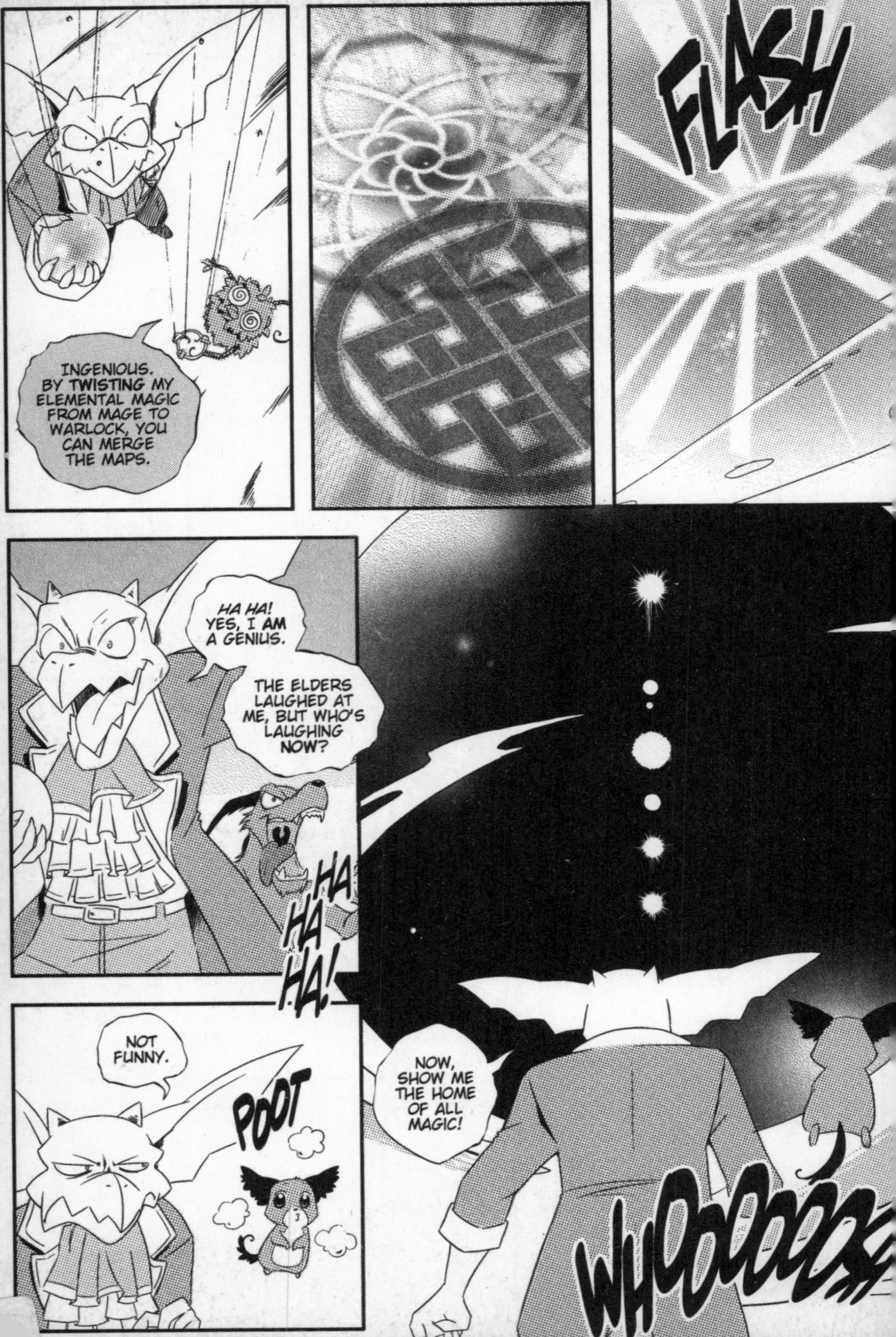
INGENIOUS. BY TWISTING MY ELEMENTAL MAGIC FROM MAGE TO WARLOCK, YOU CAN MERGE THE MAPS.
FLASH
HA HA! YES, I AM A GENIUS.
THE ELDERS LAUGHED AT ME, BUT WHO'S LAUGHING NOW?
HA HA HA HA!
NOT FUNNY.
POOT
NOW, SHOW ME THE HOME OF ALL MAGIC!
WHOOOOOSH

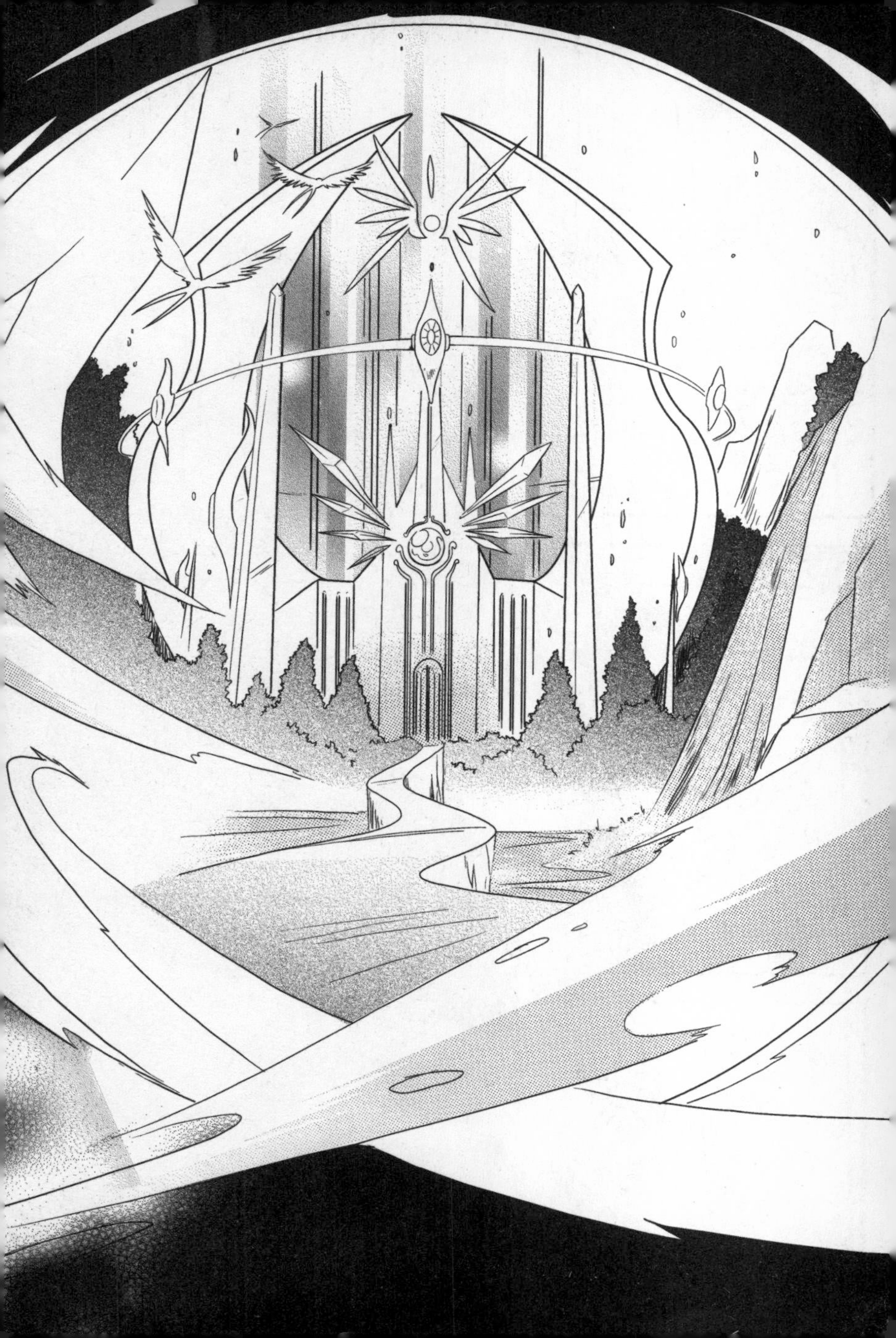

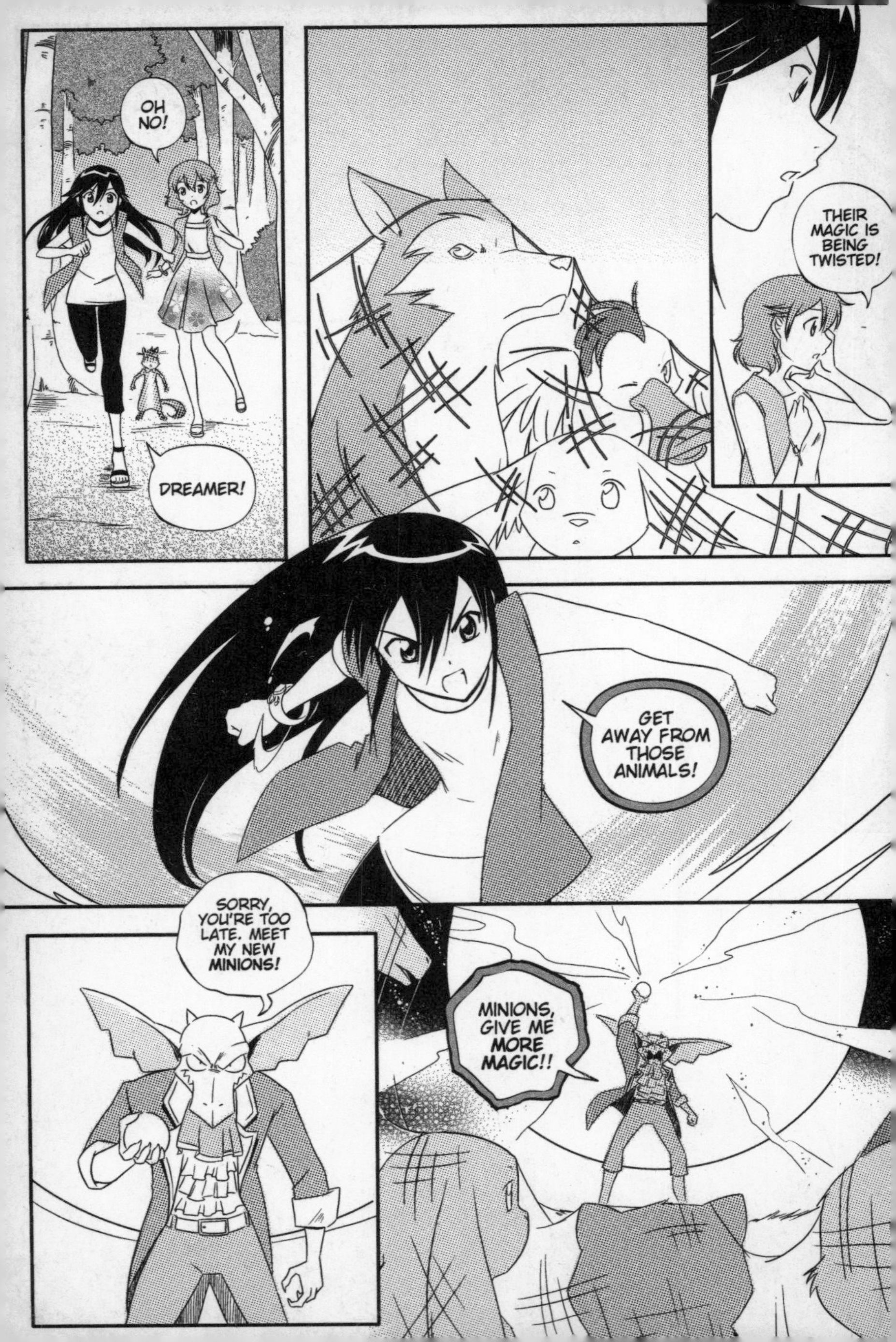
OH NO!
DREAMER!
THEIR MAGIC IS BEING TWISTED!
GET AWAY FROM THOSE ANIMALS!
SORRY, YOU'RE TOO LATE. MEET MY NEW MINIONS!
MINIONS, GIVE ME MORE MAGIC!!

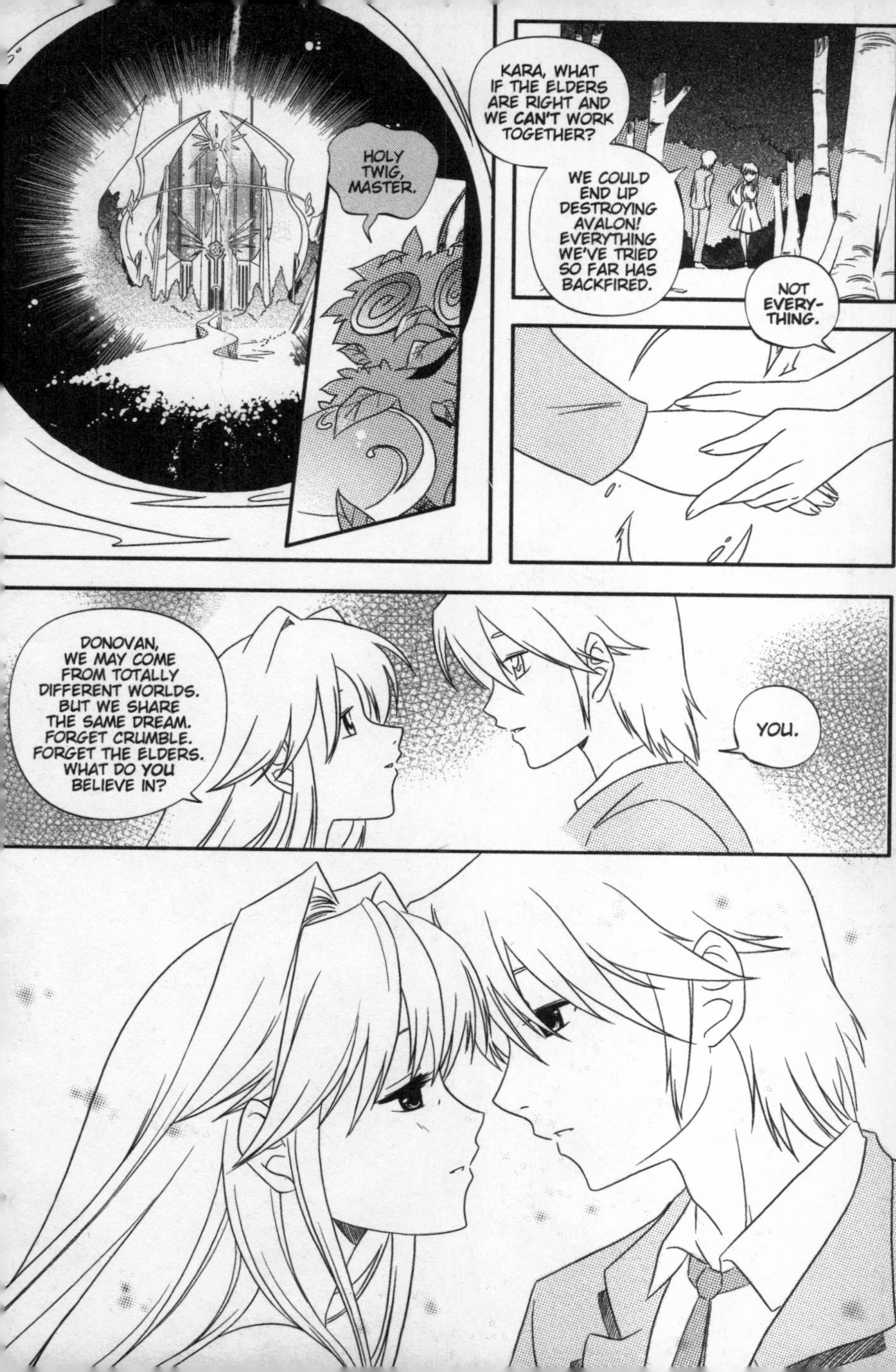
HOLY TWIG, MASTER.
KARA, WHAT IF THE ELDERS ARE RIGHT AND WE CAN'T WORK TOGETHER?
WE COULD END UP DESTROYING AVALON! EVERYTHING WE'VE TRIED SO FAR HAS BACKFIRED.
NOT EVERY-THING.
DONOVAN, WE MAY COME FROM TOTALLY DIFFERENT WORLDS. BUT WE SHARE THE SAME DREAM. FORGET CRUMBLE. FORGET THE ELDERS. WHAT DO YOU BELIEVE IN?
YOU.

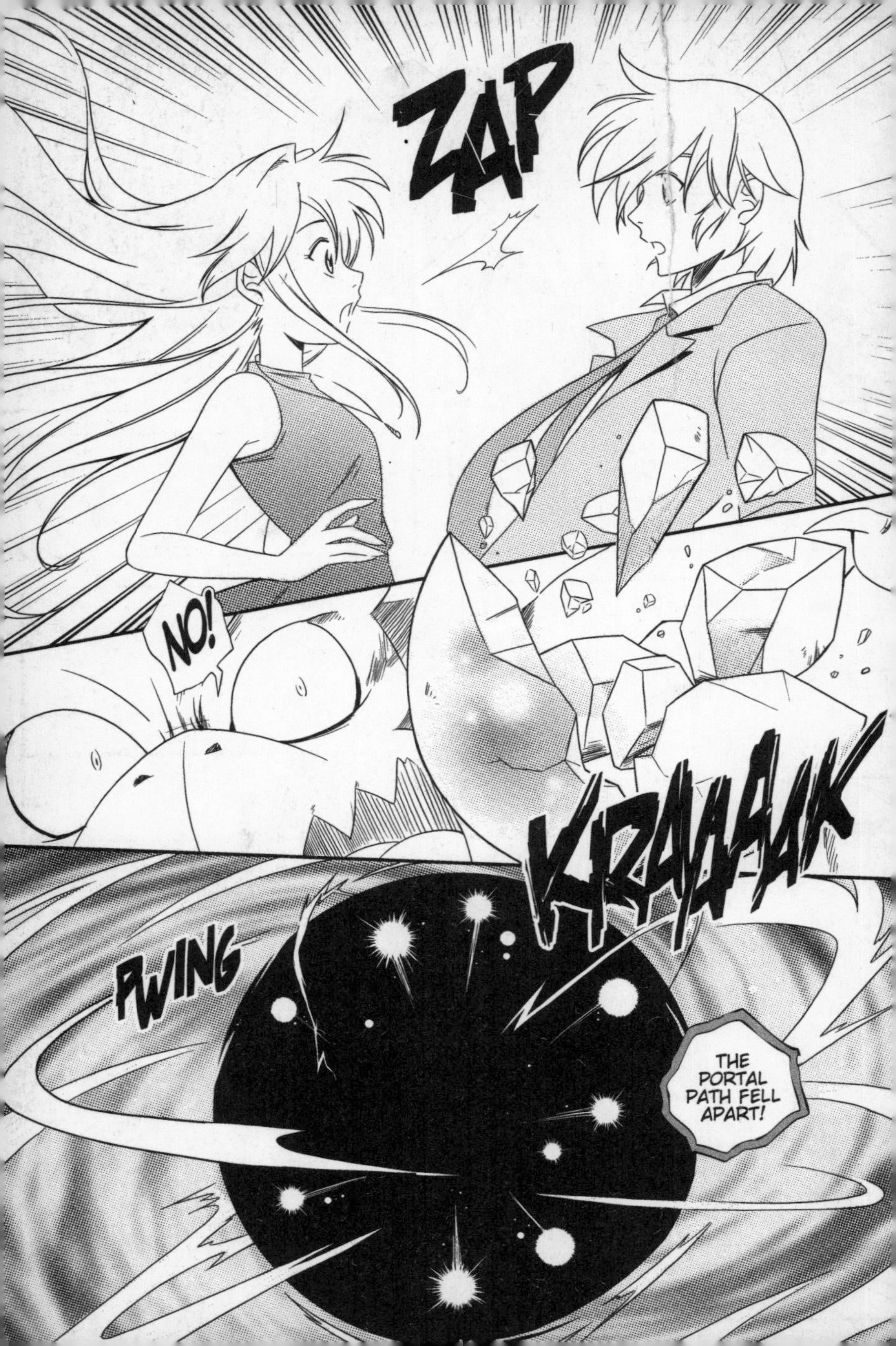
ZAP
NO!
KRAAAAK
PWING
THE PORTAL PATH FELL APART!

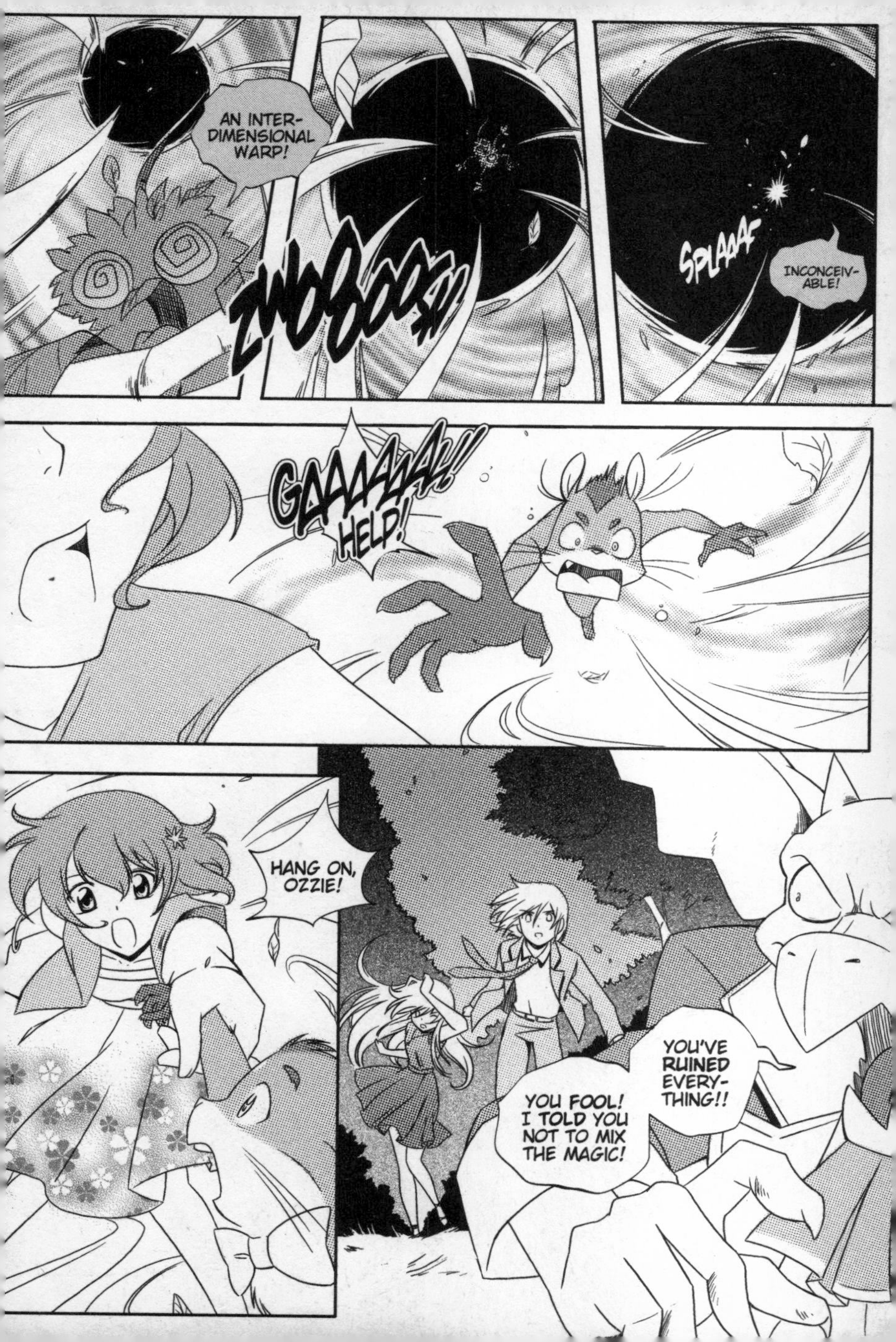
AN INTER-DIMENSIONAL WARP!
ZWOOOOOSH!
SPLAAAF
INCONCEIV-ABLE!
GAAAAAAH!! HELP!
HANG ON, OZZIE!
YOU'VE RUINED EVERY-THING!!
YOU FOOL! I TOLD YOU NOT TO MIX THE MAGIC!

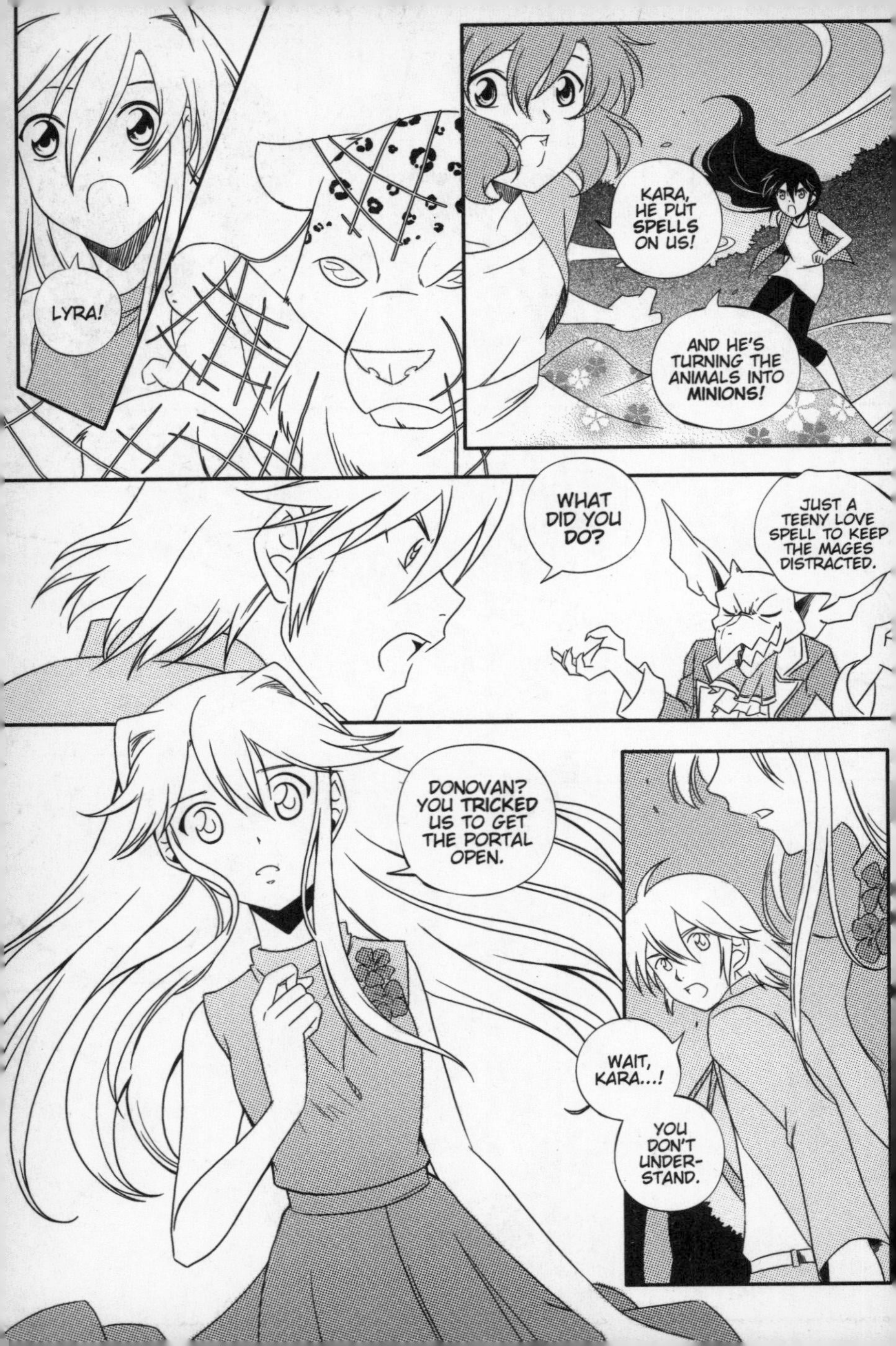
LYRA!
KARA, HE PUT SPELLS ON US!
AND HE'S TURNING THE ANIMALS INTO MINIONS!
WHAT DID YOU DO?
JUST A TEENY LOVE SPELL TO KEEP THE MAGES DISTRACTED.
DONOVAN? YOU TRICKED US TO GET THE PORTAL OPEN.
WAIT, KARA...!
YOU DON'T UNDER-STAND.

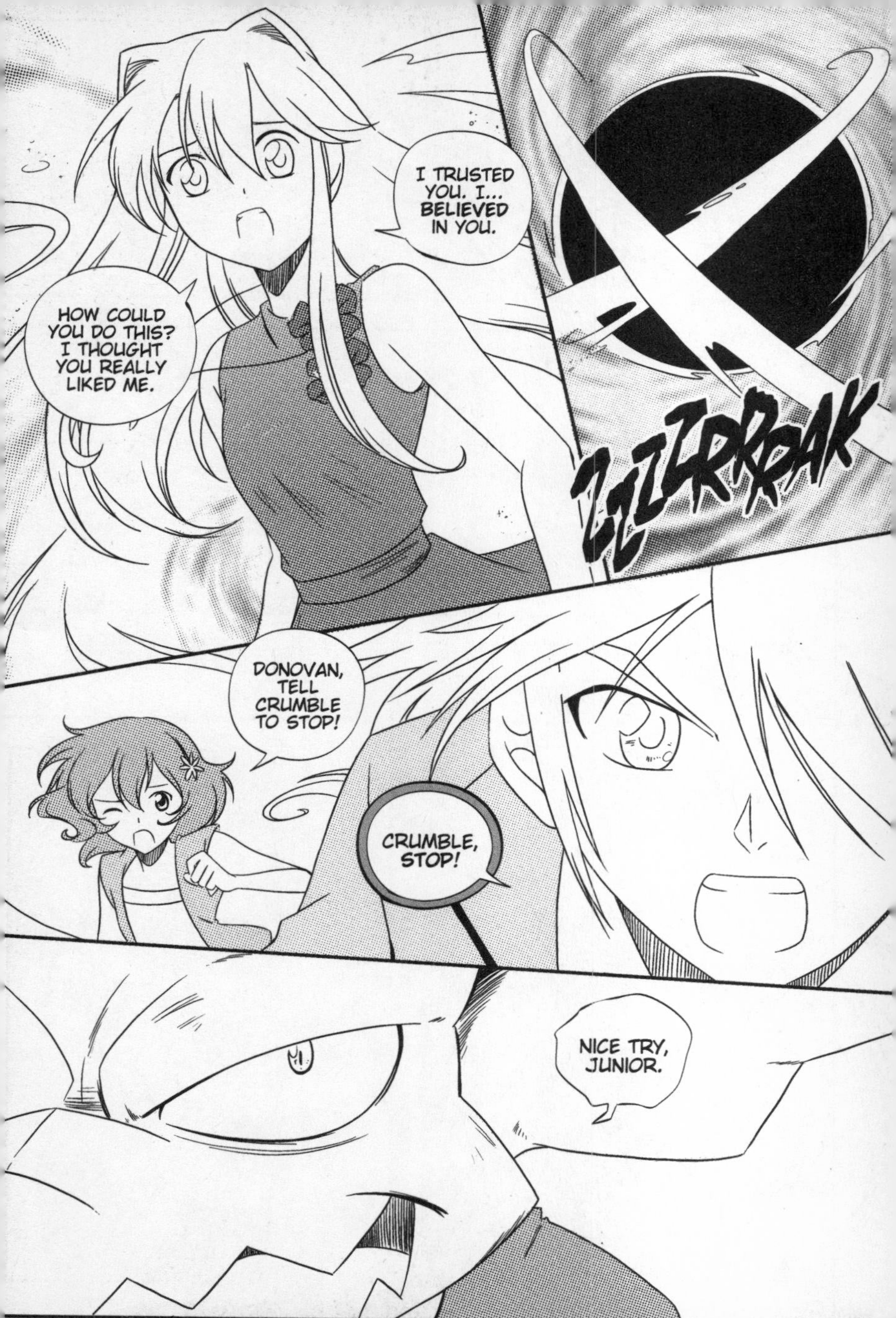
I TRUSTED YOU. I... BELIEVED IN YOU.
HOW COULD YOU DO THIS? I THOUGHT YOU REALLY LIKED ME.
ZZZZRRRRAK
DONOVAN, TELL CRUMBLE TO STOP!
CRUMBLE, STOP!
NICE TRY, JUNIOR.

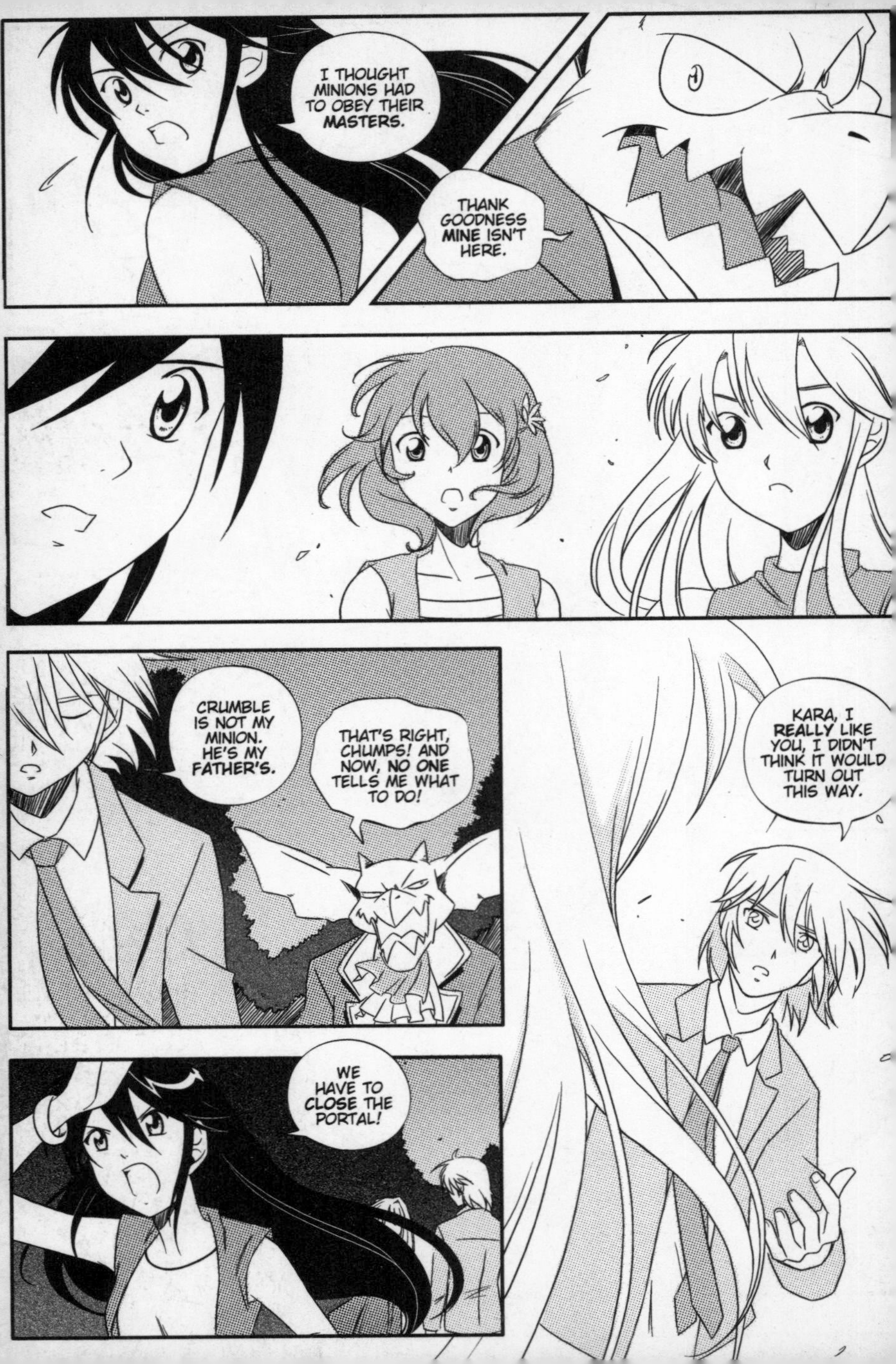
I THOUGHT MINIONS HAD TO OBEY THEIR MASTERS.
THANK GOODNESS MINE ISN'T HERE.
CRUMBLE IS NOT MY MINION. HE'S MY FATHER'S.
THAT'S RIGHT, CHUMPS! AND NOW, NO ONE TELLS ME WHAT TO DO!
KARA, I REALLY LIKE YOU, I DIDN'T THINK IT WOULD TURN OUT THIS WAY.
WE HAVE TO CLOSE THE PORTAL!

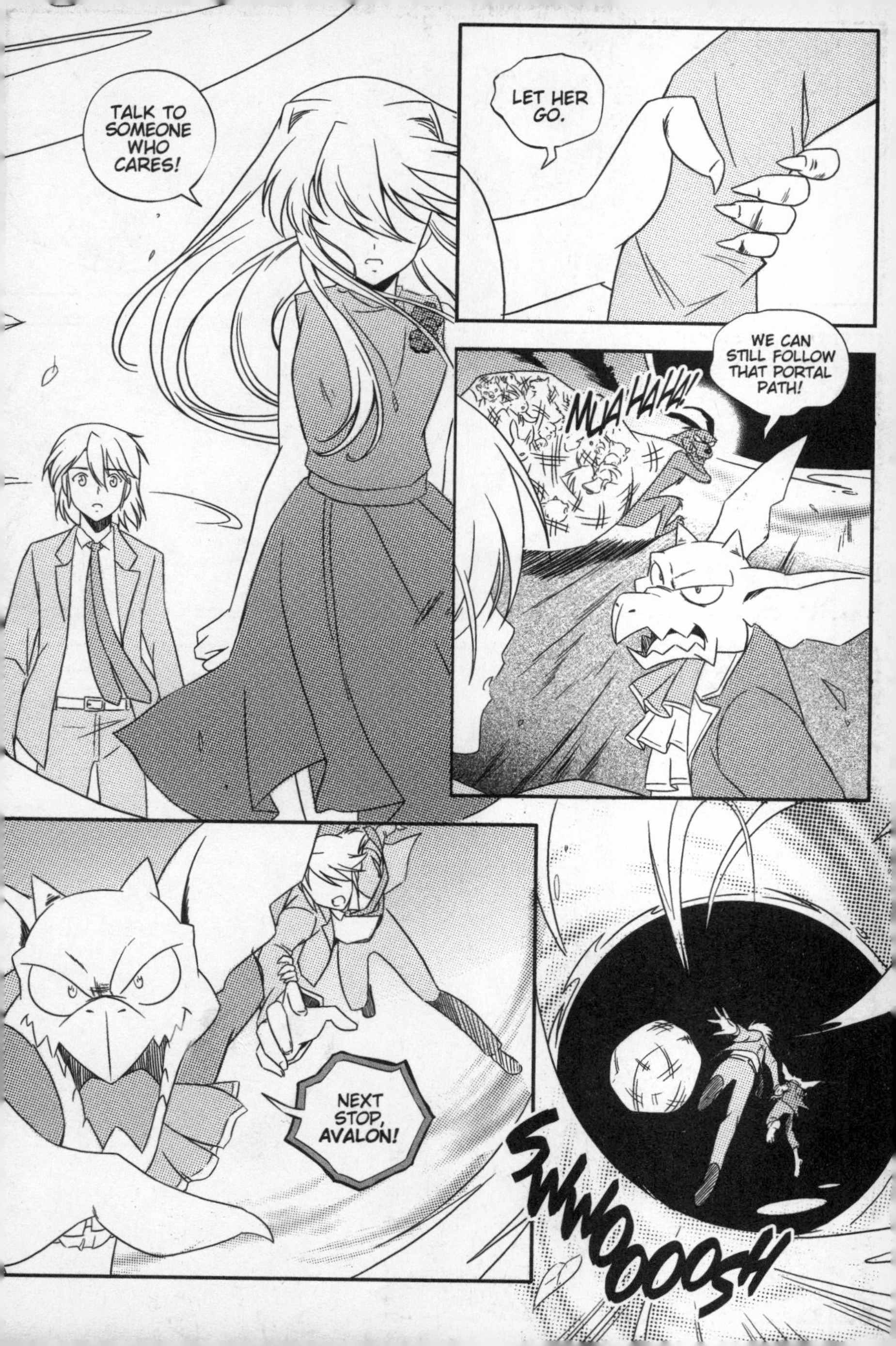
TALK TO SOMEONE WHO CARES!
LET HER GO.
MUA HAHA!
WE CAN STILL FOLLOW THAT PORTAL PATH!
NEXT STOP, AVALON!
SWWOOOOSH

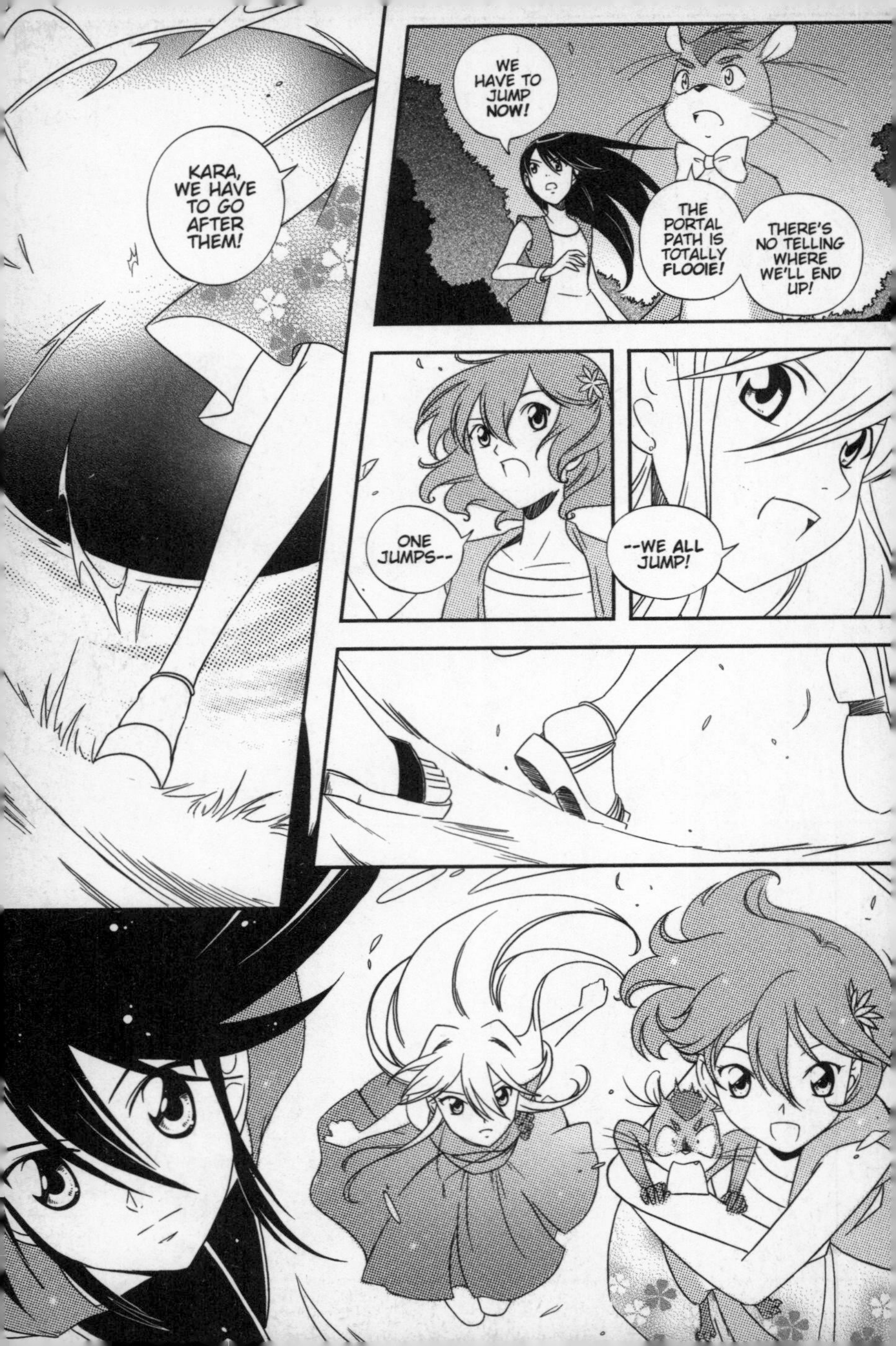
KARA, WE HAVE TO GO AFTER THEM!
WE HAVE TO JUMP NOW!
THE PORTAL PATH IS TOTALLY FLOOIE!
THERE'S NO TELLING WHERE WE'LL END UP!
ONE JUMPS--
--WE ALL JUMP!

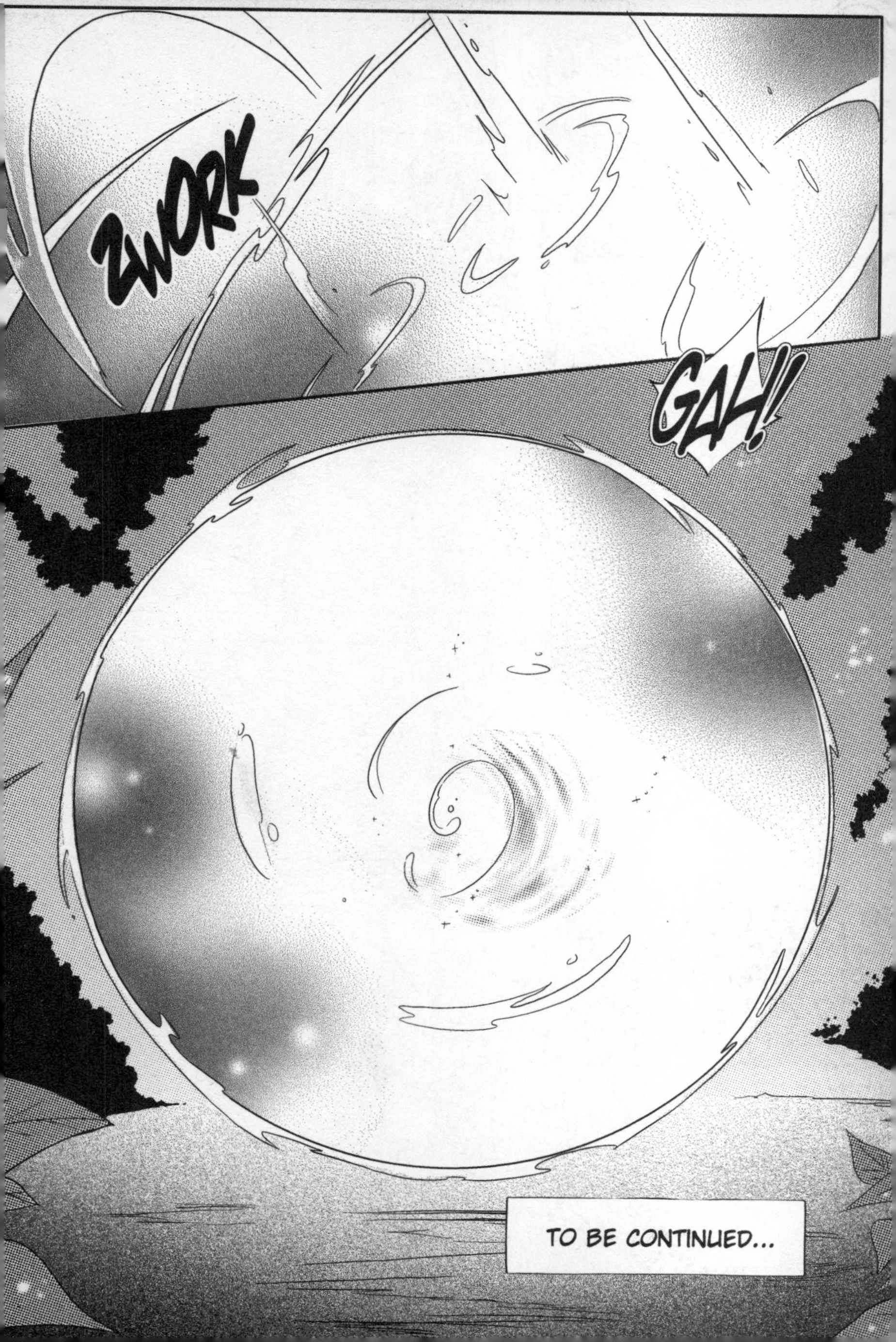
ZWORK
GAH!
TO BE CONTINUED...

The race to find Avalon is on! This time it's up to the warrior mage, Adriane, to lead the charge across the magic web and rescue the animals of Ravenswood before they are turned into evil warlock minions. The mages will need all the help they can get to stop the warlocks, including the mistwolf pack and a group of ferocious dragons. But even that may not be enough to save their friends and protect the home of all magic: Avalon.

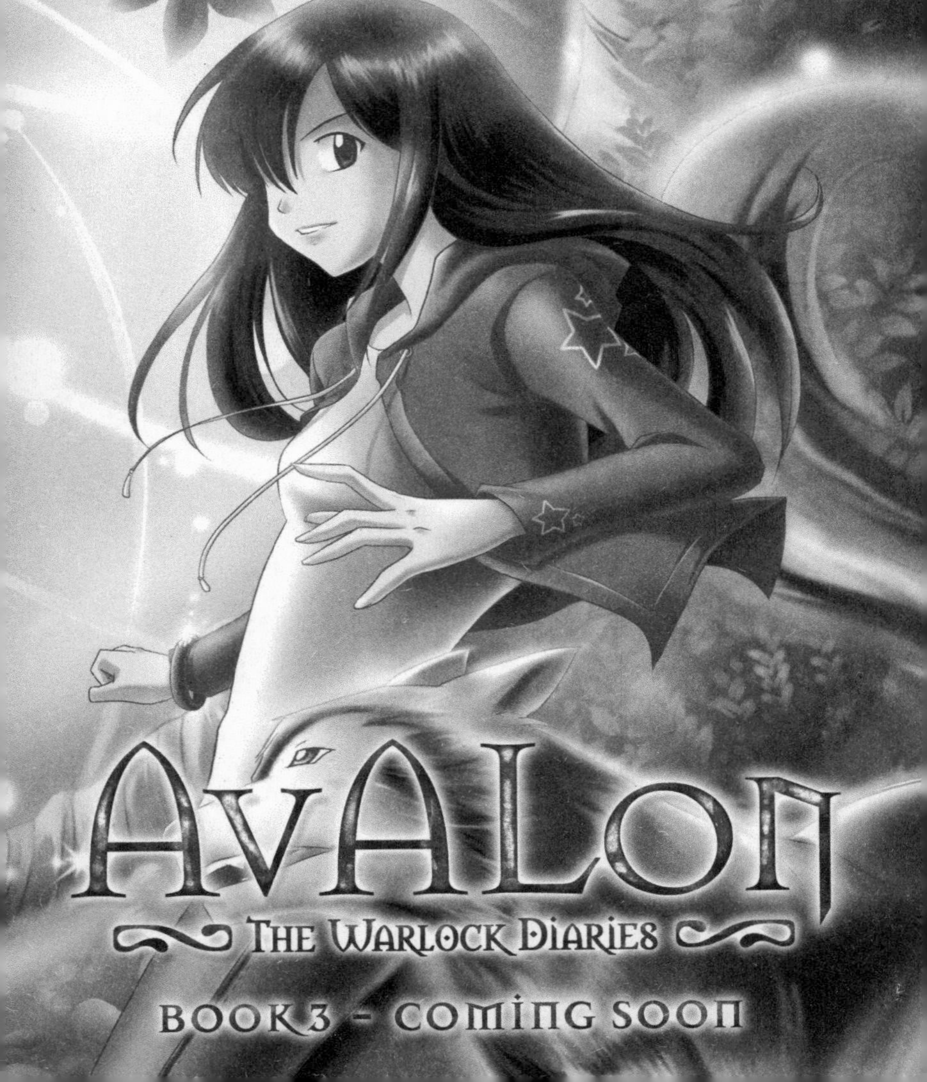
AVALON
THE WARLOCK DIARIES
BOOK 3 - COMING SOON

AVALON

■ Sketch Art Gallery ■
PART 2

DONOVAN

WARLOCK

donovan
- is he supposed to dress like a normal kid, script mention he dress 'weirdly'.

Donovan

Teenage warlock rebel who wants to prove to the Elders that warlocks and mages can work together to find Avalon and save the magic web. With the help of his minions, Donovan uses ancient spells and potions to make magic.

CRUMBLE

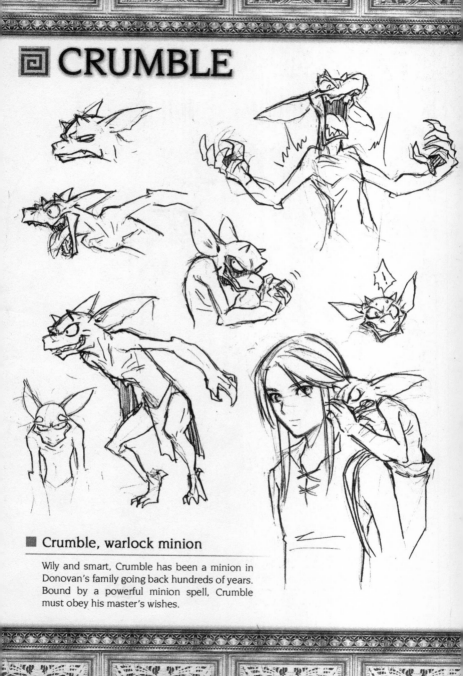

■ Crumble, warlock minion

Wily and smart, Crumble has been a minion in Donovan's family going back hundreds of years. Bound by a powerful minion spell, Crumble must obey his master's wishes.

FRIZZLE

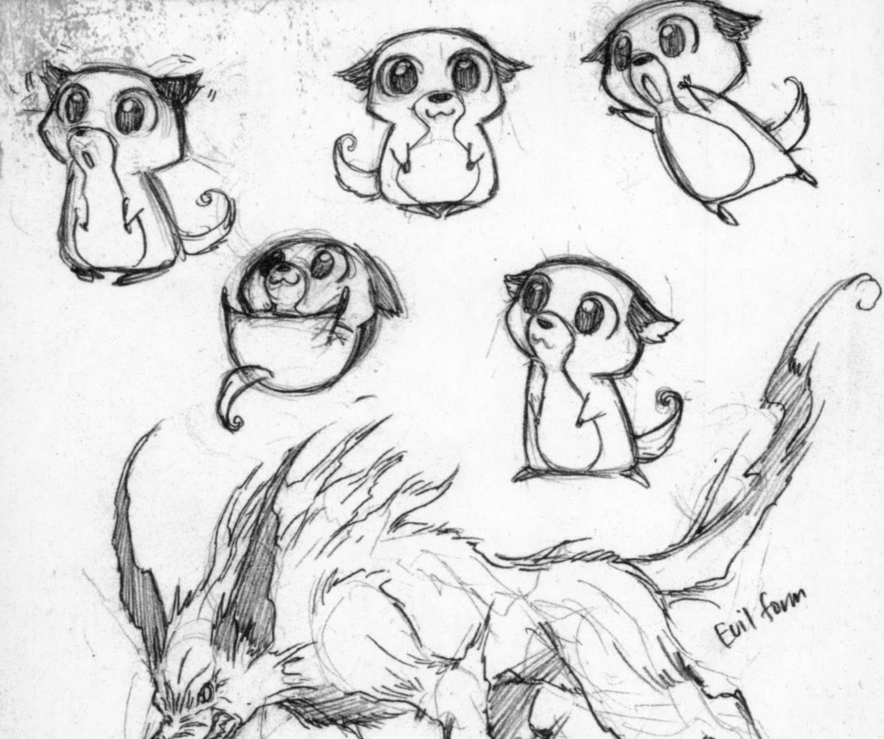
Evil form

Frizzle, warlock minion

Frizzle is a shapeshifting minion recently bound to Donovan. Frizzle enjoys making magic with Donovan and unlike most minions, he is fun-loving and likes to improvise.

DREAMER

GROWL

size comparison

Dreamer, mistwolf

Orphaned on Aldenmor, Dreamer was given to Adriane by the mistwolf pack mother, Silver Eyes. Raised by Adriane in Ravenswood, Dreamer has a deep bond with the mages and animals. Like all mistwolves, his bloodline goes back thousands of years, enabling him to tap into memories and visions of the past.

LYRA

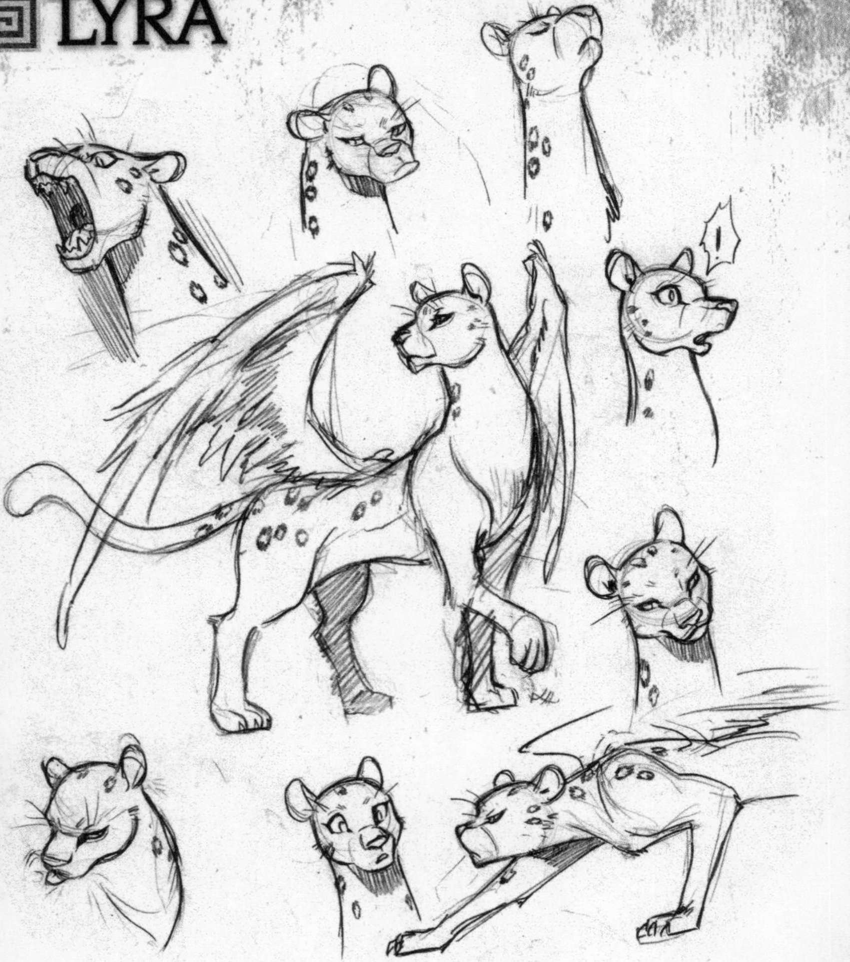

Lyra, magical flying cat

A magical, winged, leopard-like cat from Aldenmor, Lyra is dignified and very smart. She is extremely intuitive and can sense things no one else can. A fierce fighter, she is very protective of her bonded mage, Kara. Only mages can see Lyra's beautiful golden wings.

GOLDIE

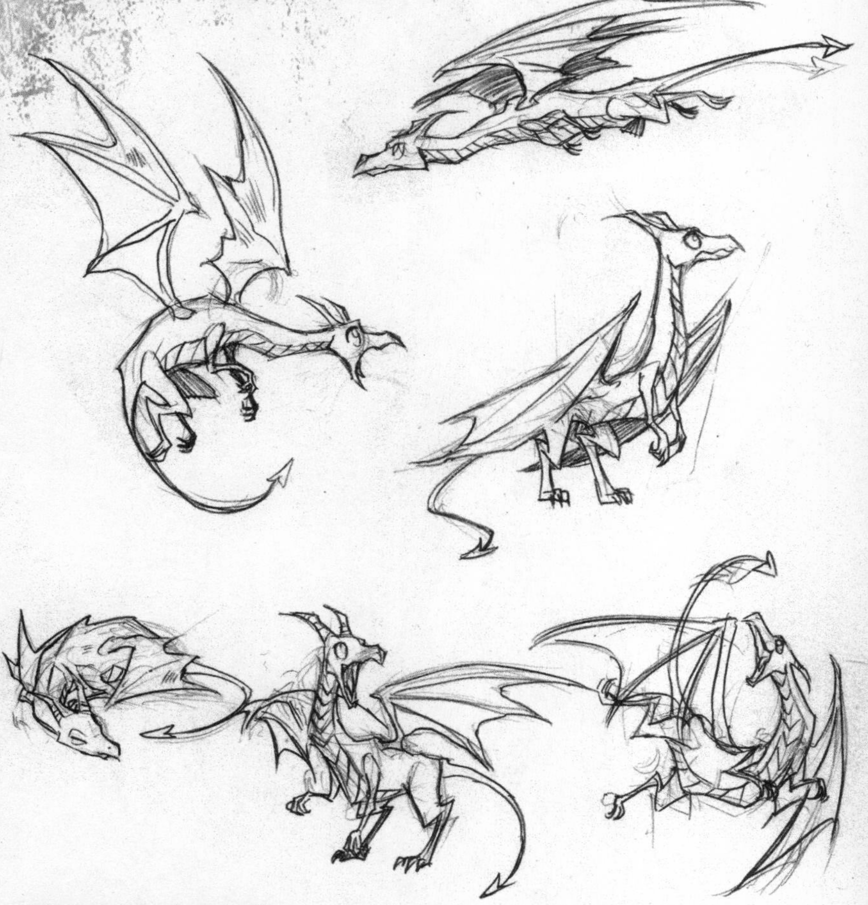

Goldie, dragonfly

Goldie and her buds always come whenever Kara calls them. Dragonflies are fairy creatures that can travel without the use of a portal. They can be used as dragonfly phones to help mages communicate with each other. Goldie has a special bond with Kara, having gone on many adventures with the blazing star.

MAGICAL ANIMALS OF RAVENSWOOD

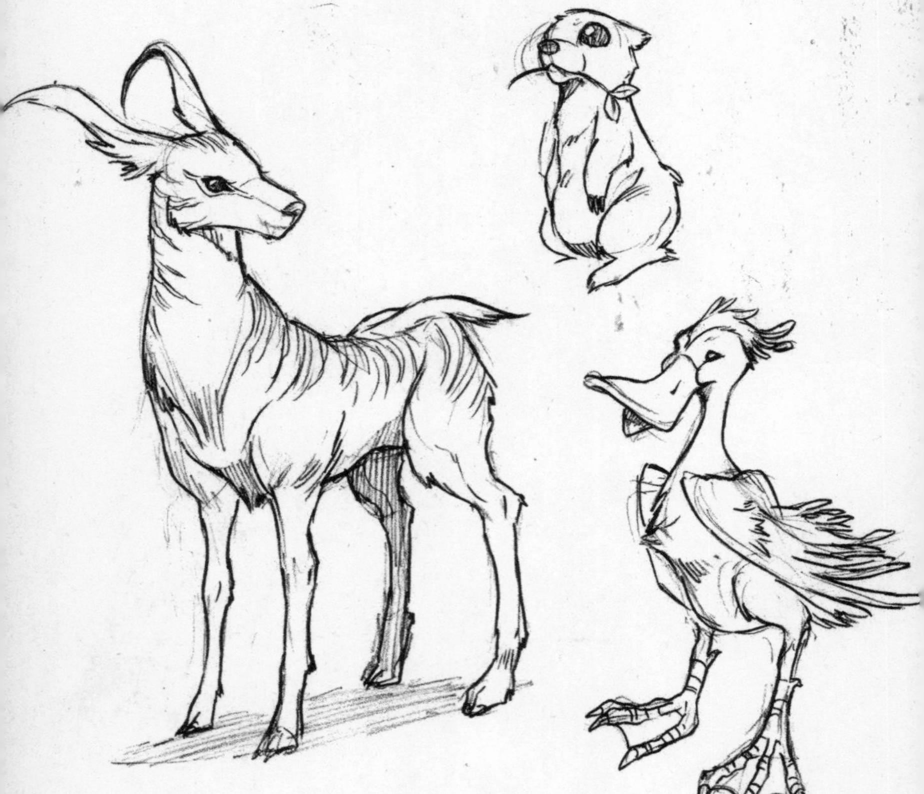

Jeeran / Wommel / Quiffle

Animals from Aldenmor who came through the Ravenswood portal seeking sanctuary at the famous animal preserve for magical animals. They now live there, helping to protect the forests and practice making magic with the mages.

FRIENDS & CLASSMATES

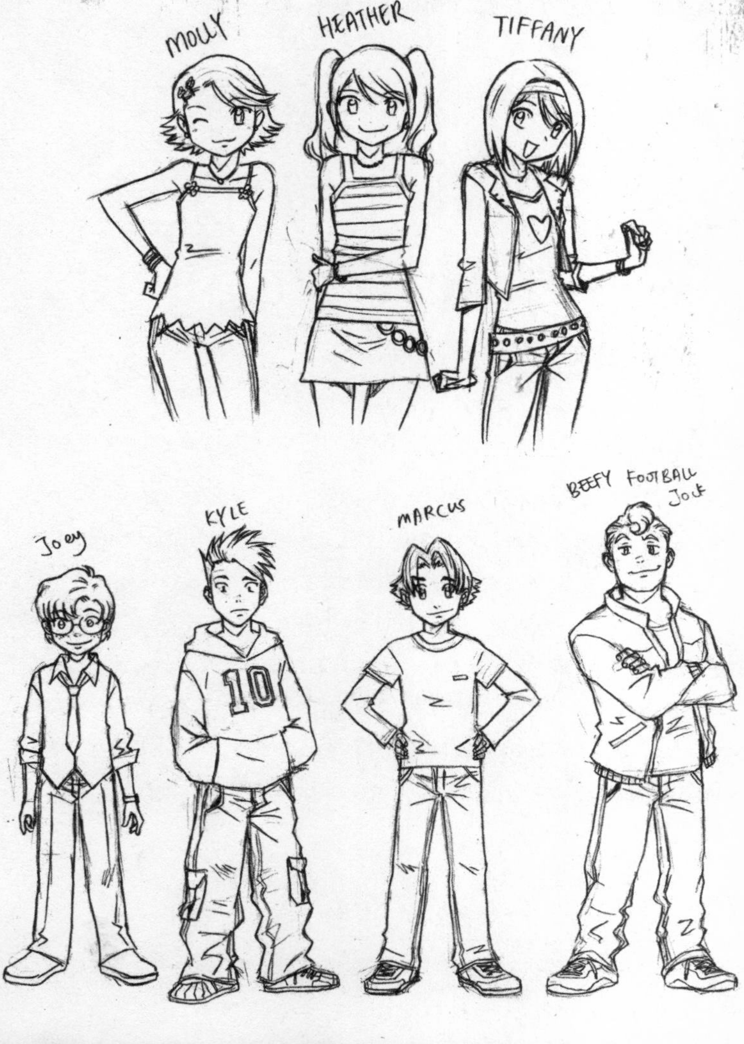
MOLLY
HEATHER
TIFFANY
JOEY
KYLE
MARCUS
BEEFY FOOTBALL JOCK
10

Circle of Friends with Rachel Roberts

Everybody say *hoot hoot!*

Oh hi, this is Rachel. Get ready for new places, new friends, and some familiar faces as the mages fly into their next manga adventure. Meanwhile, back at the Happy Trails Horse Ranch in New Mexico, a mystery is brewing for the mages' friend Sierra. Since new portals are opening all over the magic web, you never know who's going to pop in for a visit. So all you mages better keep an eye out for brimbees in your backyard, and keep the good magic flowing.

Your friend,
Rachel Roberts

Legend of the LAOA

PART 2

"I feel like there's someone missing," Sierra Sanchez said worriedly.

"Tex counted them all," Tyler Branson replied as he helped the teenage girl close the barn door.

"Yeah, so did I." Sierra's brown eyes scanned the desert that lay beyond the Happy Trails Horse Ranch. Spooked by a pack of wild animals, her horses had broken out of the corral. Her friend, Tyler, from the Twin Forks Ranch had helped her wrangle them all back in.

"You know your horses." He brushed a lock of sandy blond hair from his brow.

Sierra wasn't so sure. Something tickled at the edge of her mind, almost calling to her. She couldn't put her finger on it. But she had the strongest sense there was another horse still out there.

"I'd better head back to Twin Forks." Tyler swung onto his black gelding, Shenandoah. The horse neighed and bobbed his head, ready to jet. It seemed all the horses were skittish tonight.

"Thanks, Tyler, couldn't have done it without you and

Shenie." She patted the black horse's neck, settling him down. "You two going to be okay?"

"Probably just a pack of coyotes or wild dogs. Shen can outrun anything on four legs." He slipped his iPhone into his shirt pocket. "Call if you need anything."

Sierra nodded. "Don't forget, I've got us booked for barrel racing at the County Fair next weekend."

"Got enough room for another trophy?" He grinned.

She returned his smile. "I'm building a new shelf for Apache."

Sierra and Tyler had known each other since they were kids. Now in high school, they still shared a love of horses. She lived with her Uncle Tex, training horses and giving riding lessons to visitors at their ranch. Most of the Happy Trails horses had come from Tyler and his family, including her favorite, Apache. Twin Forks was famous for breeding paint ponies.

Sierra watched Tyler and Shenandoah gallop out the main gate. The sun dropped below the horizon, sending a last burst of pinks and purples across the darkening sky. Night was coming on fast.

She grasped the turquoise pendant on her silver necklace, a gift from her grandfather in Mexico. It always seemed to ease her fears, but tonight it wasn't working. Sighing, she turned back to the barn when she heard a soft whinny. Something was calling her. Was it in her mind or had she heard it?

Quietly, she crept behind the barn. There in the dirt was a fresh set of hoof prints, but all the Happy Trails horses wore shoes. These unshod prints led out to the desert—almost as if the mysterious horse had come to visit and then left in a hurry. A cool breeze ruffled her short dark hair. It would be completely dark soon, and whatever had spooked her horses was still out there. Sierra shivered.

She followed the tracks past the arenas and the guest cabins only to see that they abruptly stopped. There was nothing but open desert all around, no place the horse could be hiding. It was as if the horse had simply disappeared.

She looked skyward. A glow streaked across the heavens, trailing a tail of dazzling light.

Sierra gasped. "A shooting star!"

But instead of vanishing into the night, the star soared over the ranch and plummeted behind a sand dune a few hundred yards away. Sierra watched, transfixed.

Atop the dune, a lone horse stood, silhouetted against the flickering light, hooves pawing the air.

"I knew it!" Sierra blinked against the intense flare. But when her vision cleared, the horse was gone.

"Wait, come back!" She dashed into the desert toward it, her cowboy boots digging deep in the sand.

Her jewel felt warm against her neck as she scrambled up and over the dune, sliding down the other side. She leaped to her feet—and froze. The air was filled with iridescent sparkles as if a thousand fireflies danced before her eyes.

Then she heard a musical sound, strange and lilting, as the cloud of twinkles washed away. The horse wasn't there, but something else was. On the desert floor sat a small silver cat with pointy ears. Fragments of rainbow colors shimmered along his coat. It didn't look like a native desert animal and it seemed completely tame, staring at her calmly with strange, shining eyes.

Sierra slowly knelt to inspect the amazing creature more carefully. "Where did you come from?" she whispered.

"Aldenmor." A tinkling voice sounded in Sierra's mind.

She stared at the cat. "Did you just say something?"

"Meeeeeeyooooo," the mysterious cat yowled.

Sierra rubbed her eyes. "Geez, I must be really tired."

"Me too."

This time there was no mistake. The cat had spoken. "How can you talk?"

"Only those who have magic can hear me," the sparkly cat replied.

"Magic?"

The creature cocked his head, regarding her with eyes that seemed to be every color of the rainbow. *"Yes, aren't you a mage?"*

Sierra flashed on her friends from Ravenswood, Emily, Adriane, and Kara. A few months ago they had introduced her to thirty baby unicorns. She'd been emailing with Emily, and knew they were mages, users of magic. They were on a quest to save an entire world of magical animals.

"Where's your bonded animal?"

"Apache? He's in the barn."

The cat's fluffy tail twitched. *"Mages really shouldn't wander around without their magical animals. It's dangerous out here."*

An eerie howl echoed across the desert.

"What was that?" Sierra asked nervously.

"That's what I'm talking about. They must have fallen through the same portal that I did."

"Portal, as in..."

"A doorway which connects two points along the magic web," the cat informed her.

"What are they doing here?" she gulped. A sense of uneasiness filled her.

"Hunting."

Out of nowhere, six huge wolf-like creatures with black shaggy hair, pointed snouts, and glowing yellow eyes sped toward them in long loping strides.

"What do we do?" Sierra cried.

The cat arched his back, silvery coat gleaming as his fur transformed into shimmering crystal. Rings of blinding light swirled from the cat's compact body.

Sierra shielded her eyes, gasping as her pendant erupted in brilliant sparkles.

The wolf creatures yelped, stumbling away in a spray of sand and rocks.

"That won't hold them off for long," the cat warned. *"Call your bonded animal."*

"I don't understand," Sierra stammered.

Suddenly, the thunder of galloping hooves shook the dune as something barreled through the stunned creatures. In a cloud of swirling dust, it skidded to a stop. Standing before her was a magnificent red roan mare.

The cat shook his furry coat as he regarded the amazing horse. *"Ah, there you are. Here's your mage."*

The mare's deep brown eyes locked onto Sierra. *"We must hurry."*

Sierra stared in astonishment. This was the horse that had been calling to her, she was sure of it.

"What are we waiting for?" The cat leaped onto the mare's back.

In the light of the rising moon, the dark creatures were regrouping, yellow eyes flickering with malice.

There was no time to think. Sierra grabbed the mare's russet mane and swung herself on. The horse took off at a full gallop. But the wolf creatures were fast. They sprang after the horse, snapping at her hooves.

With a fierce growl, one of the monsters launched itself at Sierra, dagger teeth flashing from its open maw. She hugged the horse's neck. Her jewel blazed with light, sending the creature hurtling to the ground.

Turquoise sparkles raced up and down her arms. Sierra should have completely freaked, but somehow she knew the horse would protect her. The mare swerved, galloping up the steep incline to Stony Ridge.

"Wait, we'll be trapped up there!" Sierra shouted. The ridge ended in a sheer cliff.

"Trust me." The horse gathered speed, rocketing toward the edge. She was going right over—with her on top!

Sierra screamed, terrified as the mare leaped. For a second, they hung suspended in the air, then plummeted straight down. Something brushed against her legs. Glimmering copper wings spread from the mare's back—and suddenly they were flying!

The breath rushed from Sierra's lungs as the mare wheeled through the sky, soaring over the gully far below.

The cat casually scratched his ear as howls of frustration faded behind them.

Sierra's elation was short-lived. The pack of creatures had turned away, only to head back down Stony Ridge and make for Happy Trails.

"We have to stop them!" Sierra cried.

The mare snorted agreement. *Let's send them back through the portal.*

Angling her wings, the horse banked left and dove over the creatures. She hit the ground at a full gallop directly in front of the leader. Coppery wings sparkled once and vanished as hooves flashed across the sand.

The monsters howled in fury and gave chase.

The mare suddenly skidded and whirled around to face the oncoming predators. The beasts closed in at full speed, jaws snapping. Finally, they would have their prey.

The cat glanced at Sierra. *Go ahead.*

"What do I do?" Sierra cried.

"Focus on your jewel, send me your magic," the horse instructed.

"Now!" The cat fluffed out and blazed like a beacon in the night.

With all her might, Sierra willed her strength to the

horse. She wasn't sure she was doing it right, but her jewel responded with a powerful burst.

She felt the magic erupt behind her as they shot straight up in the air, the horse's wings open and flapping.

The monsters were coming on too fast. Unable to stop, they barreled headfirst into the magical doorway.

With a fierce yowl, the cat shrunk the portal into a point of light and it vanished.

The horse floated gently downward, gliding to the ground.

Sierra leaped off and stroked the mare's silky neck, admiring her deep copper mane and tail. "Thank you," she said.

The horse whinnied. *"I came here to find you, but the creatures followed me through the portal."*

"But why me?" Sierra asked, amazed.

"I am your bonded."

Her glowing turquoise jewel reflected in the horse's deep brown eyes. Sierra had always sensed that her jewel was special. Now she knew why.

"That was amazing!"

Sierra whirled around.

A teenage girl was walking toward them, a train of long moon and star patterned robes swirling behind her. She held a glowing handheld device—and she was green!

"A most excellent display of mage and bonded animal magic."

"Uh, hi, I'm Sierra."

"I know." The strange dark haired girl smiled. "I'm Tasha, I work with Emily, Adriane, and Kara."

"But you're green!" Sierra exclaimed.

"I recycle," Tasha replied, scanning the cat with her handheld device. The cat had transformed back into his silver furry shape and was purring like a lawnmower. "Zach told me about you. I've been searching all over but I couldn't find you on my magic meter!" The small device blinked and beeped. "But your magic seems to have stabilized."

The cat rubbed his head against Sierra. *"The mage and her bonded helped me."*

"Your healing magic must have stabilized the LAOA's portal popping," Tasha told Sierra.

"How did I do that?"

Tasha pointed the meter at Sierra. "Fascinating! You're a healer mage with elemental fire magic bonded to a flying horse." She showed Sierra several glowing lines on the magic meter. "Look, a bit of warrior, too."

"Wow." Sierra could hardly believe this was really happening.

The cat stretched his lithe body. *"When I felt the time of magic had come back, I left my hiding place, only I found out I couldn't control my magic anymore."*

"Are there other LAOAs?" Tasha asked excitedly.

"There are many of us. We have been away from home for so long. I must find my friends."

The mare lowered her head to snuffle the cat. *"How can we help the Lost Animals of Avalon?"*

"You already have," the cat replied.

"Portals are opening and closing all over the web," Tasha confirmed. "This portal here is now a key access point to the web. I have to tell the mages right away!"

"Whoa, does that mean other things are going to come through here?" Sierra asked.

"Well, be on the lookout. You never know who else might drop in for a visit," Tasha said. "But don't worry. I'll send the dragonflies to weave you a dreamcatcher. It will only let creatures with good magic through."

The cat strode over to Tasha. *"You're friends with my little brother Drake, then?"*

Tasha nodded. "I'm sure you two have a lot to talk about."

"Speaking of talking," Sierra patted the mare's silky neck, "what do we do now?"

"I can stay with you..." The red roan lowered her head shyly.

"I don't know how I'm going to explain the wings, but we'll figure it out."

"Only those with magic can see my wings," the horse assured her.

"Oh great, so everyone else is going to see a floating horse."

"Good luck," Tasha waved as the cat zapped open the portal. "You're our mage on the magical frontier. How exciting is that!"

Sierra waved back as Tasha and the cat vanished, leaving

her alone with the horse. The mare's coat gleamed like burnished copper under the desert moon.

She smiled at her bonded. "What's your name?"

The horse snuffled close. *"I guess we'll have to find out together."*

WELCOME TO A WORLD WHERE MAGIC IS REAL AND FRIENDSHIP IS EVERYTHING!

AVALON
WEB OF MAGIC

ON SALE IN BOOKSTORES EVERYWHERE!

MISSION: HUMANE

Humane means being kind and considerate of others.
A *mission* is a job or task for you to do.
We have a mission for kids who care about animals!

SPEAK UP FOR ANIMALS IN NEED!

JOIN MISSION: HUMANE!

LEARN HOW AT humanesociety.org/kids

THE **HUMANE SOCIETY**
OF THE UNITED STATES
YOUTH